THIS OLD HOUSE

ACFW Ohio Chapter
2025 Anthology

American Christian Fiction Writers
ACFW.com

All proceeds from this anthology go into the scholarship fund, to encourage student writers in Christian schools throughout Ohio.

Ye Olde Dragon Books
6909 Ackley Rd.
Parma, OH 44129

www.YeOldeDragonBooks.com
2OldeDragons@gmail.com

TABLE OF CONTENTS

Introduction

Blessed Reader,

Welcome to the first scholarship anthology from our American Christian Fiction Writers local chapter!

At ACFW, we believe in the power of storytelling to inspire, uplift, and deepen faith. Our local chapters provide a vibrant community for Christian writers, offering regular meetings, mentorship, and special events—such as book signings, retreats, and conferences—to help members grow in their craft and pursue publication.

All proceeds from this anthology, and future anthologies, will go into a scholarship fund to encourage young Christian writers. This year, our theme is "This Old House," and we were blessed with an outpouring of submissions. We also opened our doors to Christian high school students, inviting them to share their voices alongside seasoned authors. Four outstanding student stories are featured in this edition, and we're excited to continue this tradition in future anthologies.

Our members have published over 100 books collectively, and every story in this collection centers on faith—whether it's about finding it, strengthening it, sharing it, or reclaiming it. We pray these stories will encourage and inspire you in your own walk with Christ.

Are you a Christian writer seeking a supportive community? Do you long to grow in your writing and connect with like-minded believers? We invite you to join us! Our members enjoy retreats, monthly Zoom meetings, and a national conference, along with the wealth of educational resources provided by ACFW National. Learn more at *ACFW.com*.

Thank you for picking up this anthology. May these stories bless and uplift you.

Blessings,

Victor Hess
President, Ohio Chapter
American Christian Fiction Writers

A Whirlwind Wedding
and a Twisted Old House
A Tie-in to the Forest Glen stories
Bettie Boswell

Loretta climbed from the college pool and donned her multicolored robe. Joseph from the Bible would have been jealous of her favorite swimsuit cover up. Sometimes she heard others gossiping about her choice in clothing, but she didn't care. Being a single artist all her life had given her freedom to dress any way she wanted.

"Have you decided what you're going to wear to my wedding this weekend?" Honey, her friend, shook out a huge beach towel printed with lavender flowers. The gray-haired woman wrapped herself in the muted covering. Her forehead wrinkled as she waited for Loretta's answer.

"I'm not sure yet. I don't usually wear a regular dress." Loretta wasn't looking forward to calming down her color choices, but knew she needed to respect her friend.

"A nice pantsuit might work. Or you could borrow one of my dresses since we're close in size." Annabelle, Loretta's other close friend, entered the conversation.

Honey smiled.. Loretta figured it might be a bad idea to outshine the bride by wearing a bright colored caftan. She didn't want to do that to her friend, especially as a bridesmaid, who had the freedom to choose what she wore.

"That sounds like a great idea. Most of my outfits have managed to acquire a drop or two of paint. Is there a time I could come and see what you have, Annabelle?" Loretta led the way down a chilly hall to the locker room. The college had the air-conditioner blowing at full tilt, chilling the dripping women, fresh from their senior citizen aquatic exercise class.

"You can come over after I pick up Gerald from his dementia daycare group at the Senior Center. Would an hour from now work? I can get our meals to go. If you like, we can pick up lunch for you." Annabelle sat down on a bench in front of her locker and toed off her swim shoes.

"No thanks. I think I'll swing by the coffee shop and grab something sweet before coming your way. After I get the dress, I'll head to the parsonage to help the preacher clean and pack. Honey mentioned needing help with cleaning up after the bachelor." Loretta headed for the shower while the other two began drying off to change into their street clothes.

Her skin would itch if she didn't get the chlorine off before leaving the college's recreation center. By the time she'd cleaned up the others were gone. A freshly iced cinnamon roll and the local coffee shop's fruit-flavored chocolate drink were on her mind. Perhaps they might help with her stress level.

She'd never minded being single before, but it looked like her friends were both going to be busy with husbands. Annabelle spent more time taking care of Gerald these days as his dementia took over more of his thoughts. She missed her friend but understood the situation. Honey, on the other hand, had been a fellow single lady.

Honey married years ago, but no children had entered their lives to complicate things. She seemed happy in her widowed state for many years and took the time to make everyone part of her family. Would that change once Loretta's friend married Preacher Jonah this weekend? The widowed minister had come to town to locate near his family. Honey would inherit grandchildren and their parents when she married the preacher. The whole congregation might decide to capture the giving woman's attention. Would being a preacher's wife keep Honey from hanging out with her close friends? Loretta hoped not, but still found time to worry about what might happen.

A wave of loneliness washed over Loretta's heart as she drove to the local coffee shop and stood in line, waiting to get her treat. She shivered, attributing her shudders to her wandering thoughts, but the feeling of someone watching her wouldn't go away. Glancing around the room, she saw several strangers amongst the people she knew from teaching college courses or going to church. A baldheaded gentleman met her gaze and then looked down after she glanced his way.

"Can I help you, Ms. Loretta?" the barista asked.

"Yes. I'd like your hot chocolate, flavored with cherry, and an iced cinnamon roll, to go."

"We can do the drink iced if you'd like. It's a warm day out there." The former student wrapped up the bun in waxed paper and placed the sweet-smelling treat in a white bag.

"I'm good with the hot drink. You never know in May when a hot day will turn cold. Can you make my hot chocolate sugar-free since I'm getting the cinnamon roll?" Loretta accepted the bag and held it to her nose to catch the scent of cinnamon.

"Will do." The young woman began pouring ingredients into a mixing cup. "Speaking of weather, I heard a storm might be moving through on Saturday. I hope we don't get a tornado." The drink machine whirled as cherry flavoring dripped into the mixture. When it stopped, she popped the liquid into the microwave for a minute. After pouring it into a to-go cup, the barista topped the concoction with a hefty portion of whipped cream and a maraschino cherry. Placing a domed cap over the drink, she pushed it to Loretta and named the cost.

Loretta dipped into her huge purse and placed the money and a tip into the girl's hand. "I'm going to a wedding this weekend. We don't need a tornado to stir things up."

"I heard the preacher and Miss Honey were marrying. If I didn't have a shift here, I'd be there cheering them on. I love the way she plays her bass guitar. Maybe I can talk her into giving me some free lessons since she'll be the preacher's wife."

Loretta sniffed. "I imagine Honey will be busy enough keeping up with her husband." She held her purchases close to her chest and marched through the shop.

As she reached for the door, her gaze caught the stranger looking her way again. He ran a finger down the side of his handlebar moustache and smiled. What an odd thing to do. Then again, maybe she should calm herself down instead of stomping out the door like the unhappy woman she was at the moment.

She paused at the door and took a heaving breath. Doing her duty to Honey meant swallowing her concerns. Dressing in one of Annabelle's conservative dresses would only need to last for a few hours. Then she could go back to her colorful garb and her paintings. Teaching a few art classes at the college and Amber's Art Studio would provide her with plenty of young people who needed her and wanted to join her in artistic pursuits. She held her head high and flashed a smile at the stranger. There. That should give him something to think about.

~~~~

Marshal Drake watched as the woman headed to her older model sedan. Something about her had drawn his attention from the moment he spotted her walking into the coffee shop. Maybe it was her colorful blouse, or perhaps something from the past. Did he know her from his years as the preacher's kid in the relatively small town of Forest Glen? Was that why she'd smiled at him? He hoped not.

He hadn't left the best impression on the town. The smile seemed familiar. Or was it the eyes? If only he could place the person behind the face. His dad had served the church as minister from the time Marshal entered kindergarten until eighth grade. There had been several close friends, mostly guys. A few girls had trailed after his group of friends in junior high, but he had his mind on other things than girls. His involvement with those boys was something he tried to forget.

The church board gave Dad a lot of grief over some of Marshal's choices back then. A straight-laced deacon caught Marshal and his friends painting graffiti on the man's garage one Halloween. Dad dealt with the
~~~~

fallout for more than a year before moving on to serve a different church. The separation from his friends impacted his life. Though he'd communicated with the old gang for a while, he chose relationships after the move that kept him out of trouble. His older sister hadn't been happy about the situation he'd put the family in either. She had a crush on a college student doing an internship at the church. Patricia had taken Marshal's sketchpad and hidden it from him as a punishment for forcing the move. He never saw the notebook again and she refused to reveal what happened to it.

After moving, Marshal had played it straight during his high school and college years. He focused his talent for drawing into a commercial art career. He'd done well and enjoyed retirement until his wife passed a year ago. The anniversary of her death had spurred him to travel to some of his old haunts and explore the country. After distributing valued family antiques to his grown children, nieces, and nephews, he had sold his house and furniture. He'd replaced his home with a travel camper and started his journey to explore his past and future.

Ironically, his sister's grandson had recently taken the position of youth minister for The Church of the Rock. When Patricia confided that Kaleb would perform a wedding at their old church on May 17th, Marshal decided the occasion might be the perfect time to check out the old place. He hoped the angry deacon was long gone. The man would be over 100 if he still lived. There was little chance of meeting the grumpy guy.

Marshal smoothed down his moustache. A white hair from his upper lip lingered on the tip of one finger. Wrapping the hair in a napkin, he leaned back in his chair as he thought of his childhood. He no longer resembled the red-haired, smooth-lipped, freckle-faced boy who ran through the neighborhood with his gang of buddies. He did wonder if any of them might be around. At the time, they were good friends, even if they did lead him into trouble. Gerald, Marvin, and Jimmy corresponded with him for the first year, but the letters stopped by the time they entered their final high school years. He hadn't heard from them since.

Marshal cleared his table and carried his trash to the receptacle by the door. Debating between taking a walk through town and heading back to his empty camper, he chose to stroll down the sidewalk. Different businesses occupied the area, but the ancient storefronts looked much the same. He stopped at the familiar dime store building where he'd bought cheap pieces of candy as a child. Instead of touting sweets, toys, and knickknacks, a high-quality furniture store now filled the space. A young couple bounced on the edge of a mattress displayed in the front window, reminding him of his days as a newlywed. The honeymoon, two kids, a collection of dogs, one snarky cat, and an empty nest filled the time before his past year living as a widower.

He walked back to his parked truck and drove to the edge of town where The Church of the Rock sat next to the old parsonage. A vintage red mustang and truck sat next to the old house, his childhood home. Most memories were good ones. He often wondered how long Dad would have stayed there if Marshal hadn't gotten him in trouble with the board. Dad had assured him that he was glad to move on.

The next church had offered his parents the chance to own their own home instead of living in a parsonage. Mom had been thrilled to have her own accommodation where no one would worry about her housekeeping. She loved her art, too. Young Marshal no longer had to worry about making a mess while painting. With his sister in college, Mom had created a bedroom studio to share with Marshal. They'd enjoyed creating in the little room. Dad's ministry at the new church lasted until he retired at the age of seventy-five. Marshal's parents lived with him and his wife, Sheila, their last couple of active years before entering a care facility.

Marshal parked in the church lot and watched an older couple bring out boxes and place them in the truck. They must be Preacher Jonah and his bride. Kaleb had mentioned they'd be moving into Honey's home after the wedding. Retirement was on the horizon for the older minister, who'd hinted that Kaleb should put his resume in for the senior position when Jonah's retirement became official.

After loading the truck, the couple headed his way. Marshal had been caught staring again. Releasing his seatbelt, he got out of the car and stepped forward to greet them.

"May we help you?" Preacher Jonah offered his hand.

"I'm Kaleb's great-uncle Marshal. I came to support him as he does his first wedding ceremony." He shook the minster's hand.

"He mentioned you might be coming. I'm Jonah and this is my fiancé, Honey. We're looking forward to having our young preacher friend do the honors."

"I see you're packing. I'm pretty good at moving boxes." Marshal rolled his shoulders and held out open palms.

"Come on in. Kaleb mentioned you might like to see the old house since you once lived here." Honey reached for Marshal's elbow and propelled him toward the parsonage.

"I would enjoy taking a look around and helping you with the boxes." Marshal stepped away and reached for a carton sitting near the truck. He hefted the box into the truck bed.

Jonah nodded as he stepped onto the porch and made his way toward a propped open door. "That sounds like a plan. Kaleb and one of Honey's friends are supposed to arrive soon to help. You can join the crew. You can also help your great-nephew make some decisions about furniture. We're trying to talk him into moving out of his apartment and into the parsonage. He can have any of the things I'm leaving behind. Otherwise, what is left, from beds to easy chairs, will go to auction after our honeymoon."

~~~~

Loretta draped two dresses across the foot of Annabelle's bed. The muted colors didn't do anything for her. However, she'd found a couple of loose shifts that looked comfortable. If she added one of her favorite scarves, either dress would be tolerable.

"Have you made a choice yet?" Annabelle lifted the dresses and held them side by side. One was green and the other a light blue. "If you wore one of these, and I wore the other, we would look somewhat coordinated."

Loretta had never coordinated with anyone, but her friend had a point. "I can do that, but let me figure out a scarf for each of us to wear. I can only take plain dressing to a certain point."

Annabelle laughed. "I will accept your scarf, if you accept my dress. So, which one is yours?"

Loretta heaved a dramatic sigh. "I suppose the green one will have to do. It matches my eyes." She never dreamed that finding something for Honey's wedding would be an issue. "Or I could wear one of my jungle print caftans." She wiggled her eyebrows.

Annabelle's mouth fell open. "Just because Honey gave us the freedom to wear our own choice of clothing doesn't mean we want to draw attention to ourselves."

Loretta shrugged and lifted shaking hands. "Sorry. I was kidding. This is Honey's time to take center stage."

"Did you eat anything besides sugar for lunch? Your hands are shaking like a leaf. I picked up an extra meal at the Senior Center, figuring you weren't behaving yourself." Annabelle frowned and waved Loretta toward the kitchen.

"You are a wise and considerate woman, my friend. I could use some protein." Loretta stuffed her trembling hands into pockets and followed her friend to a small dining table near the stove.

Annabelle opened her refrigerator and retrieved a Styrofoam container. "Do you want it warmed up?"

"No. I'll just fork the food up cold. I need to get over to the parsonage and help Honey clean up after they get Jonah's final boxes loaded." The still mildly warm meal provided the protein she needed. Her doctor had warned her about making sure she ate right to avoid taking medication. She really did need to make better choices. Between bites, she thanked her friend for taking care of her needs.

"I wish I could help with the moving process, but it's time for Gerald's afternoon nap and I can't leave him alone." Annabelle yawned. "I could use a few winks myself. He was restless last night."
~~~~

"Sweet dreams. I'm off to do some cleaning and tossing." Loretta folded the green dress over her purse and headed toward her sedan.

A few minutes later, she pulled up to the church and parked near the parsonage. She recognized Honey's mustang. A truck filled with boxes occupied the other side of the drive. Two more vehicles occupied church parking spaces closest to the old house. One must belong to Kaleb, the youth minister. The other had out-of-state vanity tags reading 'ARTING 1' near an empty trailer hitch on a large pickup truck. Hmmm... Maybe she'd get vanity tags when her next renewal arrived.

Her ancient sedan door squeaked as she shoved it closed, announcing to the world that she'd arrived. Honey peeked out the open door of the parsonage and waved a dust rag in the air.

"You're just in time for cleaning duty. I've got a dust mop with your name on it."

"Thanks a lot." Dusting had never been a priority for Loretta, but she'd give it a try for the sake of her friend.

Honey pushed the mop into Loretta's hands. "Actually, I'm hoping you can reach a little higher than me and run this across the picture frame hook rail that runs around the upper part of each wall."

"I can handle that. By the way, who's here with the out-of-state tags?" Loretta lifted the mop above her head and began cleaning the slim wood rail on the upper part of the wall. She hadn't seen a similar hanging device since childhood.

"That would be Kaleb's great-uncle. He and Kaleb are in the cellar sorting tools that were there before Jonah moved in." Honey winked. "He's a handsome man. If you want to go down and dust down there, I won't tell on you."

"I know all about Kaleb, but I think he might be a little young for me." Loretta turned the conversation around with a snicker.

"You know I wasn't talking about the youth minister."

"I know. I'm too old for romance." Loretta's snort turned into a cough as dust particles filled the air.

Honey cleared her throat and put fists on her hips.

Loretta felt a pang of guilt as she looked at the frowning future bride. "Ooops. Sorry about that. I guess you've found your second love. I never found a first and doubt anyone will be interested in an opinionated woman like me." She lowered her dust mop at the exact moment Kaleb and his great-uncle stepped through the basement doorway below her descending duster. A cloud of debris puffed out. Speckles of dust rained down on the bald head of the man from the coffee shop.

"You." The man sputtered as he wiped his eyes and moustache.

"Make that a double ooops." Loretta started laughing and couldn't stop. The man in front of her looked like a befuddled Monopoly man. All he needed was a dark suit and top hat.

Soon everyone in the room began chuckling, including Kaleb's great-uncle.

"Could I trouble someone for a cleaning cloth? It seems I've been attacked by a dust mop." His smooth voice soothed something in Loretta's heart.

The twinkle in his eye looked familiar. Most likely the familiarity came from her reaction to him gazing her way at the coffee shop, but that didn't seem to explain something deep in the past. Loretta shook her head to clear her thoughts.

Honey stepped between Loretta and the great-uncle. "Follow me to the kitchen. There's water and hopefully a roll of paper towels to wipe with. We're down to dust rags at the moment."

He snickered. "A dust cloth might be what I need, but I will welcome the paper towels."

"I'm so sorry." Loretta trailed behind them after leaning the mop against a wall.

"No worries, Mrs. ..."

"It's Miss Loretta. I'm one of Honey's friends and you are Kaleb's great-uncle."

"You can call me Marshal. I'm sorry for staring at you earlier. Do we know each other?"

"I don't think so. Have we met?" Loretta watched as he wet a paper towel and scrubbed the dirt from his head. His cleaner visage revealed no clues to any familiarity.

"Did you grow up around here?" Marshal asked as he tossed the soiled paper into a trash bag hooked on a kitchen cabinet drawer.

"I lived here for about a year when I was a kid before we followed my military dad to our next home. I can't recall what year. There were so many schools in so many places. I moved here for semi-retirement about three years ago when a position opened up at the college." Loretta thought for a moment. "Traveling in the summers is a hobby of mine. Maybe we've crossed paths on a trip overseas."

A sad smile crossed his face. "I've never traveled abroad before. Someday I'd like to, but since my wife passed a year ago, I've been visiting places from my past."

"Am I guessing correctly that you lived here at some point?" Loretta looked him in his gray-blue eyes. The man was handsome in his own way.

"I did. I spent several years in this very house."

"I don't recall a Marshal on the list of ministers when we had our anniversary." Loretta had illustrated a cover for the booklet the congregation gave to those who attended the celebration last autumn.

"My dad was Bill Drake. We were here for about nine years. I was just a kid." A frown briefly crossed his face before a smile replaced it. "Did you come to church when he was the minister?"

Loretta shook her head. "We didn't go to church back then. I wouldn't have met you in a place of worship as a kid. I found the Lord during my graduate studies. I've been faithful since then." She paused as her thoughts slipped back to the vehicle tag on Marshal's truck. "I studied art at a college in Virginia. I saw ARTING on your tags. Maybe we met at an art school or event."

"My education was in California. After that, I went straight into a commercial art career in Chicago." Marshal looked puzzled.

"That can't be a connection. My art focus centers on painting portraits, landscapes, and exploring modern art with bright splashes of color. I encourage my students to enjoy the process of creating." She carefully observed the man's face, trying to figure out any relationship.

Honey's commanding voice interrupted their conversation. "Speaking of being creative, I could use some creative help with dusting and I'm sure Jonah could use help unloading boxes over at my house."

"Well, it is nice to meet you, Miss Loretta. I better go follow Preacher Jonah to Honey's house to unload." Marshal's smile did something strange to Loretta's heart. She fluttered her fingers at him and felt like a teenager.

Honey pushed the dust mop back into Loretta's hands. "Let's get this done so I can have a day of rest before my wedding."

~~~~

Loretta dabbed at her humid brow as she stood outside the church on Saturday. Lifting a prayer, she hoped the weatherman's predicted storm would wait until after the wedding. A few raindrops fell as clouds rolled across the sky like they were rushing to a sale at the mall craft store. She'd picked up several packs of prime quality canvas at those events. She'd hoped to have time to use one of those canvases for a portrait of the bride and groom, but they'd been too busy to accommodate a sitting. She'd have to snap a picture or two at their reception to complete her wedding gift. For now, they'd get an IOU.

Honey and Jonah's short romance, from Christmas to May, resulted in the whirlwind wedding taking place in two hours. She hooked the borrowed dress and printed scarves over her shoulder and entered the building as a whoosh of wind pulled the door from her grip. The dress fluttered in the strong breeze.

"Keep it open. I've got another basket of goodies for the reception." Annie from the historical museum rushed up the church steps. "Are you still able to help me set up?"

"I've got nothing better to do. I don't want to wear my bridesmaid dress any longer than needed." Loretta pulled the entry door closed and deposited the dress in the designated classroom before heading
~~~~

downstairs to the basement fellowship hall.

"Here are some vases and flowers that need to be arranged and then set out." Annie placed the disorganized collection in front of Loretta.

"I've got this." Creating an appealing arrangement soothed Loretta's artistic soul as she sorted and chose floral colors that complimented one another, creating small bouquets for each table. By the time she finished, the aroma of sausage coming from Annie's treats warming in trays made her tummy rumble.

Loretta approached the spread and admired the variety of desserts, vegetables, and meaty finger food. "I see you went beyond Honey's simple request for a few desserts."

"I wanted to make sure there was plenty for the whole congregation and outside friends." Annie laid serving spoons and tongs near each dish.

"Speaking of outside wedding guests, did you ever hear the name Marshal Drake? He's the youth minister's great-uncle and says he used to live here as a child."

"I doubt I would know anyone the age of a great-uncle. Besides, my family always attended the downtown church." Annie paused and arched an eyebrow. "It sounds like he might be in your age bracket. Is he handsome?"

"In a Monopoly man kind of way..." Loretta fanned her face and looked down at her watch. "I better get ready for my other duties today. I hope they run the air conditioner for the wedding."

Annie laughed as Loretta headed to the dressing room.

~~~~

Marshal stood at the back of the sanctuary and studied the stained-glass windows he'd admired as a budding childhood artist. The colors and stories depicted had entertained him many Sundays. Especially on days when he'd already heard pieces of his dad's sermon during the preceding week and didn't want to listen again. He'd hoped to see the windows on a sunny day during his visit, but the threatening clouds hovering outside darkened their hues. Worry about possible storm damage to his camper flickered across his mind. A distant rumble did nothing to take away his concerns.

A middle-aged man escorting people to their seats interrupted his thoughts. "Would you like to sit on the bride or groom's side?"

"Either side works for me." Marshal followed his escort midway up the aisle to a pew already occupied by an older fellow and a much younger man. He acknowledged his pew companions with a nod. "I'm Marshal Drake. Thanks for sharing your pew with me."

The older gentleman glared. "You're not Marshal. You're his old man. I'd know you anywhere. Why'd you make my buddy leave town? We had fun times."
~~~~

The younger man interrupted. "Sorry. My Grandpa gets a little confused. I'm Daniel and Grandpa is Gerald."

"Gerald Barnes?" Marshal couldn't believe he'd found his old friend.

"Yes. That's Grandpa's name." Daniel raised his eyebrows.

"Gerald, it's me. I'm still Marshal, but I've gotten older. I guess I do kind of look like Dad, now that you mention it." Marshal laid a hand on Gerald's arm.

Gerald snorted. "You sure about that, Mr. Drake?"

"I'm as sure as our password. Do you remember 'double-bubble-dare-time'?"

Gerald's eyes opened wide as his voice boomed. "Hush, Marshal! Did you ever find where Patricia hid your sketch book? I hope she didn't see our secret coded message. We'll be in big trouble if she figures out what we did last week."

Daniel shushed his grandpa, while curious people swiveled to look at the trio. Thunder roared from outside the building as a soloist stepped to the podium, drawing their focus back to the wedding taking place.

Gerald leaned closer to Marshal. "Let's go have some fun after church."

Marshal nodded and placed a finger over his lips as a sweet melody filled the air. The music was a song he'd not heard before. The woman sitting in front of him whispered something about the piece coming from a musical Honey had been involved with. Interesting... He'd have to ask Kaleb about that event.

When the soloists finished, the processional began. Instead of flowers, each of the attendants, both men and women held a chunky lavender colored candle. The soothing scent filled the auditorium as each participant made their way to the front. Loretta, the woman he'd met the day before, wore a light green dress with a bright multicolored scarf looped around her neck. The other older woman had a similar outfit with a more subdued scarf.

Gerald raised his hand as the second woman passed by. "Hi, sweet Annie. Are we having something good for supper?" The woman smiled at Gerald and nodded.

Marshal's focus kept returning to Loretta. Even after the bride and groom took their places, his gaze returned to the woman. There was something about her eyes that seemed so familiar, but he couldn't place where he'd seen them before.

His great-nephew's preaching voice broke into his thoughts. "You may now be seated."

"About time." Gerald's grumbles echoed through the auditorium. Muffled laughter filled the room.

Kaleb began by reading the traditional wedding ceremony from the minister's manual. "Dearly beloved, we are gathered here today to join in marriage Jonah Farmer and Honey Beekerman."

"Did he say she was a honeybee?" Gerald leaned over to whisper in Marshal's ear. "I've seen her with my honey, Annabelle. Those ladies sometimes get into trouble like us."

Quiet snickering reached Marshal's ears from the pews behind and in front of where he sat. He started to lift his finger to his lips again when a gust of wind shook the windows of the church. The swish of rain coursing down the roof and the outside walls of the church was deafening.

Gerald leaned forward and cupped a hand near his right ear. At least he didn't say anything out loud.

Kaleb spoke louder over the noise until the lights flickered and then went dark. "The time has come to say their vows." He paused and lifted the manual closer to his eyes. "I may need to borrow a candle."

Several people laughed as Loretta lifted her candle toward Kaleb.

Preacher Jonah stopped her. "No worries. I've got this part memorized." He led the echoed vows and then added some words of his own.

His bride, Honey, had her say, too, and then they proceeded with the final words of the marriage ceremony.

Kaleb pronounced Jonah and Honey husband and wife at the same moment a roaring sound filled the air. A siren blared.

"Everyone to the reception hall in the basement," Kaleb announced.

People headed downstairs.

"Good. Now we can eat." Gerald allowed Daniel and Marshal to lead him to the basement.

Marshal noted the new addition of a ramp leading to the downstairs hall. It made the journey easier for Gerald's hobbling steps.

Sirens continued to blare as everyone found a secure spot to sit. The wedding party placed their candles around the room for minimal lighting. Bunsen burner candles under warm food also provided subdued illumination while keeping plates heated.

A woman standing near the food table invited people to come and enjoy the refreshments. "We might as well enjoy the reception goodies. We've all been through a few mid-west tornado warnings."

Several people chuckled. Everyone formed a line behind Honey, Jonah, and the wedding party. Marshal and Daniel followed the crowd through the line and helped Gerald choose some favorite snacks.

"Do you still like pigs in a blanket?" Marshal knew those had been Gerald's favorite when they were kids.

"I don't recall not liking them." Gerald looked at Marshal. "How did you know my favorite food, Mr. Drake? Can Marshal come out to play after supper?"

"Sure. Maybe you can visit at the parsonage after we eat." Marshal answered without correcting his old friend. He realized he wouldn't mind another visit to the old house, knowing the preacher would move his last belongings out after the honeymoon. Since his great-nephew now had the parsonage key, he'd ask Kaleb about checking it out before he left town.

The basement lights flickered back on. The crowd cheered when the siren went silent.

After the bride and groom shared their cake, parishioners began to filter out. One of the early departing guests rushed back into the fellowship hall.

"Hey, Preacher Jonah. Something is wrong with the parsonage."

Marshal strode to the nearest exit and headed toward the parsonage. Daniel and Gerald followed close behind. The building looked mostly intact, but bricks from the chimney littered the roof and yard. Miraculously, the roof seemed intact except for right around the area where the chimney for a centrally located shaft had blown asunder during the storm.

"We need to check the interior." Marshal ran to the front door and shook the knob. Nothing moved. He'd have to wait for the key.

"Did you lose your key, Mr. Drake?" Gerald had followed Marshal and managed to climb onto the porch. "I want to go see Marshal."

"Someone's bringing the key now." Marshal gave his old friend a pat on the back.

Kaleb pushed through the gathering crowd with the key and opened the door. As they entered, Marshal spotted a few bricks scattered around the base of the living room hearth. His family had never used the condemned chimney. The church had closed the drafty flue with a metal plate long before the Drake family arrived. That shield now lay on the floor strewn with fallen bricks.

Marshal waved toward the stairs. "There's another fireplace connected to this chimney on the second floor. We need to see if that room has damage."

His sister had bragged many times about how she decorated the mantelpiece for holidays. She'd often reminded him about Santa coming to her bedroom first at Christmas because of the fireplace.

Kaleb and Jonah rushed up the stairs. Honey climbed up the steps behind her new husband. Marshal started to follow.

Gerald grabbed his arm and held him back. "Look. I see Marshal's sketchbook. Can you help me get it, Mr. Drake? Marshal has been looking for his book."

Gerald pointed to a dusty page hanging down from the damper above the firebox. Marshal leaned deep into the space and wriggled the old book free. "You're right, Gerald. It looks like I've found the long-lost drawings."

Gerald smiled. "Will you make sure Marshal gets them back? We don't want Patricia to find out we told the gossip girls about her crush on that guy at your church."

"I will." Marshal laughed at the memory. He rubbed grime from the cover of the book on the side of his pants leg. Patricia must have stuffed his sketches down the shaft in her upstairs bedroom. He'd give her a call tonight and let her know he'd found out her secret hiding place after all these years. Flipping through the pages, he spotted several colored pencil drawings he had sketched as an assignment for a school art class.

One featured a girl who'd only been in class a few weeks before moving away. Her eyes were intriguing to draw because of an interesting speckle on one of her green eyes. When the teacher had asked the students to draw a portrait of the person sitting across from them, he'd felt the flush of a first crush wash across his neck. The girl's cheeks held a bright pink as he captured her face and multicolored top with his penciled lines.

Gerald leaned closer. "Are you still crushing on Loretta? She moved away a year ago and now you're moving too. I'm going to miss you, Marshall."

"I've missed you, too, Gerald. I'm back now, and so is Loretta." Marshal felt relieved that Gerald finally acknowledged his true identity and solved the mystery of how he knew Loretta. "I'm going to the church to see if I can find her right now. You can come with me if you want."

Gerald smiled. His eyes seemed to focus on his grandson, Daniel, before returning to look at Marshal with a blank stare. "Hi. Do I know you?"

Marshal returned Gerald's smile. "We've been friends for a long time. I'll be seeing you again. I believe I might be staying in the area for a while."

Daniel wrapped his hand around his grandfather's elbow. "I think we'll head home for now. Feel free to come and visit my grandparents any time."

The younger man led Gerald away as Marshal tucked the notebook under his arm and made his way back to the reception hall.

~~~~

Loretta stayed at the church as the others ran to check out the damage at the parsonage. She hated that the old house had suffered damage. Maybe she'd paint a picture of the way it used to be for the background behind Honey and Preacher Jonah's wedding portrait. She tugged at the uncomfortable dress. Since everyone rushed away, she'd make a quick exit of her own to put on her comfortably bright street clothes.

It only took a few minutes to change and make her way back to the basement to help Annie with her cleaning efforts. The busy woman had already packed up most of the food in disposable containers by the time
~~~~

Loretta returned.

Annie brushed her hands on the serving apron she'd worn. "Honey and Jonah suggested taking leftover food to the soup kitchen downtown. I've taken care of everything except the top layer of the wedding cake. They should keep that in the freezer for their first anniversary."

"I agree." Loretta surveyed the messy room. "I'll start cleaning the tables while you box up their cake." She gathered up the bouquets she'd assembled and placed them on a shelf near the kitchen. "We can put these out for the church services tomorrow." She grabbed a dampened rag and began wiping crumbs from tables. Annie joined her and they made quick work of the mess.

Loretta stretched her back while she waited on Annie to locate a vacuum to finish their chore. She turned. Someone was staring at her again. Looking at one of the entrances to the basement, she spotted Marshal.

"Are you watching me for some reason?"

He walked closer to her, lifted a sketchbook beside her face, and grinned. He lowered the book and held it open to the portrait of a young girl. Loretta gasped. It was her image.

She looked into Marshal's eyes. Recognition engulfed her mind. "Did you used to have red hair and freckles?"

"Yes." Smile lines crinkled at the sides of his eyes as his lips tipped upwards.

Her face warmed. That red-haired boy had made her nervous in a sweet way. She still had an occasional thought about his awkward teasing and wondered what had happened to him after they moved. He'd made an impression on her. From later life experiences, she realized his efforts were probably an attempt to flirt.

The fact that Marshal was grinning and winking at the moment only confirmed her thoughts.

Loretta placed a hand over her rapidly beating heart. "I always wondered what happened to you after we moved."

Marshal took her free hand in his. "I'd love to tell you all about my life since then. Would you like to come to church with me tomorrow? I'd love to take you out to eat afterwards. I'm available if you are."

Loretta nodded. It was all she could manage, other than smiling and taking his other hand in hers. Was it too soon to start thinking about another whirlwind wedding? Only time would tell.

~~~~~

Dear Reader,
I hope you enjoyed Loretta and Marshal's reunion. You may
~~~~~

recognize Loretta from my last book in the *On Cue Series* published by Mt. Zion Ridge Press (*On Cue, Free to Love, Hoping for Treasure*.) In *Hoping for Treasure*, Loretta revealed herself as a take charge person in the midst of a touching situation. She, Honey, and Annabelle were major players in a short Christmas story called *Stolen Gift Exchange*. If you like a little suspense in your life, please check out *Hidden Names*. Loretta's home plays a role in *Hidden Names*. Look for the second and third books in that series to become a reality in the near future.

If you have little ones in your life, I would love for you to check out my children's books. See the website below for a full listing.

I am thankful to my wonderful critique partner, Ann Cavera. Many thanks go to Michelle Levigne for her amazing editing skills and willingness to take on this project. A thank you goes to my swim buddy, Pat, for sharing her story of an unbelievable, but true, family wedding full of storms, snakes, loss of electricity, and other tornado disasters. I decided to leave the snake out of this one for the sake of my snake-hating husband, who tolerates my hogging the computer to write fictional tales. The ultimate glory for my writing goes to God, the true creator of all things.

Blessings,

Bettie Boswell
https://sites.google.com/view/bettieboswellauthorillustrator/home

Doorways
Moriah Mulligan
Student Finalist
Delaware Christian Schools

The door — teal and bright as the sky. It's the first thing you see when you look at it. That's why my mom bought the house, she used to say. She wanted to match the sky. I heard Dad say once it was because it matched Ma's eyes. I liked the way Ma smiled when he said that.

There's a little table in the hallway when you walk in. Ma would decorate it with seasonal decor — always buying more every year like we would run out if she didn't. There was one decoration she would never change. It was a bright hand-painted rooster figurine. My older sister, Bella and I would play with it when we were little. I lost it once. Last spanking I ever remember. Dad loved that rooster; I loved it too. I would turn it over in my hands and trace the initials carved on the bottom. *Papi.* That was what we called Grandpa.

"Careful! Careful!" Ma had yelled at Dad and me as we strained our backs to haul a sofa through the front door.

I smiled at Dad. We had made a bet that Ma would lose her ever-loving mind watching us struggle through the hallway.

"Oh dear Lord!" she had screamed.

"If you're gonna faint, hon, don't watch!" my dad yelled. "Put it down, son, I need to readjust my grip here — "

We set it down slowly and he used his shirt to wipe the perspiration beading on his porous skin. It was a hot mid-summer day and not one breeze came through the open door. After catching our breath, we got ready to take it to the living room, bending down to get a hold on the couch. *Rrrriiipppp!* Dad's eyebrows shot up from over the opposite sofa arm and he turned as red as the wine-colored furniture we carried. Letting go of the couch, he shot up to attention like a rigid military man.

"Let's take a pause for a minute, I need to go get some water."

Ma and I watch him saunter away with a gaping hole in his britches — his tighty whities showcased for the world to see. We tried to hold in our laughter...we really did, but to no avail. We laughed till our sides hurt and then snickered the rest of the day. Dad was so embarrassed we didn't move that couch out of the front hallway until Christmas. Then Ma decided she liked it better in the hallway anyway and had us move it again.

I feel sorry for our carpet. Bella and I abused him. He endured countless milk spills from eating cereal in front of the TV, accidents from our dog, crumbs, gum, dust, and the chronic family problem of neglecting to vacuum. But maybe he deserved it, you know? He may possibly be the ugliest living room carpet I have ever seen. No offense, Mr. Carpet, sir — it's just true.

Sometimes I would peek into our dining room when I was little, like I'm doing now, and wonder why we never used it. It sat in lonesome silence with its cabinet of china sitting in the darkness. We used it once — when Bella brought over her date for Senior Prom and Ma got a little giddy. She wanted to show off, I guess. Suppose it worked out, Bella's married to the guy now. Wish Ma would've done that for me...

I love that smooth, shiny, granite island countertop. I'd stare at it when Ma was making me PB&Js and try to imagine pictures out of the streaks and blocks of color. I always thought that blob right there looked like an elephant; that one right there is a pencil; and that one over there always reminded me of a monkey, but looking at it now, I don't know why. When Grandma was over we'd make sugar cookies and she'd make me roll the dough out or I wouldn't get any. Those were the best sugar cookies in the world — soft, buttery, with the slightest crust around the outside that would melt away when it hit my tongue. This was the spot where I was when I heard Papi had died. Dad told us after dinner, while we stood all around this countertop. It had been the first time someone had died in my life. That was the first time I had heard my family quiet all together. The first time Bella was rendered speechless. The first time I saw Dad cry. He sat at the kitchen table all night. Staring at the hand-painted rooster.

Once Bella and I snuck downstairs at midnight and ate animal crackers in the pantry. We thought it was a naughty thing to do when we were seven and nine. It was in the dim yellow kitchen light we made a pact to never tell our parents. They were always adamant about our bedtimes. To this day, I have no idea if Dad and Ma ever found out. I wish staying up till midnight was still naughty.

We have two spouts in our kitchen sink. One is for regular water, and another smaller one for drinking water. I remember once in eighth grade Bella had invited one of her high school friends for homework. She was the only friend of my sister's who would talk to me. I liked her. She once asked me for water. I fumbled around the kitchen, ecstatic that she had asked me, the awkward younger brother, for a glass of water. Bella teased me about it for days after. Her friend moved away that spring. I wonder how she is doing now...

Dark, expressive woody grain runs lengthwise down the table in our kitchen. Except for that side. The tree fibers stop. Abruptly. Yellow wood pokes through the bashed-up stain. It was my fault. I tripped trying to carry too many things at once. My school books, my dinner, my hockey helmet, and my glass of orange juice all toppled over at astonishing speed toward the unassuming table. Story of my life. I always had the overconfidence that I could carry it all—and it came back to give me splinters later.

Dad's angry yells always stung and hit where he meant them to—right where it hurt most. It was twelve or something at night, I don't really remember; late enough that Bella and Ma were asleep when it happened. I'm glad Dad hadn't woke them up after I had called to tell him I wrecked his car—his reaction was enough to deal with that night. Over and over, he reminded me how I could have been responsible for serious injury or worse—all because I ran a red light. Everything he said added to my shame, like pouring liquid on an already soaked towel; adding to the heaviness of it all and watching my tears stream down because I was unable to hold it all in. There came a time when he stopped yelling at me and left me to wallow in my mistake. I stopped at the bottom of the stairs, unable to walk up and go to bed. It seemed impossible after a night like that.

That sturdy hand landed on my shoulder as I stood there and his deep voice, tender and suddenly not as sharp as before spoke:

"I'm glad you're okay, son." Dad's gentle words always stung and hit where he meant them to—right where it mattered most. I remember breaking down and crying as he gave me one of his strong bear-like hugs. After a while my sobbing stopped. He suddenly asked, "Did I ever tell you about the one time I backed up into your grandpa's pickup truck?"

I looked at him, surprised, and he gave me a smirk as we both sat down on the bottom step of the stairs and I began to hear all about my dad's misadventures. That was quite possibly the best worst day of my life. Now, lingering on the bottom step, I find it difficult to go up again.

Everyone walks up stairs differently. Some go flat-footed, some on their toes; some land their foot on the edge of the stair, some in the middle; some use the banister, some trust their balance. When I was littler I crawled up stairs on all fours because I was convinced it got me to the top faster. I guess I can't do that now, people would give me weird looks, seeing as I am no longer nine. I'm going up the stairs slowly now. Today, I would rather take my time.

I can't explain it, but I used to have an irrational fear of going into my parents' bedroom at night. Why? I don't know. I just remember having to admit I wet the bed when I was six once, and standing at the edge of the darkness, trying to will myself to go in there. I couldn't do it. Call me a coward, but I couldn't face the darkness—or maybe it was my parents. I slept on the couch that night and had some explaining to do in the morning.

Why do they put Jacuzzis in master bathrooms? Nobody I know who has one has ever used it. My parents never did—not that I know of, anyway. They never let me use it either. I suppose just knowing you have one makes you feel more luxurious or something. At least, that's the only reason I can think of to justify having one if you're never going to utilize the thing.

The only time I ever went into my sister's bedroom was Christmas Eve (and, well of course, today). I'd always sleep in a sleeping bag on the floor so we could see who could stay up the longest. It's up for debate, but I'm confident I had the longest winning streak.

My bedroom. My sanctuary. My haven. My place of peaceful solitude. Those four faded misty blue walls. That obnoxious Spider-man bed covering (as if I haven't aged a day over twelve). Before I left for college, Ma assured me my room would be the same when I came back. Nothing beats the feeling of walking into your own room. That feeling as if you belong; as if the room wouldn't look the same if you weren't in it; as if it missed you while you were away. Except that Ma lied. It's empty without the hockey trophies, the miniature car collection, the old movie stubs, the Pittsburgh Penguin posters, the many Star Wars Lego sets displayed proudly atop the dusty dresser. All my things there—in that lone box sitting on the floor.

It's weird walking through a place you'll never be again. Everything has a certain somber wilt to it. A foreboding sense that from here, things change. As I take my box past our bedrooms, past the useless Jacuzzi, down the stairs, past that bottom step, past our bashed-up kitchen table, over that ugly living room carpet (the only thing I'm glad to see go), through the foyer, past the hallway couch, I can't help but wonder what happens to the things I leave behind. Will I remember the snack runs Bella and I would steal at midnight? Will I remember the way the countertop looked? The way Grandma's cookies tasted? The smell of our dining room table sitting solus in the dark? The messes Bella and I made on that carpet? Will I remember Dad's sheepish expression when he ripped his pants? Or the time I lost Papi's wooden rooster?

"Is that everything?" Bella asks as I place my box inside the trunk of an overburdened minivan.

"That's the last of my stuff," I reluctantly reply. Bella, Ma and I linger in the front yard and drink in that house of ours. Quaint yet chock-full of memories. I suddenly find myself pining after those times, longing to be back, to experience them just as vividly. It's scary to think of forgetting them.

A man with a black suit walks across the lawn and stands expectantly next to me. I reach into my back pocket and pull out a worn golden key, handing it to the realtor who reaches to receive it. I look at the worn key that presses against my palm, feel the grooves as I run my thumb across it, hold back stubborn tears suddenly stinging my eyes. Something sharp pricks my heart as it leaves my hand.

"It'll be up on the market tomorrow." The man smiles. I nod, trying to return the expression, if only for Ma who watches silently with puffy eyes.

Slowly Ma, Bella and I enter the car. I watch the house in the rear-view mirror as I hesitantly move forward. Shining back at us is the door: teal like the sky.

"I love that door," Ma whispers affectionately.

"It matches your eyes," I respond. Ma smiles faintly, but not like she used to when Dad was here.

The End

Moriah Mulligan started writing when she was nine years old and hasn't stopped. Outside of writing, she leads a busy life as a highschooler in Delaware, Ohio. She enjoys making music, singing and playing multiple instruments. Her other hobbies include drama, competitive Irish dance, reading and running. You can contact her at *moriahmulligan.D4@gmail.com*. Moriah is excited to refine her storytelling skills and looks forward to pursuing more writing opportunities in the future. To God be the glory!

Friday Night
Sarah Choi
Student Finalist
Cuyahoga Valley Christian Academy

Nina Lovat did not believe in ghosts.

But she did watch a lot of movies that involved them. She enjoyed being scared.

Right now, though, at 9:00 p.m. on a Friday, she had put her horror marathon on hold for a critical decision. SweetTart Ropes, or Sour Patch Kids? Or both? That was the question. The sweet filling or the sour sugar coating? Fortunately, or unfortunately, Sheetz had plenty of options.

"Tough choice, huh?" a male voice said.

She looked up to see a smiling man in his thirties standing next to her, with a dark buzzcut, bright blue eyes, and a chipped front tooth.

"Yep," said Nina. She grabbed packs of both candies and hurried away down the aisle. Her keys jingled reassuringly in her pockets. Maybe it was a bad idea for a seventeen-year-old girl to be out this late, but she had a mission.

She paid for her candy and headed outside.

"Wait, miss!" The man was approaching her.

Her heart leapt. Irrationally, she told herself. She hadn't even left the glow of the Sheetz's fluorescent lights.

"Here, you dropped this," he said, holding something out to her. She took a cautious step forward — it was her library card.

"Oh, thanks," she said, taking the card.

"No problem. Good thing it wasn't your driver's license, right? Well, have a nice night!" he responded with a cheerful smile, walking away toward his car.

Nina got in her own vehicle and pulled away from the station, heading away from the light toward home. She liked the route — there were multiple unlit stretches, which only contributed to the dark and pleasantly eerie mood. Radio on, candy to enjoy later. She rolled the window down just a crack to allow some air in from the cool night.

Darkness, fresh air, all the nice things.

Suddenly, her headlights began to flicker, the car slowing slightly. She swerved and steered to the side of the road. And then the car stopped completely, and all the lights went out, and the darkness wasn't so nice anymore.

Nina reached for her phone. It was dead.

"Crap," she muttered. "No, no, no."

Don't panic, Nina. That's how people die in horror movies. But how do they stay alive? Phone doesn't work. Lights are out. Everything's dead…SOS button.

She reached up and pressed the button, heart pounding.

A second passed. Nothing. Did she press it hard enough? This button still worked when the car was dead, right? That was the point. And then, to her instant relief, a cool female voice spoke:

"Hello, what's your emergency?"

"My car stopped working. I think it's dead. I'm on the side of the road."

"All right, we're tracking your location. We'll send someone over. Please remain calm and stay in your car."

"Okay."

"Are you alone?"

"Yes."

"All right. It's going to be okay. Has this happened before?"

"No," said Nina, but there was no response. She waited. The call must have dropped or something. *Weird*, she thought as she sat there, wondering how long it would take for help to arrive. But at least someone answered the call.

Suddenly, she saw a light. She looked up, fear filling her. There was a person walking toward her car, their outline barely visible behind the glare of a flashlight.

As the person got closer, they directed the beam of the flashlight up so that Nina could see their features, though they were distorted by shadow. The person appeared to be a young man with pale hair and dark eyes. He stopped directly outside her window.

She huddled back in her seat. What did she do now? Did he have a weapon?

"Hello, miss?" he said, leaning down to peer in.

She was going to die, going to die out here, going to be murdered. "What do you want?"

"I'm sorry to scare you, but you need to come with me."

"What?" Nina looked up at him, then back down.

"I can't explain, there's not much time, but you're in danger."

Of course I am.

"There's a man out here tonight who's dangerous. He's crazy. He's around this area, and you can't stay in your car here."

Yeah, of course I'm believing you. "A dangerous guy?"

"Yes. I've seen him. He's about this tall," he indicated by holding his hand a bit lower than the top of his head. "Dark buzzcut, blue eyes."

A pause. Nina felt cold. "Did he have a chipped front tooth?"

"You've seen him, too. He's around here. You can't stay in your car."

But should she trust him? Nina had seen a man who fit that exact description, but that didn't have to mean anything. This guy could be his henchman or something. Maybe he wanted to lull her into a sense of safety, then take her somewhere where no one would hear her screams. Or maybe he was just some druggie looking for who-knows-what.

"Why should I trust you?" she asked.

The guy stood silent for a few seconds. He twirled the flashlight, making the beam of light circle in the dark. "I don't know," he said. "I don't know, but I've seen this guy, and I know he's dangerous. He's insane. And he's around this area. You've seen him, too."

He looked up sharply. He turned, and Nina craned her neck to see what he was looking at. Off in the distance, there was a faint glow of headlights.

"Please," said the guy.

The lights were getting closer.

Nina took a deep breath, trying and failing to calm her nerves. She grabbed her keys, phone, and wallet, and stepped out of her car.

"Come on." He set off into the grass. He kept the flashlight in front of him; Nina stayed close behind, her heart racing.

Where had this guy come from? Why should she believe him? More likely than not, that car coming down the road was someone who could help her. Why was she now running through the darkness with this guy who was probably some serial killer?

The guy, pausing for a second, turned the flashlight around and swept it in an arc in front of him, but Nina couldn't see his face in the dark.

"Where are we going?" she asked.

He didn't respond. Off in the distance behind her, where the flashlight was pointing, the headlights were slowing.

"Come on," he said. "He probably sees your car." He turned and continued to run.

She considered not following, but she didn't feel like being left in the dark in the middle of a field, so she sprinted to catch up with the light. Once she caught up with him, Nina noticed that the guy wasn't moving as fast anymore. He was pointing the flashlight at something up ahead.

"There," he said. Nina was thoroughly out of breath, but the guy didn't seem to be tired at all. She looked where the beam was directed and saw a lone house a little ways off.

The guy continued walking toward the house. She followed warily.

They were approaching the building from the side, so they wandered around to the front. It was old — peeling blue paint, sagging front steps, some windows with old curtains pulled closed behind them and some boarded up.

"What is this place?" asked Nina. She wondered if maybe she had driven by the building before, but didn't recognize it in the darkness. Or maybe she wouldn't have noticed it at all — why would a random derelict house hold any meaning for her when she was safe and sound with a working car and phone?

"I don't think anyone's home," said the guy. "Come on, we should see if we can go inside."

Nina balked.

"Please," he said, turning to look at her. "This isn't a trap."

"I'm sorry," she said, feeling a lump rising in her throat now that the adrenaline of running had worn off. "I'm not sure why I'm here."

"I promise I won't hurt you," said the guy. "I know that sounds stupid. But please. You can't go back to your car just yet. It's not safe."

What was this nightmare? Nina felt fairly sure her life was about to end right here, right now. And yet something was telling her she could trust this guy. She didn't know what — maybe she really was dreaming, but that didn't seem likely. She followed him up the steps.

The guy stood in front of the door, gazing at it strangely.

"Do you think it's locked?" he said.

Nina reached out and turned the knob. The door opened without much difficulty; she stepped inside, the guy following, and she shut the door behind her, careful not to make too much noise. She flipped the switch next to the door. To her surprise, the lights cut on, illuminating a bare room with dust lining the walls and floor and an old light fixture hanging from the ceiling. The space had a musty smell like an old church or grandmother's house, just not nearly as reassuring.

Now able to see the guy in the old light, Nina took in his appearance. He couldn't have been much older than her — eighteen or nineteen at the most. He had short, straight blond hair and dark brown eyes and was wearing jeans and a jacket over a dark t-shirt. He certainly didn't look threatening; slight shadows darkened under his eyes, his hair messy, and yet he stood alert like a deer who had just heard a strange noise. Since he didn't look like he was hiding a knife or a gun, Nina tried to think more logically again.

"What were you doing?" she asked. "I mean, you said there was a crazy guy and it wasn't safe for me to be in my car. Why were you just out walking?"

"I wasn't—" The guy stopped. He blinked a couple times, looking rather confused. "I wasn't." He didn't continue.

"So what were you doing?"

"I saw you and knew you needed help."

"But how did you know? How did you know about this man?"

The guy was staring past Nina with a faraway look in his eyes.

"I met him. I was riding my bike down the road earlier, and I saw his car pulled over. I stopped to see if he needed help, but he pulled a knife on me and threatened me. We got in a fight and he hit me on the head, I think, because I passed out and woke up in a ditch. He must be deranged enough that he just left me there, but he stole my bike. I guess he must have lost this flashlight, though. That was convenient, 'cause I lost my phone. I wasn't hurt, so I just started walking and saw your car. I figured you needed help. I guess I just thought it'd be more likely that you'd be in danger, not another crazy person. And he's still out there. You've seen him."

Nina wasn't sure the story made sense, exactly, though the guy spoke with an air of fear that seemed hard to fake. The man might have been insane, but why would he just leave a witness on the side of the road? She wanted to ask more questions, but then the guy walked over to the door.

"I think he's gone now," he said. "Did you call someone? For help?"

"Yeah. They should get here soon."

"Okay. Let's go."

He stood there watching Nina, who moved forward to open the door. He stepped outside, turning his flashlight back on. She followed him. As she left the dull smell of the house and reentered the cool night air, she felt a strange, uncomfortable sense, like she was leaving a safe place behind. But that was nonsense, right? The house was creepy, anyway. They walked down the steps, then hurried back across the grass toward the road, the guy seeming to know exactly where he was going.

Soon they were back at Nina's car, which looked unfamiliar in the dark.

"Here we are," said the guy. "Look, someone's coming."

Nina looked up to see headlights approaching once again. This time, as the lights got closer, Nina could tell they were emitted by a truck.

"Well, that's good," said the guy. "Hope your car gets fixed. Take care. I'm Malcolm, by the way."

"Thanks. I'm Nina."

He gave her a quick smile and began to walk away. For a second, she wanted to call out, to ask him questions such as why he was heading straight into the darkness that supposedly contained crazy people and potential murderers. But by the time she shielded her eyes against the glare of the lights, he was gone.

~~~~~

One week later, it was a dull Friday night, and Nina was flipping through channels trying to kill time—she had found some true crime documentary, but there were commercial breaks about every five minutes.
~~~~~

And—she didn't quite want to admit it—the story about some crazy guy who followed a girl's car hit a little too close for comfort. She paused on a news broadcast, where a reporter with a severe bob haircut was speaking to the camera.

"—police are still trying to find the killer."

Nina's heart thumped.

"The body of nineteen-year-old Malcolm Sands was recovered from a ditch last Friday before sundown. He had been stabbed in the chest multiple times, and the body is thought to have been there for at least a couple of days."

A picture of a young man flashed up on the screen. Nina felt a chill go down her spine. She recognized that face, those dark eyes and that pale hair.

"Oh no," she said. "No."

He didn't make it after all. That crazy guy must've found him again, and who knew? Maybe it was Nina's fault, maybe he had been caught right after he walked away from her, maybe—She didn't want to think about it.

But something was off. Nina couldn't quite put her finger on it, but something didn't make sense at all.

She had been at the Sheetz on Friday, she knew that. But the body had been found before dark and had supposedly been there for some time. But she had left the Sheetz well after dark... Something wasn't clicking. Someone had to be wrong. Maybe they were all wrong, but she doubted that.

The guy had told her who the killer was. Was she supposed to do something about that? Tell the police? What evidence did she have, though? Would they believe a seventeen-year-old girl with no proof except her own experiences? Would they believe her if she told them she had met—

Until now, Nina Lovat did not believe in ghosts.

The End

Sarah Choi is a graduating senior from Cuyahoga Valley Christian Academy. She has been telling stories since she was little. Currently, she enjoys participating in her school's award-winning Academic Challenge program and Speech and Debate team, where she competes in Informative Speaking. She also plays piano and likes to read and write fiction when she gets the chance. When she graduates, she would like to study in the field of engineering. She hopes someday to publish a full-length novel.

Heist at the Lightkeeper's House
Penny Frost McGinnis

Unable to sleep, Zach Hudson, the local naturalist and protector of wildlife, hiked to the nearby lighthouse for some quiet time. Perched on a rock beneath the great light, he watched the water crash to shore. His love for the lake had grown from years of studying the fauna and flora in the region. He let his shoulders relax as he listened to the sounds of the lake's rise and fall. At midnight, the deafening sound and forceful wind from the angry waves diminished any distractions.

He wrestled with his future as he closed his eyes and prayed. How did twenty years as a naturalist on the shores of Lake Erie, Ohio, translate into a new life in Seldom Seen, South Carolina? Sure, his cousin begged him to move, and a tempting job offer sat in his inbox. While steaming summers offered little appeal, excitement welled in him at the thought of new plants and animals to study and the opportunity to educate students about the environment. To anyone who knew Zach, he came off as a geek, but he didn't mind. He'd grown into himself over the years and accepted who he was.

An hour later, with feet wet from the lake water, he trudged home to his cottage near the lighthouse. Fifteen years ago, he'd secured the lakefront rental on the mainland and loved his view of Abbott Island, about twenty minutes away by ferry. How would he choose between a lake or mountain view out his window?

~~~~~

Seven o'clock on Sunday morning, a knock at the door startled Zach. Dressed for church, he plunked his coffee cup on the table and answered. A police officer he recognized from his work at Abbott Island's nature preserves tipped his cap.

"Good morning. Are you Zach Hudson?"

Zach nodded. "Yes."

"I'm Officer Levi Swenson and if you don't mind, I'd like to ask you a few questions."

Zach waved his hand to the open living space. "Sure. Come in and sit. Would you like coffee?"

Levi lowered to the sofa. "No, thanks." He pulled a notepad and pen from his pocket.

In the chair opposite the couch, Zach sat and crossed his ankles.
~~~~~

"This won't take long." Levi cleared his throat. "We've had an incident in town. Will you tell me where you were last night between midnight and one in the morning?"

Zach scrubbed his hand down his bearded chin. "I took a walk to the lighthouse, sat on a rock and watched the waves for about an hour, then walked home." He squinted at the officer. "What's going on?"

Zach scribbled on his notepad. "Someone robbed the lightkeeper's house last night at the time you were there. We saw you on the security camera as you walked onto the property, then the camera went dark."

"I hate to hear they were robbed, but I didn't see anything or hear anyone. The water roared last night." Zach pushed his shoulder-length hair behind his neck and wished he'd tied it back.

"Whoever did this stole money and some antique pieces the volunteers had collected." He tucked the pad and pen in his pocket and stood. "Since you were on the grounds, stay close. You are a person of interest."

Zach tugged himself from the seat. "I didn't do anything. Why even consider me?"

Levi walked to the door. "You were on the property when the robbery took place. We have a timestamp from the video of when you arrived and no way to know when you left." He opened the door. "I'll be in touch."

Zach plopped on his cushy couch, stunned by the officer's news.

~~~~~

The sun shone the next morning, making the water sparkle like diamonds. Zach had climbed out of bed Monday morning at six and ran three miles. At eight, he boarded the ferry to Abbott Island, a fifteen-minute ride. He leaned against the side of the ferry and watched the lighthouse and his cottage on the shore fade away.

How could Officer Swenson accuse him of burglary? He'd lived in the area for twenty years, not counting the summers he had spent on Abbott Island with his family. He worked for the state as a naturalist and had, as far as he knew, an excellent reputation.

When the ferry docked, Zach rode his bicycle to the natural resource office to clock in. He planned to photograph and document the lakeside daisies today. He'd studied them for years but never tired of their beauty. Then, he'd check on birding sites and clear any debris on the trails.

As he walked up the path to the station, Ranger Alexa Papadakis met him. He'd befriended Alexa when she joined the rangers a year ago. Her dad, Johnny made the best Greek and American food in his restaurant on the island.

"Morning, Zach. It's good to see you. How's your day going?"

He forced a smile. "I'm doing okay. How about you?"
~~~~~

Her Greek heritage showed in her glowing olive skin. "I'm fine, but I sense you aren't."

He figured he needed to talk to someone besides himself. In the year he'd known her, she never gave him reason to doubt her. "Got a minute?"

"Sure, what's up?"

He led her to a nearby shelter, and they sat at a picnic table. A piney scent settled over them.

Zach folded his hands in front of him. "Two things. I'm considering a move to South Carolina, and I'm in trouble with the law."

Alexa jumped from her seat. "Whoa. What?" She paced across the concrete. "You're moving and haven't told me, and you did something illegal?"

He waved his arms in the air. "No, no, no. I've done nothing wrong. They think I have. Sit down, please."

She perched on the wooden bench and tapped her fingers on the table.

"Saturday night, someone robbed the lightkeeper's house in town. I happened to be on the property at the same time it happened. I didn't notice or hear anything because the lake was so loud, but Officer Swenson said I'm a person of interest. Wrong place, wrong time sort of thing. If I can't figure out who did it, I might be out of a job altogether."

"This isn't good." She tapped her chin with her finger. "I haven't seen Levi since he and Charlotte married and settled on the mainland. He works part-time as a police officer while he's going to college. I need to talk to him. That's all."

"No. You speaking to him wouldn't help. It might even make me look more guilty, like I asked you to pull some kind of strings for me. I need to figure out who did it." Zach wrung his hands.

"Then I'm helping you." Alexa placed a hand on his. "I know people on the peninsula. We can figure this out together."

"Thank you."

She drew her hand away. "Now, tell me about this potential job."

Zach scratched his head and cringed. "My cousin lives near Seldom Seen, South Carolina, and he sent me information about a naturalist/educator position. I applied, thinking I'd never get an offer, but I did. It's in my email. The offer is great, and I'd love to study their natural setting, plus teach people about creation. Can you imagine all the wildlife and plants? It's a naturalist's dream. The money is fair, and they provide a cabin."

"Sounds like you've decided."

"Yeah, but I can't do anything until we get this robbery solved. I don't want to leave a place I've loved so much under a cloud of suspicion."

~~~~~
~~~~~

Wednesday morning, Alexa and Zach stood on the lighthouse grounds. Tourists, early for the official season, milled around the rocky shore. A sign printed in red letters hung on the lightkeeper's house door. "Closed until further notice."

Alexa eyed the ground around the entry. "Good thing we both had today off. Let's look around." They circled the keeper's house. "Lots of footprints, but they could be anybody's." She studied the building. "We need suspects." A fishy smell lingered in the air.

The wind whipped Zach's ponytail. "Where do we begin? With a volunteer, maybe?"

"Mrs. Beckleman or Mr. Palmeroy. Take your pick." A laugh escaped Alexa. "There are a few more, but those two treat their volunteering as a job. I know they manage the gift shop in the keeper's house and make sure the tourists are treated well, but the park service takes care of the maintenance and runs the tours." Her gaze moved to the top of the lighthouse. "Those two do handle the money in the shop and keep the lighthouse in the public eye."

Zach considered the older folks who volunteered their time. Mrs. Beckleman, who peered over her glasses at people, and Mr. Palmeroy, with his argyle sweater vests, spent the off-season raising money for lighthouse projects. "Well, one of their family members may have known how much cash they had collected."

Someone cleared their throat, and Zach pivoted to the noise.

Levi gave them both a stern look. "What are you doing here?"

"It's public property, Levi." Alexa placed a hand on each hip. "Have you found out anything about the robbery that will help Zach?"

"You know I can't talk about an ongoing investigation."

Alexa moved closer. "Are there other suspects?"

Levi took off his cap and ran a hand through his hair. "What I can tell you is someone stole money and two antique lanterns. They weren't worth much, but the money was substantial. We're considering a few suspects." His gaze fell on Zach. "You're not off the hook."

Levi stalked off.

"I guess he told me." Zach stared at his back.

Alexa waved her hand in his face. "We'll figure this out. Who might have disregard for the lighthouse and not care if they hurt the volunteers?"

They walked along the sidewalk made of bricks people had purchased, with their names printed on them, to a bench near the water and sat.

A sailboat bobbed across the lake. "I've seen a couple of teenagers peer in the windows when the building isn't open. They live down the street from me."

"Maybe someone who is friends with the volunteers took advantage." The lake churned and spit water on the rocks.

Zach looked at Alexa. "I overheard someone in the coffee shop yesterday say Mr. Bennett, the groundskeeper, has been struggling financially." A seagull swooped overhead.

Alexa jumped from the bench. "The coffee shop. Brilliant. We'll hang out and eavesdrop." She grabbed Zach's hand and pulled him behind her.

The sweet smell of caramel and coffee fragranced the coffee shop. They perused the offerings for the day then ordered their drinks and pastries. Alexa chose a table in the center of the bustle and they both sat. "Better to listen."

"I suppose so." Zach bit into a cranberry walnut scone. "Man, these are good. Even if we don't hear anything worthwhile, at least I'll enjoy eating."

"Mr. Palmeroy and his wife just walked in." Alexa nodded to the door, then sipped her latte. "I'm going to invite them to sit with us."

"Not a good idea. Then we can't hear everyone else."

"Yes, but we can kind of question them." She used finger quotes to emphasize her point.

The couple crossed the room, and Alexa waved at them. "Hi, Mr. and Mrs. Palmeroy. Want to sit with us?"

The older couple shuffled to the table. "Thanks for asking." Mrs. Palmeroy took the seat beside Alexa. Her husband made his way to the counter.

"We haven't seen you in a while." Mrs. Palmeroy clutched her purse.

"You know me. I'm always working or helping Dad and Henry at the restaurant."

"How are your dad and Marigold? I haven't talked to them since Marigold sold crafts at the winter fair."

Alexa rested her cup on the table. "They're both good. I think she'll set up at a booth for the craft event at the school."

"And Henry?" The older lady winked at her.

A wide grin crossed Alexa's face. "He's great."

Mr. Palmeroy carried steaming cups of coffee and a cinnamon roll. After he joined them at the table, he split the roll in half and handed his bride a piece.

Alexa leaned into the balding man, who sipped on his coffee. "Mr. Palmeroy, what a shame about the robbery at the lightkeeper's house."

The man sputtered coffee on himself, then dabbed at the spots with a napkin. "Oh, yes, Miss Alexa. It breaks my heart that anyone would steal from us. Thankfully, it was a small amount of money."

"Oh. We were told it was a lot of cash." Alexa raised her eyebrows.

"Well, you can't trust everything you hear. I was told we had less than five hundred on hand. Of course, we'll miss the lanterns. The descendants of the original keepers donated them last year. Not worth much money, but priceless to us." He stabbed at the cinnamon roll.

Zach rested his cup on the table. "Any thoughts on who might have known the money was there?"

Mrs. Palmeroy wiped her mouth with a paper napkin. "We did, and Mrs. Beckleman and those sons of hers. I'm not sure who else she told. She's a bit of a blabbermouth."

"Please excuse my wife." He rose from his chair and wrapped what was left of the cinnamon roll halves in a napkin. "We should go." Before she spoke again, the couple tottered out of the café, coffees and roll in hand.

"Interesting." Alexa nibbled on the last of her scone. "Mrs. Beckleman's boys are in their forties, and from what I've heard, don't have great reputations. Marigold told me she spoiled them, and they've never matured. Wonder if they needed money."

Soft jazz music hummed in the background. "When did Marigold tell you about them?"

"Yesterday evening, I was chatting with her and Dad and digging for information." She grinned at Zach.

"You love this, don't you?"

"Maybe." She rose from her chair. "Let's get out of here."

~~~~~

Zach and Alexa hiked along the sidewalk toward Zach's cottage. The lake had calmed, and white clouds billowed across the blue sky.

"Don't glance across the road." Zach spoke in a low tone.

"Why?" Alexa craned her neck to see what he saw.

"I said don't look." He raised his hands, then dropped them. "Those are the boys I told you about. They hang out by the lighthouse every time I'm there."

Two young men with mullets laughed as they strode along the walk.

Alexa poked Zach with her elbow. "Want to follow them?"

"Not really." He stopped.

Alexa placed her hand on his back. "Come on. How else will we get you off the hook?"

The two of them stayed on their side of the road and continued walking in the same direction as the boys. When the two young men veered down an alley, Alexa and Zach followed. They wove in and out of shrubs and hid behind trash cans. At the end of the alley, they watched the young men slide into an outdoor shed. After a minute or two passed, they slunk to a window and pressed their heads against the building.

"Can you hear anything?" Zach backed away and rose to a higher squat to peer into the window. "They're counting money, at a table. No,
~~~~~

they might be playing cards. I can't tell."

A door banged open. Alexa and Zach scurried behind the building. A woman stepped into the alley. "Reggie and Rowan, lunch is ready." The boys shoved through the shed's door and ran to the house.

"Now's our chance to check the shed." Alexa darted to the door. Zach followed. How he'd gotten himself into this mess remained a puzzle, but if he wanted to maintain his reputation, he had to find the crook.

Inside, a dank smell enveloped the room, and a weathered wooden wheel once used to hold heavy cable had been converted into a table. A stack of playing cards rested in the center, with a hand in progress on either side. A few coins scattered around the table gave the appearance the boys might be gambling their lunch money.

"Looks like a card game." Alexa searched the perimeter inside of the building. "Here's a lantern, but it's modern. Runs on batteries."

"So much for our suspicions." Zach nodded to the door. "Let's get out of here."

They trotted down the alley and stopped at the end, resting with their hands on their knees. "I'm not as young as I think I am." Zach breathed in.

"Yeah, I forget you're an old guy."

"Haha. Forty-three isn't old, but I thought I was in better shape."

"I know what you mean." She straightened and stretched.

"What about going to the library? We can figure out what the lanterns looked like, since we haven't seen a picture. They're old, so they might be in the lighthouse literature, or in an article about the donation. One of the resource officers told me they added items to the keeper's house a couple of years ago. You've met Angie. She leads the tours of the lighthouse." Zach bent to tie his shoe.

"Great idea. Yeah, Angie's a sweet lady. She helped me when I first took the job as a ranger."

In the library, Miss Rolands batted her eyelashes at Zach, then led them to the archives. "We've digitized the last five years of local newspapers. You can search on the database for those, and you'll find the lighthouse collection on the back wall." She paused. "Zach, if you need any help, let me know." With a finger wave, she exited the room.

"There's one lady who will be sad for you to leave." Alexa punched him in the arm.

Zach glared. "She's nice, but not my type."

"So, you have a type?" Alexa grinned.

"How about we search instead of talking about me?" He plunked into an oak chair and logged onto the computer.

Alexa pulled dusty books about the original lighthouse from the shelves. The two researched for an hour.

"I found the donation article. The photo is grainy, but they're holding the lanterns. The description says it's punched tin with remnants of red paint." He clicked open another page. "A few sellers have them for about one hundred dollars, a piece."

Alexa leaned over his shoulder. "Not worth much to the thief, but pretty cool for the keeper's museum. I hope they get them back."

"Me too." Zach clicked out of the archived newspapers and stood. "Not much more we can find here. Thanks for your help."

"You're welcome. We'll figure this out." Alexa led the way out of the building. "I can come back Sunday."

"In the meantime, I'll keep my eyes and ears open." Zach waved goodbye to his friend.

~~~~~

Sunday morning, with no word from Officer Swenson, Zach stepped out his door to the sound of rain. A tap-tap on the porch roof reminded him to grab his umbrella. He hiked along the walkway to join his friends at church. Alexa had told him she'd ferry over from the island in the afternoon, in hopes they could snoop some more.

Inside the church, Zach slid into his regular seat, about midway back. Three rows ahead of him, he spied Mrs. Beckleman and two men. Her sons, no doubt. Many Sundays he'd chatted with her, but her sons seldom attended. Interesting.

Zach fidgeted through the sermon. What if the police didn't figure out who stole the money? He had no alibi, and the camera caught him at the lighthouse. He couldn't lie about it, since he'd already told Levi he was there. Besides, he wasn't a thief or a liar. When the last song played, he stepped into the aisle and made his way to talk to the lighthouse volunteer.

"Good morning, Mrs. Beckleman." Zach reached his hand out.

"You're the last person I want to speak to. Why would you take money from a non-profit and then show your face at church?" She twirled around. "Let's go, boys."

The two men smirked at Zach and followed their mother out.

Outside, the sun shimmered through the clouds, and a rainbow shone overhead. *Thanks, God, for the beautiful display. Can you help me with this mess?*

Instead of his usual trip to the lighthouse, he walked to a nearby pier. How could Mrs. Beckleman believe he stole from the museum? He'd known her for years and never once gave her a reason to doubt him. What about her sons? Their hair hung in greasy strands and their shirts needed ironing. Maybe she had dragged them out of bed to come to church. They lived with her, and neither had ever married. Their work on the water, catching fish and taking folks on tours kept them busy.
~~~~~

At the pier, Zach settled on a bench and listened to the sound of waves bump the wooden piling. He leaned his head into his hands and asked God for wisdom. After bending God's ear, he walked along the edge of the wooden planks and glanced into the water. A flash of red caught his sight. He knew not to disturb the metal vessel he watched float in the milfoil plants. He tugged his phone from his pocket and snapped photos, then dialed the number Officer Swenson had given him.

Within half an hour, Levi pulled into the lot. Zach met him and directed him to the item he'd found. Levi took photos and secured the area. He retrieved a pole from the car and fished out the metal. He laid the item on the wooden planks and brushed off the plant residue. "Looks like we have a lantern." Before Zach responded, Levi lay down and stretched out on the wood and checked beneath it. "I see the other one down here." Zach handed him the pole, and Levi retrieved the second one.

"These look like the ones on the computer." Zach stared at the lanterns.

"What are you talking about?"

"I read the article about the donation to the keeper's museum." Zach spoke too soon.

"You found them?" Levi wiped the pole with a towel. "You didn't plant them here, did you?"

"No."

"What? Are you here thinking again?" Levi packed the lanterns into an evidence box.

"As a matter of fact, I was. I walked around the dock before I headed home, and the red color caught my attention." He lifted his umbrella from where he'd placed it on the bench and stepped away.

"Stay close and try to stay out of trouble. I want this solved as much as you. If you see anything else let me know." Levi stalked to his car.

At his house, Zach dialed Alexa's number. No answer. He leaned his head on his recliner. Half an hour later, a knock on the door woke him.

Alexa's face peered through the glass. He opened the door. "Hey, come in."

"Were you napping?" She lowered herself onto the couch. "I thought you'd be searching for more clues."

He recounted what happened at church and the pier.

"Oh, man. That stinks."

"Yeah. It does." Rather than let the circumstances knock him down, he wanted to keep digging. "I'd like to learn more about Mrs. Beckleman's sons. They fish off the pier and have a boat docked nearby. Want to take a tour?" He rose from his chair. "I'll wear a hat and dark glasses. Hopefully, they won't recognize me."

"Sounds like a plan. Let's go." Alexa joined him at the door, and they walked to their next mission.

At the dock, they spotted the two brothers working around their boat. They owned a pontoon with ten seats for passengers. Two people stood near them. Alexa and Zach moseyed behind the couple waiting their turn. After a few minutes, the brother who appeared older spoke to the group. "We need at least two more people for this to be worth our time. We're happy to wait if you are."

Zach leaned into Alexa's ear. "He's a delight."

Alexa covered her laugh with a cough.

Ten minutes passed before a family of four joined the venture.

"You can board now, twenty for adults, fifteen for the kids." He held out his hand to collect the cash.

After all the passengers boarded, Zach and Alexa found seats as close to the brothers as possible. Despite their nearness, the noise of the engine blocked the brothers' conversation. About a half mile from shore, they cut the engine.

"Thought you'd like some time to enjoy the water without the noise. If you want to swim, you have to wear a life jacket."

The family with children donned life jackets and jumped in. The other couple stood alongside and watched, and Zach and Alexa moved as close as they could to the brothers without being obvious.

The younger brother cast a line into the water. He glanced at his brother. "Figure I might as well get some fishing in. Make a couple of bucks from my catch. By the way, you broke my other rod last time we fished. You're gonna have to buy me a new one."

"Yeah, right." The older brother kicked the younger one in the leg. "You ain't getting a new rod from me." A raucous laugh bellowed from him. He sobered and a frown crossed his face. He leaned into his little brother. "I'm not sure why I trusted you with it, but where'd you stuff the cash? We can't give Mom any until the scuttle has died down about the robbery, or she'll figure we did it. She's in the middle of the mess." He cleaned his fingernails with his pocketknife. "At least the cops think the nature guy did it. Hope they arrest him."

Zach tugged his ball hat further down on his forehead.

"Mom burned him after church today, which by the way, was a good call on your part. She was mighty happy we went with her." His arrogant chuckle made Zach's stomach ache.

After the boat docked, Zach and Alexa hurried ashore, then jogged to Zach's house. Inside, Alexa pulled out her phone and dialed the number for Levi. "You need to come to Zach's house. We have information."

Zach opened the door for Officer Swenson twenty minutes later. Dressed in shorts and a T-shirt, he stepped inside. "We're sorry to bother you again, but we overheard something you may want to know."

Alexa spilled the story of the brothers and waited for Levi's reaction.

He rubbed his hand over his chin. "From what you're telling me, it sounds like they should be suspects, but it's not enough for me to get a warrant. Since it's coming from you, it's hearsay. Trust me, I believe you, but a judge won't go by word of mouth. We need valid proof. I have a few things I've been checking out. Let me work on it." He stepped to the door, then turned back to them. "You could have gotten hurt today if they had found out you were listening to them, not to mention you endangered the other passengers. I don't mean to be harsh, but leave the police work to the professionals, okay?" He exited the house.

"Guess we're in trouble." Alexa sank into the couch cushion. "We've got to make the evidence stick or get them to talk."

"Didn't you hear a word he said?"

"Yeah, but I don't want you to get blamed."

Zach shook his head. "Thanks, but I don't want you to get hurt."

~~~~~

Monday morning, Zach's phone rang. Dressed in his uniform, he lifted the phone from the table and answered. When he hung up, he took a deep breath, trod to the bedroom, and changed into jeans and a T-shirt. His boss had requested he lie low for the week, in hopes this situation would clear.

He flopped on his bed and closed his eyes. What now? If Seldom Seen, South Carolina caught wind of this, he'd lose his opportunity to move. Right now, he wanted nothing more than to leave Lake Erie and this mess behind. The email said they had given him two weeks to accept the job. His time dwindled.

He lay on the bed and stared at the ceiling. What if he spent time in jail for something he hadn't done? How could Mrs. Beckleman believe he stole the money? The Palmeroys didn't. He'd talk to them.

After lunch, Zach rode his bike to a lane outside of town. The Palmeroy's cottage, one of the oldest ones in town, stood on the banks of the lake with a perfect view of the lighthouse. Mrs. Palmeroy's yellow and purple pansies greeted Zach.

He tapped on the screen door, where he saw Mrs. Palmeroy wipe her hands on a kitchen towel.

She pushed open the door. "Hello, Zach. Come in."

He stepped back in time to the 1950s kitchen. A red Formica table with chrome legs and matching upholstered chairs stood in the center of the linoleum covered floor. Wallpaper sprinkled with cherries carried on the red design. "Thank you. Is Mr. Palmeroy here?"

"He's not, but he'll be back soon. Let's sit at the table. I'll get you something to drink."

She poured lemonade for both of them, then sat across from him.
~~~~~

"Can I help you?"

"I'm not sure." Zach sipped the cold drink. "This is good. Thank you." He glanced at a photo on the wall. "Are those your children?"

"Yes, Roy and Arthur." She pointed to another picture. "These are our grandkids. The little dickens sucked our pockets dry." She covered her mouth with the tail of her apron. "I didn't mean for that to come out."

"No worries. I know kids can be expensive."

She stood, paced across the room, then stopped at the window and stared at the lighthouse. "You have no idea. I worked at the school well past retirement age, slaved over those stoves, and fed those mouths every day. It was exhausting. When I finally retired, both boys moved away and left us with an empty bank account." She sniffed and pulled a handkerchief from her pocket. "I saw you at the lighthouse the other evening. You must have watched me cut the cable on the camera, break the window, and go in."

Zach stood and inched toward her. "No, I didn't see you."

"Of course you did. You know I stole the money. You saw me." Her back stiffened. "When Harold told me how much cash the Lighthouse Society had collected for the coming season, I had to get my hands on it. I grabbed those two lanterns to throw the cops and Harold off my trail."

She spun to face Zach, who towered over her. Hysterical laughter echoed from her mouth, then a glassy-eyed stare glared at his face.

Zach reached to calm her, but she jerked away. "Now I've done it. I've told on myself and to the person who should take the blame." Before Zach could stop her, she reached for a rolling pin and swung it at him. He dodged her swing, then grabbed the wooden weapon from her hands.

Mr. Palmeroy charged into the room. "Joleena, I heard you through the screen. What have you done?" He wrapped his arms around his wife and motioned for Zach to leave and call the police.

Outside, Zach dialed the police. Mrs. Palmeroy's voice vaulted out the door, from sobs to hysterical laughter. His heart hurt for her, but he had to clear his name. Besides, Mr. Palmeroy told him to call.

After Levi arrived and searched the house, he stepped outside. "We found the money in the Lighthouse Society's cash pouch. She confessed everything. Said she used her husband's key but broke out the lower windowpane, so it looked like someone had broken in. I'm sorry we gave you a hard time, but it's part of the job. If we don't follow the clues, we fail the investigation."

"No worries. I'm glad it's all resolved, and I can go back to the woods tomorrow, where there's peace and quiet." He shook Levi's hand.

Around six in the evening, Alexa and Henry stopped by Zach's house. They carried in an armload of food.

"Time to celebrate." Alexa set the table with plates and silverware she brought.

"Alexa, without your help, I wouldn't have had the motivation to find the real culprit. I couldn't picture Mrs. Palmeroy breaking in and stealing, but her husband said she hasn't been the same since her boys and their families moved east of Cleveland. I hope the judge isn't too hard on her. They recovered all the money and the lanterns." He sat at the table.

Alexa sat and Henry said a prayer, then dished out the moussaka. "I hope you like this. It's one of Johnny's specialties."

"I'm sure I will. Thanks for coming with Alexa."

Henry grinned. "We spend as much time together as we can."

Alexa patted Henry's arm then turned to Zach. "Enough about us. Any news about Mrs. Beckleman's sons?"

"Yeah. They were selling drugs but didn't want their mom to find out. The police had been watching them, but Levi couldn't tell us. In the meantime, they caught them dealing."

"At least our covert operations paid off." Alexa passed homemade bread around the table. "So, is this a double celebration? Cleared from the crime and a new job?"

"Yep. I sent my acceptance email before you got here, and I'm telling my boss tomorrow. I won't leave until mid-summer, but I can't wait." He spooned a bite into his mouth. "Wow, this is delicious."

Alexa raised her glass of water. "Here's to your new career in Seldom Seen, South Carolina."

"Yes!" They clinked their glasses. "Here's to hoping there's a lot less intrigue down there than I've seen here lately."

The End

~~~~~

Reader, there won't be less intrigue. Follow Zach Hudson to Seldom Seen, South Carolina and meet Lyndie Lavender as they solve unexpected mysteries in the upcoming Seldom Seen Mystery series.

If you're intrigued with Abbott Island, check out **Home Where She Belongs, Home Away from Home***, and* **Home at Last***. Three friends, one island, romance, mystery, and the promise of hope. You'll love it there.*

Penny Frost McGinnis

Penny Frost McGinnis, author of the Abbott Island series and picture book, ***Betsy and Bailey: No One Will be Just Like You***, would live in a lighthouse, if she could. Instead, she and her husband are content to
~~~~~

live in southwest Ohio and visit Lake Erie every chance they get. She adores her family and dog, indulges in dark chocolate, and enjoys fiber arts, and baseball. Her life's goal is to encourage and uplift through her writing.

Her Perfect Home
Gina Bishop

In the 1940s

Tunie Miller sleepily grasped a damp corner of the heavy old quilt that nearly covered her head. A large droplet from the ceiling fell with a wet splat, hitting the top of her head and trickling through her hair, then down her face, pooling a bit in the rounded high collar of her faded flannel nightgown.

She listened to the wind whistling and whirling outside the old house, as the autumn rain was persistent on the leaking roof. She groaned, pulling away the sodden corner of the quilt, the bedsprings loudly protesting as she got out of the iron bedstead, and pushed it a couple of inches away, making an awful racket as it scraped the wooden floor.

She pushed aside the threadbare bed sheet strung across the doorway and went through the narrow hallway to the kitchen. In the near darkness, she took down a battered metal pan from a hook in the wall and picked up a couple of clean rags.

"What's all the noise! What are you doing up in the middle of the night?"

Tunie looked up to see Mom glowering from the doorway of the back bedroom.

"There's a leak in my room, and I pushed the bed away. I'm putting down a pan where the water's coming in."

"Patch it before you go to school," she mumbled as she turned to go back to bed.

"Might be raining when I leave, and don't have a ladder to get up there."

"Hit's almost over now. Ladder's in the shed, Clay come in late."

Why couldn't Clay do it? She already knew the answer. *Mom would say he's got better things to do than getting on a wet roof when I'm here to do it.*

She put down the pan with the old rags and jumped back into the bed to escape from the damp cold.

An hour later it was impossible to sleep with the combination of voices coming from the kitchen, and the strong, overwhelming smell of coffee, cigarettes and bacon. She pulled off the damp quilt and almost tripped over the nearly full pan of water just a few inches from her feet.

No one paid any attention to her as she emptied the pan just outside the front door and stopped at the hand pump in the kitchen to get some fresh water and pick up a sliver of the homemade soap.

She passed Mom standing over the stove in her ratty old chenille robe, and Clay sitting at the table in his usual long-sleeved blue shirt and faded overalls, a cigarette in one hand, peering over a newspaper spread out over most of the kitchen table.

She quickly dressed in one of the hand-me-downs from her older sisters, both of whom had quit school in 1940 and run off in quick succession. They both had big ideas to work in a factory and get a husband. The family grapevine was that they were either working in a restaurant or a drugstore; and barely getting by.

The long-sleeved green and black plaid dress was more than a bit worn, and she had brightened it up a bit with a pleated green ribbon to the center of the white collar. She rolled up thick black knee socks, and black lace-up shoes that had two layers of cardboard in the soles, as they were nearly worn out. She picked up the small hand mirror, while looking at the movie star's picture she had tacked up next to the newspapers that covered the walls and combed her shoulder-length brown hair back, fastening the brown plastic barrettes on each side.

Mom was now taking a pan of oatmeal off the stove and put it in the middle of the table, pushing aside the small plate of bacon, and not disturbing Clay, who was buried in his paper, dropping his ashes mostly near a cracked saucer as he drank his coffee.

They didn't look up as Tunie went outside and got the ladder out of the shed. She quickly found the black roof flashing on a shelf, along with a hammer and some nails. She climbed up on the damp roof and quickly hammered in the rough, tar-like material, carefully made her way back down, and put the supplies back in the shed.

It was getting late, but she was hungry and helped herself to some oatmeal. After looking under a couple of spread-out newsprint pages, she saw that the bacon was gone, but there was now a pan of warm, half-burned biscuits, and a large knife in the opened jar of strawberry jam that her grandmother left for them a few weeks ago.

She ate the oatmeal with some of the jam on it quickly, and had to wait on a biscuit until Clay had picked out what he wanted from the pan.

"Ladder in the shed?" Clay said, reaching over to pull out a couple of biscuits. "That hammer and nails better not be on the roof or out in the wet grass."

"It's all put away," she said, reaching for a couple of the burned biscuits to put in her lunch pail, then got up to gather her schoolbooks.

"What a waste of time," Clay mumbled as he stubbed out a cigarette in the saucer, and didn't lose a beat as he reached into his front pocket to light another one.

"Oh, you mean going to school?" Mom chuckled as she flicked the ashes from her cigarette.

"Whaddya they need to know? This one'll have to work, too gawky and plain to catch a fella." Clay laughed as he pulled another cigarette from the pack in his shirt pocket.

Tunie didn't bother to glance back as both Mom and Clay laughed, and shut the front door behind her

~~~~~

"Where were you? You missed the meeting for the school party," Hazel Taylor said as Tunie joined her for lunch at a table in the small school cafeteria.

"The roof leaked in my room right in the middle of the night," she said, taking some of the burned biscuits and dried apple rings from her lunch pail.

Hazel unpacked some crumbly oatmeal raisin cookies and pushed them over to her.

"I had to repair the leak before I left for school," She picked up one of the oatmeal cookies.

"You were up on a slippery wet roof in that dress?"

"Yes, and the front hem is still a little damp."

"Is your father around? Why couldn't he do it?"

"Clay? He's there."

"You call your father Clay? I don't remember you telling me that before," Hazel said.

"Yes, well, he isn't there very much, sort of drifts in and out, a week on, two weeks out. My sisters always said he didn't deserve to be called father," Tunie said, putting the leftover apple rings in her lunch pail. "As long as one of us was ever around he never did anything around the house."

"That seems so strange. I always called my parents Mama and Papa. And my mama always calls my papa 'Mitchell dear,' and my papa always calls my mama, 'Beautiful Clara.'"

"That's never happened in that old house. I've never heard them say a loving word to each other or to me that I can remember. They're always arguing or mad about something or other. Ever since my sisters ran away, one right after the other, I've dreaded going home and living in that house. It's awful. I'm sorry I said anything at all. It's kind of depressing, I know. Thank you for being my good friend," she whispered, as Hazel reached over and gave her a hug.

"Sorry, I forgot you were alone. Didn't your sister Amanda leave last year?"

Tunie nodded as she picked up her lunch pail.

"You're welcome at my home anytime, you know that," Hazel said
~~~~~

as she began to gather up her books and lunch pail. "We need to hurry, social studies starts in just a couple of minutes. Don't worry about the school meeting, I'll share my notes with you. You're still coming over tomorrow morning, aren't you?"

"Yes, I'm really looking forward to it. Thank you for inviting me and letting me stay overnight." Tunie smiled as they walked down the hallway together.

"You have any trouble getting permission from your parents?" Hazel said as they walked in their classroom.

"Clay's working a job in town, he won't care, and Mom's cousin Wraejean is coming for a visit this evening and staying for a couple of days, so the less I'm around, the better. I'll see you tomorrow morning."

~~~~~

"Where you going, girl? You're not having no breakfast with us?" Wraejean asked as Tunie got her coat from the hook beside the door.

"She's staying in town with her school friend, going to a church meeting, she says," Mom said, walking into the kitchen.

"Church meeting!" Wraejean coughed and laughed as she lit a cigarette and sat back in her chair. "Always beggin' for money. How old is this one, Edna? Ain't she sixteen or more?"

"Seventeen, but looks like a kid. Not like her sisters, they all filled out, but she's like a plucked chicken!"

"Scared of her own shadow."

Tunie picked up her tote bag from the floor, went out the front door, and could still hear both the women laughing as she opened the gate and walked away from the old house.

She walked past the trees, over to the mostly burned-out old log cabin that still had an old stone fireplace. Slinging her tote bag over her shoulder, she picked up the long tree branch that she had fashioned into a walking stick and began the hike up the hollar to take the free bus to town to Hazel's house.

The curtain was going up for her play, being the playwright, the director, and all the actors at the same time. She put the walking stick on the back side of the bus shelter, boarded the bus, which had become the stage, and transformed it in her mind into a beautiful house, with doors on all the rooms, and a lovely porch swing. She would be a mother who welcomed her child when she came home from school and hugged her and told her how beautiful she was. She would marry a wonderful man who wanted their child to be well educated. Their child would be happy to call him Father.

She wanted to end the play when she flung open her closet door to see it jammed full of store-bought brand-new dresses. But the play ended abruptly when her stop came, and the bus doors opened. She walked two
~~~~~

blocks to Elm Street, happily walking to the Taylors' house with the bright green shutters, and with a big front porch. She saw Hazel waving and calling to her from the doorway. Tunie practically ran up to the front porch, jumping the three steps up, to see a nice porch swing and a couple of flowerpots on either side of the door.

"Right on time! We need to get to work, Tunie, and get those pies made." Hazel smiled as they walked in the house together to see Mr. Taylor coming down the front staircase.

"Hi, Tunie, how are you this morning?" he greeted her.

"Hello, Mr. Taylor. I'm doing fine," Tunie said, looking down at the nice blue rug in the hallway instead of at him.

"How are your parents?" Mrs. Taylor said, peering in from the dining room.

"Oh, fine I guess," Tunie said, as she and Hazel went into the kitchen.

"You hungry? We have some leftover toast and jelly," Mrs. Taylor said as she folded the dishrag and hung it over the sink to dry.

Tunie shook her head. "No thank you, I'm fine."

"I'm so glad you're staying with us tonight. Hazel tells me that you have a lot of experience making pies," she said as Hazel began to get out some pans.

"My grandmother taught me everything she knew."

"Do you have some good recipes that you're willing to share?"

"I don't have anything written down, but I'll be glad to share what I know, and write it down as best I can."

"I hope we do well at the contest!" Hazel exclaimed as she began to gather spices from the cabinet.

"This is the first time our church is doing something like this. I understand that a lot of people are entering their very best," Mr. Taylor said.

"I never was in a contest before," Tunie said as she put on an apron over her head. Hazel tied it in the back.

"This might be your time, Tunie. Well, enjoy girls, I'm happy to volunteer to be a taster if you would like that." Mr. Taylor chuckled as the girls began to get to work on their pie entries.

"Your mother and father are nice. I like coming to your home, it's so beautiful," Tunie said. *With doors to every room,* she thought as she unwrapped some butter.

"I guess I do have a great mom and dad. This house was a kit from mail order, and there are thousands of other houses just like it all over the place." Her friend smiled.

"Maybe it's like a thousand other houses, but it's wonderful to me. When do we have to be at the church?"

"Oh, plenty of time, about 12:30," Hazel said, looking up at the clock on the wall, now showing just a few minutes past nine o'clock.

"Well, that should be plenty of time to get the pies done and cooled." Tunie smiled as she began to cut the cold butter into a bowl of flour to form the dough.

She easily rolled out enough dough for the crusts for four pies, two apple and two blackberry. Hazel mixed the ingredients after Tunie measured them out. She spent extra time making a fancy crisscross top for each pie, and fashioned intricate dough leaves to accent the center of the pies, finally brushing the tops with a little milk, and sprinkling over a bit of granulated sugar before putting them in the large oven.

Tunie excused herself to freshen up from the pie making.

"Join me in the parlor when you're finished," Hazel said.

She opened the bathroom door and marveled at the indoor plumbing, the flowered wallpaper, and the fluffy towels, a lovely room that had no gaps in the walls stuffed with rocks and old newspapers.

"I combed through my hair a couple of times. Do you see any flour?" Tunie said as she walked in the parlor.

"Your hair looks fine. My mom said she would be checking on the pies and let us know when it's time to go," Hazel said as she handed Tunie a stack of magazines.

The next hour passed quickly as the girls paused at nearly every page to admire all the beautiful clothes.

"Girls, I didn't want to disturb you while you were so busy studying the latest fashions. I took the pies out a few minutes ago. Tunie, thanks for making the extra apple pie, as I'm sure we'll all enjoy it if Mr. Taylor doesn't eat it all!" Mrs. Taylor said as she paused in the parlor doorway.

"You're welcome, Mrs. Taylor. I was glad to do it," Tunie said. "What exactly is this big church meeting all about anyway? You never really said other than the pie making contest,"

"Well, there's a lot of music, and testimonies, and then the preacher gets up to speak," Hazel began.

"Testimonies? What is that?"

"People get up and talk about how God has helped them and blessed them."

"Oh, I see," Tunie replied, feeling uncertain.

"People are bringing wood carvings, quilts, and of course pies. It's all in good fun, but it sure would be nice to win." Hazel laughed.

Mrs. Taylor had provided nice new-looking stainless-steel pie pans and covered them with new clean tea towels in a blue and white checkered print. Mr. Taylor put them carefully on an old towel in a large cardboard box and drove them all over to the church a couple of miles away.

The church building was large and old, with a very long room that Hazel called a sanctuary, but Tunie had no time to look at it. They went past it, downstairs to the basement, a very large room with long tables and folding chairs set up. Off to the right side were large tables already full of a selection of quilts, each one more beautiful than the last. The table near the other corner had carvings of bowls, large spoons and forks, animals and birds, a flute, and even a small chair. On the other side of the room was the pie table. The girls took numbers to label their entries and placed them beside pies of all sorts and kinds.

Mrs. Taylor had brought a large, covered roaster pan filled to the brim with fried chicken and put it on the large table in the back with all the fine dishes that Tunie looked at in delight. Hazel kept steering her past all that, saying they needed to get upstairs so they could get a good seat.

The music in the meeting was wonderful, with a violin, piano, and flute, and a lot of singing, mostly new to Tunie. The testimonies were numerous and interesting, with a lot of people laughing and crying as they talked about God and what He had done for them.

How did they get to know Him in the first place? she wondered.

The preacher was a short, elderly man, probably in his early seventies. His dark blue suit was a bit baggy for his small frame, and instead of shouting like she had heard preachers did, he had a very gentle, soft-spoken way about him, and talked about God like he had known Him for many years, like a lifelong friend.

Tunie glanced around from under lowered eyelids. Nearly all the people around her had their eyes closed and heads bowed. She glanced straight ahead and ducked down as the elderly preacher was praying and now looking straight at her with gentle, twinkling eyes and a friendly smile.

When the meeting ended, the full crowd of people made their way down to the basement, where the judging was now finishing up for the quilts, the wood carvings, and the pies.

"First prize for both the apple and blackberry pies!" Hazel hugged Tunie and pointed to the blue ribbons on their pies.

"Congratulations!" Mrs. Taylor said, giving her a hug too.

"You did all the work, so you deserve all the prizes!" Hazel laughed.

"But I made them with your supplies and in your kitchen," Tunie whispered. Hazel just shook her head. "I've never won anything before," she said as the people applauded all the winners.

"Well, come on up here and get your prizes, everyone, and bring your entry cards with the numbers on them," an older woman called out.

Later, Tunie still couldn't believe it, as she sat at one of the tables with Hazel and the Taylors, looking at the beautiful gifts on her lap. A beautiful dusty rose quilted tea cozy, a large silky head scarf in a red and green tartan design, and blue imitation leather book with silver letters on the front that said *New Testament with Psalms*. She gently fanned it open and saw red letters on some of the pages.

"Look at this, Hazel." Tunie pointed to the printed pages. "Red letters among the black ones."

"Those are the words that the Lord Jesus spoke," Hazel said as Tunie gently smoothed her hand over the pages.

~~~~~

The girls spent the evening after the church revival listening to a couple of radio programs, then went up to Hazel's room to look through a large pile of fashion magazines and catalogs.

"This is the outfit that I want to get for graduation," Tunie said, pointing at the page in the mail-order catalog.

"A dark blue suit with a white-collared ruffle trim. Yes, that's the latest fashion with the white buttons on the jacket going up one side," Hazel said as they huddled together.

"Look at this," she said turning over a couple of pages. "A dark blue felt hat with some small white flowers on it. A blue and white shoulder bag and matching spectator heels. And this over here, gold, or gold-like hair combs, and pearl earrings. I'd wear it with my class ring, once the senior order comes in,"

"This is perfect and will go well with your brown hair and eyes. But it's expensive. Mama is planning to make a new suit for me for graduation. How are you going to pay for it?" Hazel asked.

"My part-time jobs being a mother's helper for my two neighbors and running some errands for old Mr. Clemson. Hopefully I'll have enough by then."

"Aren't you still paying the layaway on the class ring?"

"I just made the last payment earlier today. Just a few months longer, and I'll have enough for everything. And the second Principal Disney hands me my diploma, well, I'll be going…" Tunie trailed off.

"Going? Going where?" Hazel said, turning to her.

"My cousin Juniebelle, she lives up in Clancyville, about four hours on the bus," Tunie said.

"What? Do you mean for a visit? A family occasion? Your parents are going?"

"No family occasion. Mom and Clay wouldn't go even if there was an important occasion. I want to get out of that awful house, and all the people who live there."

"I didn't think it was all that bad for you. I don't want you to go, Tunie. I would miss you so terribly much," Hazel said, hugging her.

"I'd miss you too. Mom and Clay keep bringing up that I don't need any more school, that I've had more school than any of them and my older sisters, saying it won't do me any good to finish. They keep talking to me about getting a job in town because Clay is having back problems. Ever
~~~~~

since my older sisters left, I dread going alone to that house."

"Tunie, no, that's terrible that you dread going home. Does he have a bad back?"

"Not that I can see. He likes to hang out over in town at his cousin's house when he's not painting houses, as far as I know. I'm not supposed to know, but I overheard my grandmother say he drinks up a lot of the money he makes." Her voice lowered to a whisper. "They keep saying all the time no fella would look at me and to quit and go to work and support them."

"Tunie, you know that's not true. Everyone at school loves you, and thinks you are beautiful and smart. The girls and the guys," Hazel said.

~~~~~

In the weeks since the wonderful church meeting and the pie making contest, Tunie had a few more opportunities to earn money to grow her little nest egg safely stowed under her bed. She only had to stay in that old house a few more months, and then she would be the very first person on either side of her family to graduate from high school. She knew that Clancyville had a teacher's college, and her dream was to go there, work a day job, and go to school at night while staying at Cousin Juniebelle's home.

Tunie added a brand-new act to her private play on her way home from running a few errands for her neighbors. There were now flowery long drapes at all the windows, designer wallpaper in every room instead of the old newspapers, floor lamps instead of a bare bulb hanging from the ceiling, and two porch swings with potted flowers flanking them.

She came down the hill from the burned-out cabin, and around the bend, slowing down as she came near the falling down old wire fence, and the rusty hinges on the front wooden gate where the white paint had nearly worn off. Climbing up on the cracked front stoop, she silently declared the play was over.

The old house was eerily silent as she shut the door, and now noticed Mom's coat and outside shoes were gone from their usual place. Her footsteps creaked loudly on the old floorboards, and from the hallway she saw that the blanket strung over her doorway had been pushed aside.

She pushed the blanket all the way back, quickly glanced around the room, and noticed two of the drawers of her rickety old chiffarobe were sticking out a bit. The underclothes and socks were pushed around, and her barrettes and comb and brush were scattered around the bottom of the drawer. She glanced around, not understanding what was going on. Then she saw that the old, flowered quilt was all hunched up on her bed and the pillow had been pulled out on top.

Her treasure box was still under the bed, a large pink and white flowered cardboard hat box that her eldest sister Fannie had abandoned
~~~~~

when she ran off years before. It had dark colored twine, and she had found an old apple box bottom to set it on to keep it off the floor. The lid was not all the way on. She thought she was in a hurry when she had the box out a couple of days ago.

She lifted off the lid and saw that the carefully folded headscarf was pushed off to the side, the quilted tea cozy on the other side, and the blue New Testament on the bottom. The top was off the old metal biscuit tin, and it was completely empty. Sixty-four dollars and eighty-four cents. Gone.

She dropped the metal biscuit tin when she heard a familiar grunt and someone pushed the slightly swollen front door open. She jumped up from the bed to run to the kitchen.

Mom had set down her old brown handbag, and three large cloth tote bags on the table, and was in the middle of unpinning her dark blue felt hat when she came into the room.

"I'm going to town to get the sheriff."

"What do you need the law for?" Mom said, taking off her coat and hanging it in its place beside the door.

"My room, it looks ransacked. I had some money in the box under my bed. It's gone. Somebody's broke in here and took it," she said, reaching for her coat.

"Don't need no law. Clay took it." Mom calmly began to unpack the brown cloth tote bags.

"Clay? What was he doing in there?"

"He ran into old man Clemson who told him you'd been doing a lot of errands for him, and he had paid you, and you had told him you'd been running errands for that old couple, the Stanleys, that you were getting some good amount of money doing all that work."

"He, he went through my things?" She shifted from one foot to the other.

"I was busy cooking, but I told him to leave everything else alone and just look for the money. We was surprised, didn't know you had squirreled away that much money. I gave him some for his smokes. Look at everything I got," Mom said, smiling and proud of herself.

"I earned that money. It was mine."

"Don't raise your voice to me. Needed the money. Don't need your permission to do what I want in my own house."

"You never even asked."

"Don't have to ask you anything. You should be grateful to have a roof over your head and food to eat. Clay said we should think about getting you married off to that old man Clemson, him being a widower and all, and he's got a government pension. Wouldn't have to put up with him for long." Mom laughed as she unpacked the tote bags.

Tunie whirled and ran to the bedroom. She quickly shoved what little clothes she had in her school bag, with the barrettes, tea cozy, headscarf, and the blue New Testament. She marched out to the front room, jammed her feet in the black shoes, grabbed her coat and ran out on the front stoop.

"Where you think you're going?" Mom called out.

"Far away from this old house," she said, fumbling with the buttons on her coat. She jumped off the stone steps and through the worn-out wooden gate.

She had half expected Mom to run after her; and drag her back, but all she heard was laughing, a loud cackle and a slamming door.

Tunie marched up the hill and past the old log cabin. There weren't going to be any more plays about a wonderful old house and perfect family, because she was going to have to make do when she got to Clancyville, working for her keep, and showing everyone that she was beautiful and smart.

Tears streamed down her face as she wondered how she would pay for a bus ticket. She did think about asking Hazel to lend her the money, but her friend would try to talk her out of going.

She reached into her dress pocket for her handkerchief. Feeling the big knot in it, she remembered the little bit of money she had just earned in the past couple of days. There was just enough money in that hankie to get her a bus ticket to go to Juniebelle's. She sighed with relief as she made her way past the old elementary school and saw on the posted schedule that the county bus was due to come in just a few minutes.

She would go straight to the terminal, get on that bus and start a new life. She knew Mom and Clay wouldn't try to bring her back. They never cared that her sisters quit school early and ran away to live with Juniebelle.

There weren't many people coming her way on the street. She glanced over to the other side. Seeing Clay, she quicky shrank back into the front entrance of a watch repair shop. He stumbled a bit as he made his way along the sidewalk, the ever-present cigarette hanging out of his mouth. He stopped suddenly, bent all the way down, picked up a coin on the ground, and ambled along as he rubbed it and tucked it in his front pocket.

She pressed into the shadow near the store entrance, waiting for him to pass by. When he was gone, she slowly moved forward, furtively looking both ways, and made her way to the terminal. She hoped she would never see him again.

The terminal hadn't changed since the last time she had been there. Mom took her up to the capital to see her relations over ten years ago. The last time was when she came with her sister Amanda over a year ago. Amanda had boarded the bus to Clancyville, never saying goodbye, leaving her alone to face Mom and Clay by herself.

She would miss her school friends, her teachers, the Taylors, and Hazel. But it was her time to go and leave that old house.

~~~~~

"Yes, one ticket to Clancyville." Her tone was barely above a whisper.

"Clancyville? Well, let's see young lady." The older man was looking at a printed schedule, and then at a handwritten note in front of him. "Bus is supposed to be here in a few minutes. But we just got a call from up north of the state. Heavy rains and tornado warnings have gone out up that way. They may be late, or not here at all. They ain't going out just to get stuck in the mud someplace."

A cheerful older woman waved at him to get his attention from the other ticket window.

"My missus is here with my coffee and hopefully something to tide me over until dinner. Check back later this afternoon," the ticket master said, and then walked over to take the covered basket from his wife.

Tunie went over to sit on one of the nearly deserted long pew-like benches, trying to think about what she would do if she couldn't get on the bus. She watched the smiling older woman take out a metal thermos and a covered bowl to hand to the ticket master. She smiled in amusement as they waved kisses to each other.

The older woman walked away, shifting the basket to the crook of her arm, and stopped directly in front of Tunie. "You're going to be waiting here a good long while, my Tinsley says."

Tunie nodded, barely looking up at the woman, who was wearing a blue flowered dress, gray hair pulled up in a soft bun and a wide smile.

"I'm going to my ladies' group at the community church just down the way. Why don't you come too? We're a bunch of older ladies, but I bet we'd be more interesting than just sitting here on a hard wooden bench."

"I wouldn't want to intrude," Tunie said.

"You're more than welcome. We'll be having tea and sandwiches, and I'm bringing some brownies," she said, patting the basket. "I'm Rose Stewart by the way. Everyone calls me Rosie. I need the company, let's go together." Rosie held out her hand as Tunie gathered up her tote bag.

"I'm Petunia Miller."

"Petunia. We both have pretty flower names. People call you Pet?" Rosie said as they walked out the front door and down the sidewalk.

"Everybody's always called me Tunie."

"You prefer that?"

"Not really," Tunie said, surprised to realize that suddenly.

"Pet suits you. Pet it is!"

~~~~~

"Ladies, this is Petunia Miller. Pet, welcome to our ladies group today," Rose said as they came into the meeting room.

"Well, Pet, you certainly look familiar," an older woman said from the back, near to the tea table.

"Yes, weren't you here with the Taylors at the church revival some time back?" another woman spoke up.

"Oh sure, I remember you. The cute little champion pie maker. You beat me — well, you beat out everyone!" another older woman called out.

"Oh, I'm sorry about that," Tunie began.

"Nothing to be sorry about, Pet. I'm Martha Ellington, and I could take lessons from you. My Elmer got a piece of the apple and blackberry and raved about them for days. Where'd you learn to bake such wonderful pies?"

"My grandmother," she replied. "She taught me everything I know."

"Didn't know you were so famous, Pet. I was visiting my sister the weekend of the church revival," Rosie said as she led her over to the tea table.

The sandwiches, brownies and pots of tea were all consumed by the dozen ladies. Tunie helped with the clearing away, and soon everyone settled down, brought out their large Bibles from their handbags and placed them all around the table. She rummaged around her tote bag, pulled out the blue New Testament and placed it closed in front of her.

"Psalm 90 tells us that the Lord is our perfect parent, our loving heavenly Father," Martha said to the ladies, who were nodding at her. "In 1 John 3:1 it says that the Father's love is lavished on us. John 3:16 says that God sent Jesus to die to save the world to give us eternal life. He will dwell with us, and He is knocking on the door of our heart,"

Rosie opened the blue book in front of Tunie and pointed out the index and turned to the scriptures.

"Jesus died on the cross for our sins, He rose from the dead, and He is alive now and forevermore," Marilyn Rosemire said as the ladies around the table all murmured their approval. "Everyone who calls on the name of the Lord will be saved," she recited from 1 Peter. "He loves us and wants to save us from eternal death, so we won't be separated from Him."

"Did He die on the cross for me?" Tunie said in a voice just above a whisper.

"Yes, dear, He did," Marilyn said in a gentle tone as the other ladies looked on.

"He loves me?" She smoothed down the page, looking intently at the red letters.

"Yes, Pet, He does," Rosie replied, patting her hand. "He wants you to know Him and love Him."

"How do I do that?"

"Talk to Him, Pet. Just like you're talking to any of us. He's listening and waiting for you to talk to Him."

Tunie swallowed and looked down at her folded hands in her lap, closed her eyes and bowed her head.

"Lord, I'm Petunia. Petunia Margaret Miller. I know I've done many wrong things that I'm sorry for. Please save me, Lord, and show me what to do." Tunie opened her eyes, wiping away tears that were running down her face. Smiles surrounded her.

"Oh, I forgot. Thank You for listening to me. Oh, and Amen." She had barely finished when she was fairly encompassed by one big hug after another.

~~~~~

"So Pet, shall we walk back to the bus terminal and see if you can catch that bus?" Rosie said as the women were leaving the church to go home. "Where are you going?"

"Clancyville, to my cousin Juniebelle."

"She is expecting you, it's a special occasion?"

"It's a last-minute visit," Tunie said, looking down at the sidewalk as they walked along. "Well, that's not true. It's not a visit. It was a last-minute decision to leave."

"I take it no one knows you are leaving. Does that include your friend Hazel?" Rosie said.

"I would have written her later, to explain."

"How about school? You'd quit with only a little while to go before you graduate? One of the ladies heard you are the top student in the senior class, and of course, you're a prize-winning baker." Rosie smiled.

"Things are awful at home. My parents would be more than happy if I quit school and got a job to support them. I think they'd like even more to marry me off to an old neighbor that lives close by, just because he's got a federal pension, and they said I can't get a man any other way. My two older sisters both ran off and never finished school."

"I see." Rosie reached out for her hand.

"I had been working a long time to save money for my graduation, and was going to leave town then, but Clay and my mom took it all."

"Clay?"

"Clay is my father. I don't call him father. Can't."

"Pet, I know things do sound hard for you, and going to Clancyville is a way to get away from a difficult situation. If you decide to stay, my Tinsley and I will be right there to help you, as well as everyone at the Community Church, and of course, your friend Hazel."

They slowly made their way arm in arm, the only noise being the clatter of their shoes as they walked through the alleyway and crossed the street. They approached the terminal steps and walked up to the ticket window together.
~~~~~

"Oh, hi, Rosie, and hi, young lady," the ticket master said, looking up. "Good news, the storm passed, and I got a call that the road is fair and passable to Clancyville, and the bus is on its way and should be here in just a few minutes. I was just getting ready to run over to the church to let you know."

Tunie swallowed and looked down at the floor for a few seconds. "Thank… thank you. I… I do want to get on that bus."

Rosie brought her hand to her mouth.

"But not today. He wants me, God wants me to stay here and go back to that old house," she said, fighting back tears.

"God will go before you, Pet. I'll be praying for you as you go back. You let me know if you need anything, a listening ear, or a place to stay," Rosie whispered in her ear, then they parted.

When she was nearly home, Tunie heard the struggling engine of the old green county bus as it chugged up the hill, going the opposite direction. She passed the burned-out log cabin, left the walking stick where it was, and closed out the playhouse in her mind. There would be no more plays, no acting out the parts and wishing for a perfect family and home.

The broken down old wooden gate was stuck in the mud, pushed halfway open, and the ladder was visible through the open shed door.

"That old house. I hate it." She stood still at the gate.

"I will be your perfect home," God said in her heart.

She made her way to the bottom of the front stoop, and paused, hearing news playing on the radio, and noticed the smell of cigarettes and coffee.

"I can't go in there."

"I will never leave you or forsake you. I am your heavenly Father."

She quickly bowed her head and whispered a prayer, resolutely climbed the steps, and walked into the old house.

~~~~~

Many happy years later …

"Pet, dear, what are you doing up here?"

She turned to see her husband, Gary, peering out from the top of the attic stairs.

"I thought you were downstairs in your recliner watching a football game," Pet said as she put down the old pink faded hat box she had been looking through.

"Well, I'm used to my pretty Pet bringing me a big bowl of popcorn, and you never brought it, so I came looking for you. But you didn't answer my question. What's so important that you're up here?"
~~~~~

"Rosie called earlier to see if I could find her old sleeping bag for a college sleepover next weekend. I found it, and then I started looking at other stuff and lost track of time."

"Oh sure, I see it over there," Gary said as he went behind the large plastic boxes. "I'll just take it with me when we go back down. What's that you're holding?"

"My old childhood memory box. Things I haven't looked at in over thirty years. My blue ribbons I won for the pies. The ribbon when I made valedictorian. Those church ladies made me a navy-blue suit that I wanted so much." Pet held up an old black and white picture. "Oh, I wore it until it fell apart, I loved it that much. Those women and their husbands, and well, the entire church came to my graduation. Wonderful people. The old preacher, Pastor Smetzer, he was so kind to me. And Hazel, I haven't talked to her in such a long time, oh, since last Christmas. She did so much for me when Mom and Clay…" Pet trailed off and looked away.

"Hey, hey, Pet dear." Gary reached into his pocket for a white hankie and handed it to her. "You did the best you could for your mom and Clay, when they did nothing for you."

"Thank you, dear." Pet wiped the tears from her face.

"Selling that old house and giving some of the proceeds to the Community Church. You couldn't have done more."

"Look." She pulled the imitation blue leather book from the bottom of the box. "This book really got me through some hard times. All the letters, red and black. The Lord never left me. Never."

"Pretty Pet, why don't we go out to dinner?" He picked up the sleeping bag and slung it over his shoulder.

"It's a little early yet, Gary dear. I think I'll bake you an apple pie."

"You haven't made me a pie in a long time."

"I'm a champion pie baker, didn't you know?" Pet said, smiling.

"So, you've said."

"When it's done, we'll go to dinner, and by the time we get back it will be cooled and ready to enjoy for dessert."

"We could just buy one at the grocery store. You don't have to go to all that trouble to prove anything to me." He smiled.

"It would be a pleasure to do it for you. I am so thankful to the Lord for you and our wonderful family and perfect home," she said, closing the door behind them.

The End

Gina Bishop is a published short story author who seeks to glorify

God through her writing to encourage others in their daily walk with Him. She is originally from southwestern Ohio, and loves participating in music performance, genealogy, and travel. She has written and taught Bible studies, as well as writing articles on health and family history. She currently serves in local homeless and prison ministries.

Gina dedicates this story to her Aunt Ruth Leedy. Ruth is the inspiration for the heroine who overcame challenges, learning to love and be loved. Connect with Gina online at *ginabishop.com.*

Hiraeth – Griffin's Journey
Lynda Page

Hiraeth - (n.) A homesickness for a home to which you cannot return, a home which maybe never was; the nostalgia, the yearning, the grief for the lost places of your past.

A tall, slender traveler, dressed in Loden green from hooded cloak to knee-high leather boots, crouched by a tree at the edge of a clearing in the Dryad Forest. Griffin Edris licked dry, cracked lips and resisted the urge to rush toward the yearned-for watering place as he scrutinized the clear, sparkling stream meandering through the grassy meadow. A persistent inner nudging stayed him. He dared not ignore the impression that something dangerous lurked nearby.

He lowered his body to stretch full-length on the damp, mossy ground to absorb the sights and sounds around him. The move made him virtually indiscernible to any potential observers. The water shimmered in the noonday sun as it tumbled and swirled over rocks and around bends in an age-old rhythm, a gentle gurgling its only sound. A slight breeze rippled the water and rustled the leaves on the trees above him, reminding him of the nearly forgotten whispers of children at play. Occasionally the call of a bird broke the silence. All seemed as it should be.

Squinting against the sun's brightness reflecting on the water, only his eyes moved as his gaze carefully swept the landscape. He detected no sign of life or activity, save a few insects darting here and there. Still, he waited. The patience typical of his kind held him in place as more minutes ticked past. He was a Dwindling. One of the last remaining Elven groups still inhabiting this land. Their numbers were few, but they had survived by remaining cautious of other people groups. That habit of caution returned to him now despite his six-year absence from his homeland.

A wave of dizziness swept over him. He closed his eyes and waited for it to pass. His need for water was becoming urgent, but Griffin forced himself to remain where he was a bit longer. He sniffed. The air held a hint of something…not evil exactly. Reproach? Perhaps. Even with the prospect of encountering danger, he had little choice. He had been two days without water. Replenishing his supply could no longer be put off.

He lifted his gaze to the sky. The sun was just reaching its zenith. This was the hour he deemed to be the safest to make his approach. Wildlife generally sought water in the early morning and late evening. It was his intent to complete his task while the animals rested.

Four-footed beasts were not the only source of danger he might encounter, but the actions of the two-legged kind were much harder to predict. Stragglers and deserters from the massive Stonack Army were said to have sought shelter within the Dryad. They had no wish to be found. That suited Griffin's purpose. After finally being released from his forced conscription with that army, he certainly did not wish to cross paths with them.

Several more minutes passed before he was satisfied there was no immediate threat, though his senses warned him he was not alone.

Numerous times over the last several days he had felt another's presence—or imagined he had. The impression had disappeared so quickly that he doubted his intuition. The possibility of someone behind him on the trail was only mildly concerning. He detected no malevolent intent in the fleeting occurrences. Why someone shadowed him was puzzling, but they were not the source of his current unease. Whatever his senses were detecting lay in the meadow ahead, not on the trail behind.

He pushed the possibility of a stranger at his back from his mind to concentrate on the more pressing matter at hand.

With one final scan of the meadow and nearby trees, he pushed to his feet, pulled the hood of his cloak up to hide his distinctive Elven features, and approached the stream in a slow jog. Falling to his knees, he cupped his hands to scoop up life-giving handfuls of the icy water. Once his thirst was quenched and his parched throat soothed, he pulled two waterskins from his pack and began to fill them. Setting the first aside when it was full, he dipped the second into the stream.

Without the slightest warning, something struck him sharply between his shoulders. A startled grunt was all he managed before his body was thrust forward, his head plunging beneath the surface of the water. He pushed back against a weight holding him down, but it was no use. Dehydration and days of difficult travel had weakened him to the point his effort was useless. His lungs began to ache from lack of air. He ceased to struggle, his body going limp. He felt his life force draining slowly away, and he was powerless to stop it.

Then, just as suddenly as the blow had come, the pressure lifted, and he was free. When he came to himself he was lying on his back, enveloped in a cocoon of warm bright light. Within the glow, eyes the bluish green of beryl shone bright and familiar as a somber gaze met his. Amber, the sprite-like healer who had attached herself to him and his small group of companions during the recent war. He didn't know what name she may have been given at her birth, but he had bestowed the appellation on her the first time they met due to the amber streaks that edged her blue-green pupils. She never corrected him, so Amber she had become.

After witnessing her strange power—or magic as some called it— during many battles, he wasn't unduly surprised it was she who rescued him. Nor was he surprised she had chosen this moment to reveal her presence. She would explain later. Or perhaps not. She tended to be very circumspect. She revealed few of her thoughts and those only when she deemed them important enough to share. That trait caused him much frustration initially, but he had gradually come to accept her wisdom as he had come to accept and share her belief in the Maker.

Amber had indulged in a rare trill of laughter, showing her pleasure, when he had bowed a knee and sworn fealty to the Maker. He had derived much comfort from that decision, though his circumstances and trials had not lessened as he had hoped. If anything, they had become more intense with each battle he fought. Perhaps there was a bit of magic in that as well. He had an inward peace that defied logical explanation. He felt that same peace now encased in Amber's protective shield.

He had no perception of the passage of time before the light vanished and Amber sat cross-legged next to him in the grass.

"What happened? Who attacked me?"

She shook her head. "I could not see his face. He was unusually tall, dressed in a long, flowing robe with a cowl that kept his features in shadows. He appeared quite suddenly behind you and shoved you into the water. When I intervened, he vanished as quickly as he appeared."

"Was there nothing to reveal who he could be?"

"He wore an unusual robe. It was as black as ebony and bore the image of a silver tree. Its trunk and leafless branches were covered with hundreds of eyes like a vast host of people were watching."

Surprise caused his breath to catch. "A Sentinel. I have long doubted their existence. As a child, I listened avidly to tales of these watchers. Visitors to my father's house regaled my brother and me with stories of these mysterious rovers. I assumed the tales were exaggerated, if not merely fables invented solely to entertain children. According to the tales, Sentinels were tasked in ancient times to be the guardians of land and water.

"One tasked to protect the Dryad is logical, but I cannot fathom why he would attempt to drown me. I understood they were on friendly terms with Elves since we shared their respect for creation. Why would he attack me? I intend no harm."

Amber made no response. She did not indulge in idle speculation. Griffin found that both familiar and exasperating.

Rising nimbly to his feet, he suggested, "Once I retrieve my waterskins, we should return to the shelter of the forest. We can share a noonday meal while you tell me why you have been following me."

He detected a faint wry smile as she got to her feet and turned to watch for further threats. He bent to pick up the skins before leading the way into the trees, retracing his steps down the barely-there animal trail he had followed to the stream.

~~~~~

Amber had no answers she could give Griffin. At least none he would understand. She had impulsively followed the leaning of her heart. She no longer had a home or family. Both were long gone now. Her parents and siblings had died when their home was destroyed at the beginning of the war.

Griffin was the sole survivor of the group of Dwindling she had grown close to as she ministered to them during what seemed like hundreds of battles. The Dwindling was as near her kind as she was ever likely to find. She was a Hury, born of Faerie and man. As far as she knew, she was the last such in existence. Griffin was part of an Elven people who remained behind when the main body of Elves chose to leave this realm. Now they were alone. Having ties to the few remaining races imbued with magic gave them a kind of kinship. It saddened her that the magic had begun to fade after the exodus of the Elven elders.

Griffin's tall, slender body, silver eyes, and slightly pointed ears spoke clearly to her of his origins, but he had never spoken of his life before being captured by the Stonack Army. She often wondered if he possessed any remnant of the magic. She had seen no evidence, but she would not ask him about such things just as she would not volunteer details of her gifts as an empath or healer. These were perilous times, and it was best that personal secrets were kept closely guarded. Even words whispered in private were carried on the wind and could find their way to one's enemies. She would not risk that lightly.

Amber followed Griffin to a sheltered patch of earth beneath a stand of tall oak trees and dropped to the ground. She lowered her two packs and rummaged inside the smaller one until she found the napkin filled with berries she had picked earlier and added them as her contribution to the meal of crusty bread and dried meat Griffin offered from his store of food supplies. Once they satisfied their hunger and drank more of the life-giving water, Amber leaned her back against a tree and waited.

The question sounded only mildly curious. though that was contradicted by the expression Griffin wore. "Why were you following me?"

With a faint shrug, she said, "I have grown accustomed to protecting you."

He studied her for several moments before he said, "Our part in this
~~~~~

war has ended. Your responsibility to me is over."

Wearing a small, sad smile, she said, "I do not know how to stop." She dipped her head and admitted, "I have nowhere else to go."

When no response came, she lifted her head slightly to peer at him through the fringe of raven hair that had fallen forward, covering her face.

He wore an expression of understanding, nodding his agreement.

Griffin's easy acceptance of her emboldened her enough to ask, "Where exactly are we going?"

His eyes sparkled at her question. "Home. Home to Cymeroon. A land so beautiful it will bring tears to your eyes. Its lush verdant valleys and gentle hills are surrounded by a virgin forest. Much of my childhood was spent exploring that woodland with my younger brother." He grinned. "The Edris Forest is much smaller than the Dryad where we are now, but as youths, Gwynn and I considered ourselves great explorers."

His gaze held a far-away look as though he glimpsed something she could not see. "My father's house stands near the center of the village on the crest of a hill with a lake to its back. It has been home to six generations of the Edris family. Its thick hand-hewn stone walls are yellowed with age, but its rooms are filled with laughter and love. There is rarely a day that guests do not gather there for a meal or to consult with my father who is head of the Elven Council. My mother is a very talented gardener. Her garden draws travelers far and wide to marvel at its beauty."

"It sounds truly wonderful. I cannot wait to see it."

A shadow fell over his countenance. "Sadly, we have many long days of travel ahead of us and untold hardships to endure before reaching the haven I have ached to return to for six long years. Knowing this, I will be most grateful for your company if you are still willing to travel with me."

The decision was not a difficult one. There was no place where she would be free from evil. An encroaching darkness shadowed the lands. The gifts bestowed on her by the Maker afforded her a measure of safety, but she had no wish to continue to journey alone. Traveling together increased their chances of survival. "I will go. Tell me more of the things we may encounter."

"After so much time away, that is hard to predict. The land itself will be challenging. We must pass through the Limberlost Swamp, then the Hinderland, a dead stretch of land. It has no animals, no living trees or running streams. It is a place of specters whose voices cry out to travelers, confusing their minds.

"But perhaps the greatest danger may come from those dispossessed in the war with the Stonacks. Groups of them have banded together. They attack anyone they happen upon. They will not deal kindly with those who fought with the Stonacks, even though we were given no choice in the matter."

That news was daunting. She was so weary of witnessing cruelty and needless bloodshed. Yet she would not change her mind. Griffin was determined to make the journey so she would continue to use her gifts and skills to provide them both with whatever measure of security was within her power.

"Then, with the help of the Maker, we will do our best to avoid them."

~~~~~

Griffin began to pack away the remnants of their meal. "We should continue on our way while we still have a few hours of daylight left. We will find a place to make camp when the light fades."

Amber immediately joined him in cleaning up. "I'm ready."

He slipped the straps of his pack onto his travel-weary shoulders and glanced at Amber to see if she needed assistance. She stared back at him with her usual placid, solemn expression, ready to move whenever he chose. Her slight, willowy frame appeared completely unsuited for carrying the two packs that were never far from her. The smaller of the two, he knew, carried her personal belongings. The larger held bandages as well as vials and potions she employed in her role as healer.

They spoke little as they skirted the meadow and continued westward through the dense forest. Griffin wondered again at the presence of a Sentinel. He hoped once they put some distance between them and the stream, the Sentinel would no longer pose a threat. He remained alert for anything harmful, whether from nature or other predators. It comforted him to know Amber would also be watchful. With Amber guarding their backs, he allowed his mind to consider what awaited them.

By his estimate, once they left the forest behind, a day's journey would bring them to the border of the Limberlost. The vast swamp was majestic in a wild, untamed expanse of flora, but it was riddled with seemingly bottomless bogs and curious creatures that lay in wait for those who were careless enough to wander too far from the path. It was a place of legend and old magic. His father had regaled him and his brother with frightening tales of souls lost to its depths. Tales that had been told to him by his father and his father before him. No doubt the stories had been embellished to discourage youths from exploring the unknown and treacherous territory. Still, Griffin would not venture into it now if he had another choice.

Choice? What a capricious word. How long had it been since he had a choice about anything? That freedom had been savagely taken away six long summers ago when he had been little more than a boy of one hundred four years. The war-mongering Stonacks had invaded Cymeroon and taken him and a dozen others captive. They, with captives stolen from
~~~~~

neighboring villages, had been hauled away in chains, taken first by prison carts and then, when the terrain was too rough for the carts, forced to march across harsh, barren lands, to be trained as warriors to aid the Stonacks in their quest to conquer any people with the misfortune of lying in their path.

Griffin had learned well the skills he had been taught. He had become proficient in the use of bow and long knives, and his body had hardened, developing well-defined muscles as he spent countless hours sparring and training. His determination to survive and eventually return home enabled him to endure his conscription. Now, at last, he was free to make the long journey. The dream of seeing his homeland again had sustained him through many harrowing days and nights. To his sorrow, none of his close companions had survived the battlefield to make this journey with him.

He shoved down his bitter thoughts and did his best to concentrate on how best to navigate the Limberlost. His memories of traveling through the swamp six years ago were vague. His body had been bruised and his spirit dejected. He seemed to recall it taking two days to traverse the length of it, but that had been in a large group with a guide to lead them. He and Amber would have no one to aid them. Together they must find a way to avoid the pitfalls.

Griffin turned around quickly as he felt Amber stumble behind him. He caught her by the arm and assisted her to sit at the base of a tree. He had been moving fast, thoughtlessly forgetting how weakened Amber became after using her power. He should have allowed her more time to regain her strength.

"I am sorry. I should have remembered you required rest." He pulled out his waterskin and poured water into a cup for her.

"I do not wish to delay you." She accepted the cup and drank deeply. "I can continue."

He was filled with remorse. Amber was exhausted because she had expended herself to rescue him. "We will rest for a time. When you are recovered, we will go on a short distance to a place that is more suited to stopping for the night."

<center>~~~~~</center>

Amber regretted her weakness would cause a delay, but some time to recover was a necessity. She did not regret aiding Griffin. But the use of magic always came at a cost. For her, overwhelming fatigue left her feeling more diminished with each use. She counted that a small price to pay for having the ability to save lives.

After a brief time, Amber rose to her feet, determined not to be a burden. This time, instead of taking the lead, Griffin walked beside her. Even though he slowed his stride to match hers, every step forward seemed harder to manage than the last. She was grateful when he finally directed her to a sheltered nook beneath a rocky overhang that would protect them from predators as well as the cooler night temperatures.

Once they had eaten and gotten settled for the night, Amber wrapped her blanket closely around her shoulders and said, "Tell me about the Limberlost."

Griffin sat facing her across the small fire he had built to prepare them a hot meal. "My memory of the swamp is limited. It will take at least two days to reach the other side. There is a path, of sorts, but it is easy to stray from it without realizing it. Wandering too far afield would be dangerous. The bogs can swallow a person whole, and the creatures who make the swamp their home have survived by devouring the flesh of careless travelers. We will need to exercise care so we do not become one of those unfortunate souls."

"Then we shall be cautious."

Griffin's description reinforced her need to restore her strength. She must be ready in the very likely event her powers were needed again.

~~~~~

Amber had taken his description of the Limberlost in stride. Once she drifted into slumber, Griffin's thoughts turned once again to home. What would he find when he finally stepped foot on the land of his birth? What would Amber think of this land he loved so dearly?

He had lain awake many nights worrying about how his family had fared after the raid. His younger brother had gone with a group of friends to a distant village that fateful day, so Griffin believed Gwynn had escaped harm. He knew nothing of what had become of his parents. Would they still be there to celebrate his return? Even though Elves did not die in the manner of other races, they could be killed in battle. Surely by now, his parents believed he had departed for the Undying Land.

Griffin felt a surge of gratitude for Amber's presence. He had missed her in the days after beginning his homeward journey. Since his companions had one-by-one succumbed to the enemy, he had felt the weight of loneliness and loss. Amber was the last remaining link to his friends and the quest for home.

Tomorrow they would leave the forest. Perhaps one day he would return to the Dryad. He would like to bring his brother here to explore its mysteries.

What changes would he find in his brother? Gwynn had been a youth of ninety-three years, full of laughter and unbounded curiosity when Griffin was torn away from his family. His brother would be nearly grown now—just one year short of his majority. Had the events of that day wrought many changes to his brother? His parents? He would have answers to those questions in a few days.
~~~~~

The heaviness of sleep dragged at his eyes, so Griffin wrapped his cloak more tightly around his body and made himself comfortable on a bed of pine needles. He slept.

~~~~~

Amber awoke to a cold drizzle that had begun during the night, chilling her body. Griffin was already awake, stoking the small fire he built the evening before. She was grateful they could break their fast with a hot meal before continuing their travel. Within the next day or two they would reach the Limberlost. She and Griffin agreed they would light no fires within its borders in hopes their presence would go unnoticed by its inhabitants.

She folded her bedroll away and joined Griffin in preparing a meal while she wondered what this new day would hold. If they were successful in avoiding the bands of dispersed soldiers, their remaining time in the Dryad should be relatively safe. The way Griffin described the swamp and the barren land beyond left no doubt hazards would be abundant. Even so, she would not change her mind. She would count it her mission to aid Griffin in returning to the home he loved so much since the same was not possible for her.

She clutched her cloak tightly, pulling the hood up to ward off the rain that continued to fall. She did her best to ignore the chilling dampness that seemed to reach to her bones, taking her place next to Griffin who also huddled within his cloak.

The long day continued much as it had begun. The rain had slowed their progress enough they were forced to make camp once again before they reached the forest edge.

~~~~~

Griffin stared at the narrow break in the foliage that heralded the entrance to the Limberlost. The path, though it hardly lived up to the name, was overgrown with stunted trees that had long ago given up the fight for sunlight against the taller, stronger specimens. Their bent and gnarled limbs were covered in lichen, and their dry, brittle roots lay exposed. The early dawn light did nothing to dispel the forbidding appearance of the way before them. He took a deep breath, squared his shoulders, and spoke quietly to Amber.

"Walk behind me and stay close. We cannot risk getting separated."

Amber followed without speaking. Her steps were so light Griffin could hear no sound, but he was acutely aware she kept pace with him. She seemed to be fully restored from the lethargy of the day before. They walked for several hours, skirting around pits filled with pitch and slime and climbing over rotted, fallen trees. They maintained a steady pace despite obstacles in their path.

Griffin had halted only once, just long enough to cover his mouth and nose with a bit of cloth, miming for Amber to do the same. Steadily increasing odors permeating the swamp were so foul to his enhanced Elven sense of smell, they left him with an unsettled stomach and the inability to sniff out other potential dangers. Perhaps Amber had something in her pack that would help. He would ask when they stopped for rest and food. For now, he kept moving. His goal was to be clear of this swampland as quickly as possible.

Whirling around when he realized Amber was no longer behind him, he retraced his steps fearing she had been injured. He found her kneeling next to her pack, rummaging through its contents. With a satisfied grin, she held something out to him as he returned to her side. He accepted the misshapen object, questioning her with a look.

She whispered, "It's ginger root. Chew it to help your stomach." She broke off a small piece for herself and returned her pack to her shoulders.

There were times when having an empath as a companion was uncomfortable, leaving him feeling exposed, but today her insight was a boon. He plopped the root into his mouth and began to chew.

~~~~~

Amber could tell when the ginger began to ease Griffin's distress. The queasiness she experienced with him faded. She briefly considered using the light to aid them. It would be a simple thing to blunt their olfactory nerves, but she was reluctant to act in haste. Interfering in the ability to smell could increase the risk of undetected danger. It would be prudent to conserve her energy against a time of greater need. She would rely on the herbs and cures in her pouch for the present.

She resumed her position behind Griffin, ready to continue the journey. They did not stop for a noonday meal, anxious to make as much progress as possible this first day. Once darkness overtook them, they would be forced to stop for the night. They could eat then.

Amber cast numerous glances upward, hoping to catch a glimpse of the sun's position through the trees. She guessed it to be late afternoon. The light would be fading soon. She could tell by Griffin's behavior, he was searching for a suitable spot to make camp. She would welcome the respite. The impressions and feelings she sensed from Griffin and other living things within the bog made her very weary. Sleep would be difficult. The necessity of traveling in silence served to enhance her perceptions. They were not easily shut off, but she longed to seek whatever rest she could find.

At last, just as the shadows were making walking difficult, a dry patch of earth appeared where the foliage was more sparse. Griffin checked the stability of the ground before beckoning her to join him. Quickly divesting themselves of their packs, they set about preparing for the night.
~~~~~

~~~~~

Griffin took scant comfort from the thin ray of sunlight piercing through the trees as they prepared to begin their second day in the swamp. The previous day had been uncomfortable, but it had presented few of the pitfalls he feared. He had little hope they would be as fortunate this day. He sensed a change in the air. Something was out there. Something sentient. And whatever it was, it was aware they were here.

He watched as Amber turned in a slow circle. She seemed troubled as she gazed about, searching for something. Was she attuned to his heightened sense of danger or did she also sense a threat? She started to say something, then shook her head. Whatever had disturbed her was gone.

Griffin led out as he had the prior day with Amber close behind him. There was a restlessness about her today. He had noted the same reaction just before the Stonack army had gone into battle. Something was about to happen, and he had no idea from whence it would come.

He listened intently, turning his head from side to side to detect movement or sound that would provide them with a warning. He spun around, pulling his sword, as a muffled cry came from behind him. A wiggling, writhing vine held Amber fast. Its thick, woody length entwined itself around her body, tightening its hold on her throat and limbs, squeezing the breath from her.

With a shout, Griffin lunged forward, slicing off the section coiled around her neck before dancing back and charging again and again. A gelatinous green substance oozed from the cuts he made. He continued to feint and thrust at the vine until, with an enraged shriek, it released Amber, dropping her to the ground. Her body lay in an unmoving heap looking like nothing more than a discarded bundle of rags. Griffin rushed to her side. She was alive — barely.

He lifted her gently into his arms and carried her to a safer spot before opening her pack to find something to aid her. He checked labels and sniffed vials until he located a pungent restorative. Holding the vial beneath her nose, he was relieved when she coughed and opened her eyes.

"Annon Allen." The Elven word for "I give thanks to you," came easily to his lips as he lifted his heart to the Maker. He saw no need for their continued silence. The Limberlost inhabitants were very aware of their presence.

"How badly are you injured? What can I do to help?"

~~~~~

Amber had no words of comfort for Griffin. There was no way to hide the fact her injuries were life-threatening. The predatory vine had crushed nearly every bone in her body. Her breathing was shallow and labored, and her body felt like mush. But they were not totally devoid of hope. She was alive and awake, which allowed her to use her gift to repair the damage. She struggled to produce words to convey to Griffin what she needed to do.

"I can mend this, but it will take time. It will appear as though I am no longer breathing. That is an illusion. Bear with me and all will be well."

"Do what you must. I will not leave you."

She read fear as well as determination on his face. There was no time to explain more fully what she intended to do. She had to act now.

She closed her eyes and used her mind to call forth the light. A comforting warmth began to curl around her, filling the broken places within. Slowly the heat increased as her bones began to knit themselves together. The burning inside was no longer comfortable as the light shifted and expanded, filling her lungs with life-giving oxygen. Just as the fire within was becoming unbearable, it changed again. It gradually retreated until it once again wrapped around her like a second skin, leaving her exhausted, but alive.

When awareness returned, Griffin was by her side. His hand rested on her brow, his expression concerned. "Did the healing work? Your skin was so hot it burned my hand when I touched you."

"I am well. But I will need rest before I can travel again."

"Take as long as you need."

~~~~~

Griffin sank to the ground as his tension drained away, leaving him feeling unbounded relief. He had been afraid when Amber was injured, but that was overshadowed by a greater fear when she lay unmoving and by all appearances dead. The presence of the pulsating light suffusing her body was the only indication she lived.

This light was nothing like the light that surrounded him and Amber at the edge of the stream. That had been a protective shield, a golden glow that calmed and comforted. This light was hot and penetrating, leaping about like tongues of blue fire. He had witnessed her use of the light on his companions who were injured in battle, but it seemed to take on a larger power when she used it on herself.

He dampened a cloth and bathed her forehead with the cool water. She seemed to be in an exhausted sleep, her breathing shallow and slow. Her skin still seemed too warm, but it no longer singed his hand when he touched her. He wished there was more he could do for her. All he knew to do was keep watch and give her the time she needed to mend. However long that took.

Time was not on their side. The presence he sensed earlier, before Amber was attacked, was stronger now. It was close. And it watched them. Could they withstand another attack while Amber was still so weak?
~~~~~

Griffin drew his sword and positioned himself on the ground next to Amber. He would forfeit his life if necessary to keep her safe from whatever was lurking out there. Once Amber was able to continue the journey, a few hours would see them safely on the other side of this slimy bog. Not that it meant they were free from danger, but he was ready to see the last of this treacherous place.

~~~~~

Amber opened her eyes and looked around, a smile emerging as she caught sight of Griffin. He sat hunched nearby, a sword held loosely in his hand. His chin rested on his chest and soft snores erupted at regular intervals. He had fallen asleep while guarding her. She hated to wake him, but she was feeling much better. Her injuries had delayed them too long already. It was time to resume their journey.

Amber pulled herself into a sitting position, testing each limb. Her movements roused Griffin, who jerked his gaze to her, his face turning red.

Ignoring his embarrassment, she asked, "How long did I sleep?"

He took a moment to look around before turning his gaze to the patch of sky visible through the trees to get a view of the moon and stars. "About nine hours at a guess. How are you feeling?"

"I am whole, and ready to be on our way whenever you are ready."

~~~~~

The dawn marking their third day in the swamp was still about two hours away when Griffin began preparing a meal of crusty bread and dried venison they could consume quickly. They would resume their trek as soon as there was sufficient light to see the path. He did not plan on stopping again until they put the Limberlost far behind them.

While they ate, he observed Amber. Her fair complexion was more pale than usual, but she otherwise seemed to have recovered from her injuries. Even so, he resolved to maintain a moderate pace until he was sure she was fully restored.

She looked up and smiled as if divining his thoughts. Griffin knew she could not read his mind, but thoughts led to emotions, and she read those with amazing ease.

She smiled again and dusted the breadcrumbs from her faded dove-gray tunic before rising to repack her supplies. She shouldered the first of her two packs and bent to retrieve the second. Griffin wordlessly took it from her and added it to his burden. There was little he could do to make the journey easier for her, but relieving her of this added weight was a small service he could provide.

He set out with Amber falling in behind him. They had not gone far when the food he had eaten suddenly felt like a leaden weight in his belly. There was a tension in the air around them, an anticipation. He halted, allowing Amber to reach his side.

He whispered, "There is something on the trail ahead."

"I feel it too. Whatever is there is angry and frightened. It could be injured."

Griffin considered her words. He was loath to turn back and the path before them was surrounded by marsh and bubbly mud. They could not go around. And somehow that felt wrong anyway. If there was an injured creature, they should try to aid it. Amber was a healer. She would want to do whatever she could.

"Stay close to me." He inched forward, his steps making no sound on the spongy ground. A few moments later he stopped and halted Amber. "We are close. It is just beyond these bushes."

Amber slipped ahead of him and gently parted the branches of a thorny bush. "Oh, the poor thing."

Joining her, he saw a strange creature with its rear legs and hindquarters stuck in a bog. It had shaggy fur and a huge head. Its maw was spread wide as it growled in pain and frustration. There were cuts and open wounds on every part of the creature visible above the muck. It must have blindly run into the bog trying to escape whatever had caused its injuries.

Amber stood next to him with tears running down her face. "We have to help him."

"First, we need to free him. He will sink completely if he continues to struggle." Their task was not a simple one. Helping the creature while keeping a safe distance from its sharp teeth would not be easy. "I have an idea. Do you have a potion in your pack to induce sleep?"

She searched through her pouch, coming up with three paper-wrapped packets. "These should help. They contain Valerian, Lavender, and Skullcap. Due to the creature's size, he may not sleep, but he should be docile."

Griffin took the packets and stuffed the contents in a piece of bread from his pack. Moving as close as he dared to the edge of the bog, he tossed the bread into the open maw of the beast he believed to be an Addanc and waited.

They did not have to wait long. The thrashing movements of the animal began to slow, his agitation draining away, reducing the speed at which he was sinking. Amber shifted her gaze from the animal to Griffin.

"What do we do now? How can we free him?"

"I have a rope in my pack. If we can get it around him, we can pull him free."

"How will we get close enough to do that?"

Griffin turned in a circle, looking for anything to aid them. At first, he saw nothing. With a second look, he spotted a fallen tree. It was undersized, but he thought it would hold his weight, and it was long enough to span the pit. "We need to roll this as close to the Addanc as possible. I can use it to get the rope into position."

~~~~~

Amber had doubts about Griffin's plan. The first part should work, but she feared the sapling could not bear Griffin's weight. Since the time was short to free the animal before it was sucked beneath the mire, she assisted Griffin in rolling the log into position. Once they were ready, and Griffin pulled the rope from his pack, she stopped him.

"Allow me to take the rope? I am lighter. The log will support my weight."

She felt his struggle as he weighed his chance of success before speaking.

"It is not to my liking, but your concern is valid. We will do it your way if you agree to tether yourself to me so I can pull you back if something goes wrong."

"That is reasonable. Please hurry. The poor creature does not have much time."

Once Griffin secured a rope around her waist, Amber nimbly mounted the log and made her way to the sedated beast. Easing down to sit astride the log, she spoke softly to the animal while she looped the end of a second rope around its torso and knotted it securely.

Working together, they pulled the wounded animal free of the mire. Once they had him on solid ground, Amber used her ointments on the cuts and wounds to ease the Addanc's pain and promote healing.

The herbs she used to sedate the creature were beginning to wear off, but she could not leave until he was fully recovered. He would be vulnerable to attack while his senses were dulled.

~~~~~

Griffin tried not to think about the delay the rescue of the Addanc caused. He shared Amber's concern for the creature. It would be cruel to leave him alone and unprotected. Neither of them could do that.

They sat on the ground a safe distance from the wounded animal and waited for the sedative to wear off completely. Amber crept closer now and then to check on his progress and to administer more ointment.

The creature followed Amber's movements with a steady gaze, unalarmed by her nearness. After a time, the animal seemed to collect itself and rise to its feet, striding off into the trees without a backward glance.

Griffin laughed. "Well, I guess that takes care of that. We are no longer needed here."

"I suppose not. We should go."

Griffin was ready to get back on the trail. He hoped there was still time to get clear of the swamp before darkness fell. They would make camp and rest before entering the Hinderland shortly after first light the next day.

Furtive movements and rustling from within the foliage set Giffin on edge. They were so close to the border of the swamp that it irked him to stop, but danger had found them once more. Amber crept closer to him. He was uncertain if she sought protection or if she was preparing to extend protection to him. Perhaps both.

He crouched and signaled Amber to do the same. They needed to determine what new threat they faced. A party of six former soldiers approached, blocking their way to freedom.

Amber leaned in to whisper, "Shall I use my gift to hide us?"

"Not yet. They have not seen us. Perhaps they will pass us by."

Hoping to remain hidden and to spare Amber the necessity of using her magic, he scooted even lower, drawing her down with him. But it was not to be. One of the men caught sight of them and sent up a shout. Catching Amber by the hand, Griffin leaped to his feet and ran in the opposite direction with the soldiers at their heels.

~~~~~

Amber did her best, but she could not keep up with Griffin's longer stride. She tugged free of Griffin's hand and turned, intending to cover them with her light. Before she could act, the Addanc they had rescued loped from the woods and took a position between them and the soldiers. Rearing up on its hind legs, the beast let out an ear-splitting roar. The result was immediate. With shrieks and yells, the soldiers disappeared into the swamp.

Amber stood very still. She did not believe the creature intended them harm, but she made sure not to make any sudden moves that could antagonize him. Griffin stood close beside her, following her example.

Slowly the Addanc dropped to all fours and moved to the path. He took a few steps and turned to stare at them.

"I think he wants us to follow."

Griffin smiled. "Since that is the direction we need to go, I think we should do what he wants."

Amber led the way, keeping a respectful distance behind the Addanc. After another hour of walking, they came to the edge of the swamp. Holding out her hand toward the animal, she spoke in a soothing tone. "Thank you, my friend, for guiding us."

The Addanc glided forward and placed its massive head beneath her hand for only a moment before turning and moving back into the Limberlost.

Griffin said, "That is one of the strangest things I have ever seen."

Amber smiled. "It is the magic of kindness."
~~~~~

~~~~~

Today's events had taken a heavy toll. But that was one more hurdle behind them and one day closer to home. Now that they were free of the swamp, Griffin decided it would be safe to build a fire. A hot meal and warmth for the night felt like a precious gift.

Amber sat huddled close to the warm blaze, her cloak tucked in around her while she sipped on the sassafras tea he had prepared from the bark she produced from her pack. He observed her through half-closed eyelids. How would the strange sounds and visions they would experience when they entered the Hinderland affect her? Even though it was years ago, he had not forgotten the terror he experienced. He thought he would go mad before the horror had ended. He would spare her that if he had the ability.

He poured the last of his tea from his cup and spread his blanket on the ground. "Good eventide, Amber. We will leave at dawn."

~~~~~

A tinge of orange and yellow was just beginning to show on the eastern horizon when Amber awoke. She quickly folded and stored away her bedroll. Weary from lack of sleep, she stoked the fire and prepared some tea. Griffin's dread of this day was palpable, disturbing her rest. He was sleeping now, which was good. Amber relished a few minutes alone to prepare herself.

The prospect of battling against unseen forces with the power to affect the mind was frightening. She mentally reviewed the herbs and potions remaining in her pack, wishing she had something to provide them with a preventative. She could think of nothing to calm them without dulling their ability to think and react to threats. All she had was the light. She would use that only if there were no other way.

Griffin soon joined her as she set about preparing breakfast. "Good *morwe*. Did you rest well?"

She ignored the question and handed him a cup of tea. Neither of them had rested well. No matter. It was time to be on their way.

~~~~~

The sight in front of them was horrendous. Once healthy, growing trees had dotted the landscape. Now the vista was filled with bare, stunted skeletons, bleached white from the sun. Amber sucked in a deep breath. It could be the last normal one she drew today. The air felt as dead as the Hinderland. She was beginning to understand Griffin's dread of this place, and they had yet to step one foot within its borders. She could only imagine what evil had caused this devastation.

Her skills as an empath were not needed to detect Griffin's turbulent emotions as he stood beside her. She reached deep inside to control her own emotions. She would not be able to cope with those as well as the
~~~~~

feelings rolling off Griffin. He had experienced this place before. He had ample cause to fear what was to come.

Tension built as she waited for Griffin to take the first step into a land forsaken by any living being. She had to wonder what had become of the Sentinel tasked with protecting this piece of blighted ground. Had he been killed? She knew little of their kind. Could they die? Certainly, he had failed in his assigned task.

~~~~~

Griffin took Amber's hand in his and offered a prayer to the Maker for protection. It would not be long before their minds were bombarded with the keening and wails of unseen spirits. Visions of past failures and deepest regrets swirled around him. Those had been severe enough six years ago, but the horrors of war would multiply every failure he experienced since that time. The visions of future things interspersed with the past but were clouded with uncertainty. They were wispy and ethereal, created from someone's darkest fears. They denoted possibilities and half-truths rather than events that were sure to come to pass.

Amber did not pull her hand from his as they began walking. Her touch was reassuring. His hand tightened on hers as images of his fallen friends, lying broken and bleeding on a battlefield, filtered through his mind. He pushed back against them, replacing them with memories of living, laughing companions. That tactic was the only weapon he possessed that would be effective against this enemy. He must use good to counteract evil.

They had only a short reprieve before the next assault began. Stronger this time, as if the spirits shifted and adapted to overcome his defenses. A vision of his brother, looking just as Griffin remembered him, came to mind. Gwynn was laughing with someone. Suddenly his head came up as if someone called him. He turned to look behind just as a spear plunged into his heart, felling him in an instant. Griffin cried out in anguish. Amber caught him in an embrace. Her voice was low but urgent as she whispered words of comfort.

"It is not real. Do not be afraid."

~~~~~

For a time, the voices receded. They were not silent but rather seemed to confer among themselves. Amber assumed they were preparing for another attack. She was surprisingly unaffected by the spirits. Perhaps it was due to her Faerie blood. She could hear the voices, but they were not directed toward her. It was possible they could not separate the spirit part of her from their own. Griffin was their chosen target. The urge was strong to use the light, but she could not be certain she could maintain the shield long enough to escape this land. She must wait until she had no other choice.

She held tightly to Griffin's hand. He was so tortured by the attacks on his mind that he seemed incapable of moving forward without assistance. She led him westward, taking advantage of the lull to cover as much ground as possible. They had been in this wasteland for the better part of the day. She scanned the horizon, hoping to see the end of the deadness.

~~~~~

Griffin faltered as a new image emerged. He was standing at the eastern edge of Cymeroon, witnessing utter destruction. The lanes were empty of inhabitants and the buildings were hollowed out shells. He forced his feet to move, rushing toward his father's house. When he reached the center of the village, his worst fears were realized. The once stately home was ravaged by war. Chunks of the stone walls were missing and the roof was riddled with holes. His mother's garden had been trampled and destroyed. Only small bits of color remained to show where once vibrant plants had stood.

He fell to his knees as grief overwhelmed him. The vision had shown no sign of life. What had become of his family? Had anyone survived?

He was only vaguely aware when Amber kneeled beside him, wrapping her arms around him.

"I have to use the magic now. You cannot endure this torture any longer."

She bowed her head, and a low hum began as she summoned the light. He had never heard her use her voice to call forth the magic. The gentle rhythm of sound reached deep inside him, searching. A change seemed to be taking place within him. He felt himself grow larger, expanding. A yowl of pain escaped as his body felt as if it was being torn apart.

An enormous winged creature with the body of a lion and the head of an eagle and talons on its front feet appeared where he had been standing only a moment ago. A griffin. How was this possible? He had become the mythical creature he was named for. Had Amber brought this about with her magic?

Amber's urgent words cleared the fog from his mind. "Hurry, we must escape this place now while the magic holds. I cannot sustain it for long."

Griffin lowered his cumbersome body so Amber could mount, leaning forward to wrap her arms around his neck. With a bounce, he rose into the air, his wings spreading wide to catch the current and glide them to a safe place. In only a short time, the Hinderland was behind them. He flew in a downward spiral, lowering them into an empty field. Amber quickly slipped from his back and ceased humming, allowing the magic to fall away. Spent from the effects of the magic, they both collapsed to the
~~~~~

ground and fell into an exhausted slumber.

Long after, when he awoke, he had returned to himself. Amber lay nearby.

He did not disturb her sleep. He had much to think about. He could hardly believe this experience was real. Had he really transformed into a winged creature? That would bear thinking about later. Now, his fears led him to consider the last vision. Would Cymeroon still be standing when he finally arrived or was the destruction only a trick created by the spirits? He would know by this time tomorrow. For now, he and Amber must regain their strength.

~~~~~

Amber awoke in great confusion. Her magic had never taken that form before. She had sought only to create a barrier between the tormenting voices and Griffin. The only explanation she could think of was that Griffin possessed a latent Elven magic that had combined with hers to manifest a physical change in him. Quite possibly, he was unaware of his abilities. Whatever the cause, the combined magic had forged a greater bond between them. One that could not be broken in this life. She did not know how she knew this, but her perception of his emotions had deepened. She was not only aware of his feelings, but she experienced what he felt.

That he had become the embodiment of the ancient griffin made sense. The regal dignity symbolizing divine power and protection was familiar. Griffin were the guardians of priceless possessions. They were loyal and protective. Griffin had fought all enemies to return to what he treasured. His home and family. It had become her goal as well.

~~~~~

Griffin stood frozen to the ground, overwhelmed by the sight before him. Cymeroon had been destroyed. It was his vision, come to life. The village lay in ruins.

Without conscious volition, he turned his feet toward his family home with Amber walking silently by his side. Just as the specters predicted, little remained of the house he had dreamed of returning to.

Picking his way through the rubble and debris, Griffin pushed aside the door that was no longer on its hinges. His heart grew heavier with each step. He carefully searched each room, hoping for a clue about the fate of his family. Everything had been broken or damaged. At last, he entered the room he and his brother had shared. It had not been spared from the wanton vandalism of the rest of the house. He allowed memories to wash over him. Secrets the two had shared, the games they had played, and the treasures they had hidden.

At the thought of treasures, another memory came to mind. He quickly returned to his parents' room. Shortly before the Stonacks raided his village, his parents had shown him a set of betrothal rings they had purchased for him. He would have been selecting a mate by this age if he had not been captured. Once a match was made, he and his bride-to-be would wear the rings on the first finger of their right hands for the year-long betrothal period before the union was celebrated at a feast of their joint families.

He hardly dared to hope the rings were still here. They had been placed in a concealed cavity inside the walls. Was it possible the raiders had not found them? He barely breathed as he removed a loose stone to search the hollowed-out space. Plunging his hand into the darkened hole, he felt around until his fingers touched a leather pouch. Pulling it out, he opened it and poured two gold rings into the palm of his hand.

Tears streamed down his face as he stared at the rings. They represented the hopes and dreams of his family. He could not, he would not believe those hopes were dead. Not as long as there was a chance his family lived. If they had managed to escape, he believed they would head north to join another group of Elves who had settled at the base of a mountain where they had built a stone fortress. He must go there and see for himself if they still lived.

Amber stood by, silently supporting him in his grief. Her hand rested on his shoulder. That gentle contact was the only thing keeping him from total despair. He turned his gaze to her.

"What do I do now? My home is gone. I have no one. My family is lost to me."

"You have me. I will not leave you. When you are sad, I will cry. When you are hurt, I will bleed. When you are happy, I will laugh with you. Together we will search for your family. And until we find them, I will be your home."

He stared at her for several moments, allowing her words to sink into his heart as he realized he could not find a more suitable mate than Amber.

He promised, "And I will be your home." He selected the smaller of the two rings he held in his hand and placed it on Amber's finger, handing her the other to place on his. By the grace of the Maker, they would be reunited with his family in time to share their joy when they wed.

The End

Lynda Page lives in Central Ohio, but grew up in West Virginia surrounded by mountains and fast-moving rivers where she developed a life-long love of nature and books. Books of all kinds, often annoying her mother by being late for dinner because she had to read "just one more paragraph" before joining the family. Some of the more unusual aspects of cases she encountered while working in the Special Investigation Unit of a Midwest insurance company often find their way into her writing, primarily romantic suspense, but with an occasional foray into fantasy.

She was a double semi-finalist in the ACFW Genesis contest in 2022 and a finalist in the First Impression contest in 2024. Lynda has one grown daughter and a six-year-old granddaughter who has amassed an impressive library of her own. She can be reached at *pagesix622@gmail.com*.

Legacy of the Canal Barge
A Tie-in to the "Together" Series
Kim Garee

The Graham family of Buckeye Lake knew the old canal barge they'd turned into a house had been won in a poker game. That was "way back" in the 1800s when the Ohio & Erie Canal still operated. That was all any of them really knew of its history.

Hauled up onto a narrow strip of the canal's towpath, the once functional freight barge came to boast lace curtains, window boxes of marigolds, and some hodgepodge furniture. Over the generations, it had settled onto Towpath Island alongside a more traditional, newer family home.

By the summer of 1957, no one occupied the old barge house.

So, twenty-year-old Delia Stimpson Adams—adopted into the Graham family and its long history at the lake a decade before—decided *she* would move into the furnished barge, at least for the summer.

The early June morning was still cool as she trudged down the slope past the marina toward the lake, armed with her Remington Quiet-Riter Miracle Tab typewriter.

"Look who's not wasting any time." It was Charlie, her best friend and brother, loping out of the marina's workshop.

"You haven't left yet?"

"Forgot the rope." He waved a coil of it at Delia. "You know, Grand Canyon and all. Might need to be pulled out of some pinch." He was clad in pants with a dozen pockets for his annual hiking adventure.

"Don't let Mom hear you talk about being pulled out of anything."

"She's still triple-checking Pop's backpack. Not too late to change your mind, you know. You can come."

Delia appreciated the reminder she was welcome. Gabe Adams, Charlie's stepfather and Delia's adoptive father, would take either of them to the ends of the earth, were they inclined to go.

"Things to do," she insisted with a pointed shift of the typewriter's weight. He grinned at her wrestling match with the bulky thing but, in true brother fashion, made no offer to help. Delia had to look up to catch his grin because he had never stopped growing, while Delia had stopped almost before she got started.

"You're really moving into that old barge for the whole summer."

"I need some quiet." She didn't have to explain to her brother how little quiet was to be found at the inn or the marina their sprawling family of parents, aunts, uncles, and cousins ran on Liebs Island. Then there were the screaming crowds summer brought to the lake's amusement park.

To punctuate the lack of quiet, one of the bay doors of the marina opened with a rattle. A man taller than Charlie waved in greeting and then turned to retrieve something within.

Delia squinted. "Who's that?"

"Miles Martin," Charlie said. "*The Third*. He's mostly running the marina for the summer." It went without saying that their grandpa Hickory would still monitor the place from his rocker on the towpath. "Miles is a teacher over at Walnut Township."

"A teacher." Delia pulled a face. Teachers had rarely appreciated her brand of curiosity, and she had rarely appreciated … well, not being appreciated.

"You know it wouldn't hurt you to go up to the ballroom some." Charlie gestured in the direction of the north shore amusement park. Or he might have been gesturing at Miles Martin the Third; she couldn't quite tell. "When you're not …" Then he waved his rope-free hand at the Remington in her arms.

Delia rolled her eyes. Teachers were not the only ones who failed to appreciate her.

"I don't dance, Charlie."

"Wouldn't kill you to go out with someone."

"I've been out with *someones*. You know they never take."

'You can't be so strange right away, that's all. Can't you … ease into it a little?"

Delia was too used to that for it to sting. "That seems dishonest."

Miles Martin reappeared from the marina bay with his own armful of rope. "Good! I caught you before you left!" he called. "Switch me rope. This'll work better for what you're needing."

The men made the switch. Up close, Delia could tell the teacher was in his mid or late twenties. Even talking with Charlie about a stupid rope, she could *hear* the teacher in him, and it annoyed her.

"Thanks." Charlie admired the better braiding. "Miles, meet my sister, Delia."

"Hello," he said, stretching a big hand out for a shake, only to notice Delia's were occupied with the typewriter. He drew his hand back and studied her. "It's really nice to meet you."

"Yeah." Delia cringed. "I mean, *yes*. Nice to meet you."

"Miles, is it asking too much for you to take Del dancing a time or two at the Crystal Ballroom this season?"

Delia felt her face heat, watched Miles Martin blink in confusion, and decided she was not too mature to kick her brother right in the shin.

"Ow!"

In her momentum, she fumbled the unwieldy typewriter, only for Miles to reach over and lift the thing right into his own arms like it was a toy.

"Where does this go, ma'am?"

Delia cringed again over … so many things. At Charlie's fatheaded set-up. At her near drop of her beloved machine. And definitely at being called "ma'am" moments after childishly kicking her brother.

"She's bound for the towpath, Miles," Charlie said, and he stopped rubbing his shin to point. "She's a temperamental writer bent on locking herself away from everyone."

"How wonderful!" Miles said un-ironically, and he was studying her again.

"Brother," she said, teeth gritted. "Do have a good trip and be careful not to plummet to an early grave."

Charlie threw his head back with a laugh, then tossed a wave behind him as he moved toward a honking horn. "Thanks again for the rope, Miles. Love ya, Del."

"Yeah. Love you too." Delia worked to reclaim her typewriter from the teacher. "It's not heavy. Thanks, though."

"May I ask what you write?" His voice was gentle, kind even, as he situated the Remington back into her arms.

Delia despised this question. *What did she write?* Things people never understood.

"I'm working on a novel," she hedged, and then she bid him farewell and hurried to the footbridge that led over the old canal to the swath of towpath that was about to be her hiding place.

~~~~~

Open windows moved the early summer breeze through the old box of the barge house. Delia had just slid the first sheet of paper into the typewriter when she heard Rosie Graham Adams approaching.

"Hullooooo, the barge!"

If anyone could interrupt Delia without earning a growl, it was her adoptive mother.

"Door's open," she called, pushing back from the desk she'd arranged in front of the window facing the lake. The lakefront half of the barge was also dominated by a bed, while an added wall set off the cooking area on the old canal side.

Hickory had once lived in the thing. Aunt Emily had lived in it, too.

Now it was Delia's turn.

"I brought strawberry bread." Rosie nudged open the screen door with a plate, and she offered her usual soft smile.
~~~~~

Thanking her, Delia couldn't help but also notice the canvas tote on her mother's shoulder. This bag, with a cheerful frog painted on it by Rosie herself, undoubtedly held the latest pages of the children's book mother and daughter had been partnering on for the past two years.

Now, *The Frogs of the Bog* series of illustrated stories sold nationally and seemed to be in ever-greater demand.

Delia wrote, Rosie illustrated, and some company Gabe knew in Columbus published it. Delia barely concerned herself with that part of it.

The happy frogs in the series lived on Cranberry Bog at Buckeye Lake, Ohio, where their patchwork amphibian family entertained other families with their wholesome and humorous adventures.

The deadline for the next hope-filled frog story was already approaching.

"Mmm, bread's great, Mom. Thanks again." Delia spoke around the bite that had been pushed at her on her mother's way through. It was still faintly warm. Now Rosie returned from placing the plate in the kitchen, and Delia's gaze returned to the tote. "What's up?"

"Getting all settled in?" Rosie asked, surveying the space.

Few would look at the older woman and guess she'd raised the lanky Charlie to manhood, adopted and raised Delia to whatever semblance of womanhood she'd achieved, and had three more children still in various stages of being raised. Despite the demands of family, Rosie's pixie-like grace still made it seem as though she'd walked off the pages of some fairy tale herself.

"You didn't like the storyline," Delia guessed, resigned. She was familiar with that expression on her mother's face.

Rosie off-loaded the tote and produced the brief manuscript Delia had dropped in her studio the day before.

"It's not exactly what we talked about, Del."

That was how it worked. Rosie would do preliminary sketches (which *every*one knew made *The Frogs of the Bog* so delightful), and the mother-daughter team would talk through a simple storyline. Then Delia would type it up, and Rosie would crank out final illustrations to match.

It had worked so far.

Now, Rosie fanned the sheaf of typed pages at her daughter.

"It's a bit dark. For children, I mean," Rosie said. "Don't you think?"

"I thought you wanted Frieda Froggy to be recovering from a leg injury." Delia used her most innocent tone.

"Yes. Well." The fold of worry appeared between Rosie's brow as she looked at the words on the page.

Some part of Delia had known it would not fly with her mother, but this was a dance they still had to do with each draft.

Frieda's froggy leg had gotten stuck in a cranberry picker, Delia had written, and now the poor thing could not walk without help.

"It's the level of *detail* you included with the picker, dear," Rosie said on a sigh. As though required to defend the position, she held up the page and read aloud:

> *"As the joint of her leg gave, Frieda looked into the jagged jaw of the picker, afraid she would see it stained red from more than just cranberry juice."*

Rosie's gaze rose from the page and slammed into Delia's. "*Really, Del?*"

Delia swallowed carefully. "Who says kids don't want stories like that?"

"*I do.* I say that. Anyone with sense says that."

"That's harsh, Mom." But she couldn't stop the rueful smile that surfaced.

"Look, write whatever dark things you want to while you're hidden here in the barge, but first *please* give me a story I can illustrate without giving myself nightmares." With that, Rosie produced the roughed-up cover design for *Frieda's Summer Recovery* story, which she tacked onto a stray nail in the beam beside the desk, clearly as a reminder of the deadline.

"Maybe I don't need to include quite that much detail about how she sustained the leg injury in the first place," Delia conceded carefully.

Shouldering her tote, Rosie raised a single brow.

"I'll have it done by tomorrow." Delia tried not to sigh. She'd long since given up wishing she were more like her warm, nurturing mother.

Hair tied back in a colorful bandana, Rosie took Delia's cheeks into her palms. The corner of her lips quirked, and Delia knew there would always be one person who appreciated her, if not always her writing. "Stained red from more than just cranberry juice?"

"It didn't *have* to be blood." Delia smiled outright as she added, "I can't help it you've got such a morbid imagination, Mom."

Rosie smacked a loud kiss on her forehead and turned to the door. "Enjoy your quiet, my sweet girl."

~~~~~

It took hardly any time at all for Rosie's "sweet girl" to remove the gore in Frieda Froggy's woeful tale. Delia finished it before dark.

Afterward, she paced the inside length of the barge house in the gathering dusk, eating beans out of a mason jar and letting the shadows prompt those wondrous chills down her back.

The barge was cozy but somehow still haunting, with its heavy, rough-hewn beams of white pine stained by stories she could only guess at. As children, she and Charlie had invented a ghost for the barge, a murdered captain returned to claim his freight.
~~~~~

Though the structure had been wired with electricity decades before, Delia was reluctant to flip the switch and remove those shadows. Instead, she lit a candle for the corner of her desk.

The tale she'd been scaring herself with for months flickered to life like a film reel and had her turning to pen and paper, rather than the typewriter, to capture those first thoughts. Dropping into the chair, she let the ink flow with the scene. Her heroine, suddenly separated from her friend on the trail, saw a shadow that was not quite as shapeless as she'd like. In fact, *she knew this shape …*

The last smudges of pink faded from the lake's reflected sunset as a similar moonless dark settled over Delia's story. There was only the soft breath of the candle flame, the gentle gravel sound of pen on paper, and the slide of her own hand as it moved across the page. Far across Buckeye Lake was the distant jangle of the ballroom and amusement park, which Delia had stopped noticing years before.

She did, however, notice footsteps on dry grass.

Delia's hand stilled and she looked up into the darkness outside her window.

There it was again. More rustling footsteps, slowing. Close to the side of the barge, by her calculations.

Another delicious shiver of fear.

Someone really was out there.

It wouldn't be Aunt Emily's and Uncle Drew's kids, though they all lived in the big house next door with Grandpa Hickory. The towpath was their playground as it had been Delia's own, but a glance at her wristwatch confirmed the kids would all be in bed by now.

Besides, these were the slow, furtive steps of one person, not the rush of children.

Then the beam of a flashlight flickered across the wood of the dock outside the window, immediately going dark again.

Gasping, Delia rose clumsily from her chair.

This was not her imagination. Most things that scared Delia in life had turned out to be her imagination, but this was real, and she really was alone. Or as alone as anyone ever was on Towpath Island.

There *was* someone a few feet on the other side of the barge's outer wall.

It could not be Charlie pranking her. He and Gabe had left hours earlier. *What would her heroine do?*

Taking a careful breath, she pinched the flame out with her fingertips and crept through the kitchen to the back door and outside. Easing the door shut, she knew the darkness was on her side, as she'd run tame here most of her life. Trailing her hand along the wood siding, still warm from the summer sun, she tiptoed along the lavender that bloomed each year around the foundation.

Reaching the corner, she let out the breath she'd held, sucked in a fresh one …

… and screamed for all she was worth when the enormous figure of a man rounded the corner and walked right into her.

It took her a moment to realize *he* had screamed, too.

"What …" she tried to say, heartbeat thudding loud in her own ears.

"Sorry! Sorry! It's me!"

Though she'd only heard his voice once that very morning, Delia realized whose shadow towered over her.

"*Miles?*"

What she was learning for the first time was that Miles Martin the Third smelled like soap and boat engine oil, much like her grandpa. She'd have to remember that detail for her story.

"What are you doing here?" he asked, stepping back and fiddling with something. "My flashlight went out."

"What am *I* doing here?"

"No, no. Sorry. I didn't mean … I mean … I thought your family lived up by the inn. I'm sorry. I didn't know you were sleeping in this, this thing! I didn't mean to scare anyone."

"I'm staying in the barge house this summer."

"I thought … the bigger house." His shadow gestured toward the lit windows of Hickory Graham's home. "I thought that's where you'd gone to write. Forgive me."

Collecting herself, Delia tugged at her top and tried to pin him with a glare he, no doubt, could not see. "I guess I'd like to know what *you* are doing poking around our property late at night, flashlight or no flashlight."

He was shaking the thing in frustration and ground out, "It was a story your aunt wrote. I can explain. I promise."

As if on cue, the porchlight of the big house flicked on, and Uncle Drew was visible on the front porch. "Everything okay out there?"

"Well, looks like that explanation will happen in front of your employer."

Delia knew she sounded snooty as she marched the man across the narrow strip of island like a criminal, but she was still embarrassed about how loud she'd just screamed.

<center>~~~~~</center>

Puzzled, the family had shut off a special episode of *I Love Lucy* and gathered with Delia and Miles in the dining room.

"My great-grandfather was Durb Martin," Miles announced, both large hands spread calmly on the table.

He still hadn't touched the coffee Aunt Emily had served. It was never too late for coffee, at least where Emily was concerned.

Durb Martin? Looking around at Aunt Emily, Uncle Drew, and Grandpa Hickory, Delia waited for the man's heritage to mean something to anyone at the table.

Then it did, apparently.

"Wait a minute. Abraham Martin?" Hickory asked, his fuzzy gray brows shooting up. "*That* Durb Martin?"

Aunt Emily, used to being in-the-know, swiveled her head to take in faces. "Okay, I'll ask ..."

"He's the one who lost the old canal barge to my father," Hickory supplied.

Familiar with the lore of a lucky poker game that had established the Graham family presence at the tip of Liebs Island, everyone at the table nodded an "aha."

As the story went, at least as far as Delia knew, Henry Graham had won the freight barge but didn't care to pole the waters of the Ohio & Erie Canal. Instead, he started a marina, converting the barge into a crude cottage for him and his wife. Later, their son Hickory had married and lived there with Louisa. They had eventually built the larger house they all sat in now on the towpath, but their son brought his own bride to the barge house in 1919, and Rosie and Emily Graham had even been born there. Over the years, amenities had been added: plumbing, power, walls, a tiny attic level with extra beds.

It was difficult for Delia to imagine this teacher across the table, with his carefully trimmed beard and calm manner, might feel a connection to the old barge stronger than her family's.

Great-grandpa Durb or not.

"I have a journal he kept," Miles was explaining. "Durb Martin, I mean." He looked at Aunt Emily. "It was the story you published in your newspaper, ma'am, the one honoring the hundred-year history of that barge-turned-house, that had me putting it all together. I never knew where he'd hidden the barge until now."

"Hidden?" This from Uncle Drew, a lifelong lawman. "He *lost* it, son. On a bad hand of cards."

"With all due respect, that's the story they told, sir. Yes. But the journal points to that barge containing important ... clues. Some kind of mystery that meant they had to disguise it deliberately to save my great-grandfather's life."

Hickory leaned forward and spoke slowly. "My father saved your ancestor's life by turning the man's active canal barge into a house?"

"Yes, sir."

"Saved how? From whom?" Emily insisted.

"I'm not sure, exactly. I was hoping I could find clues of some kind hidden within the barge itself. I didn't know Delia was staying there, honest, or I wouldn't have gone over like I did." Miles made eye contact around the table. His eyes were a clear, surprising shade of blue. "Everything I've learned from the journal points to secrets that might be valuable. Ones that might even clear my family's reputation as traitors to our country."

~~~~~

The next morning, Delia wasn't exactly surprised to see her aunt pop into the inn's laundry room on her way to the newspaper.

"Morning, Aunt Emily."

She would have known she'd find Delia there with Rosie. Linen-washing day, after all, was an all-hands-on-deck endeavor for the Island Inn ladies, including the inn's long-time manager, Ruth.

"Don't you go digging around that old barge with a shovel, Del," was Emily's playful greeting as she gulped yet more hot coffee and followed it with a hiss. "You'll ruin the lavender Granny Louise planted."

"You're just jealous you don't have time to go digging." Delia absolutely had every intention of finishing the linens and spending the day knocking on the walls of her summer home. Could there be a secret compartment, perhaps?

"The whole thing seems very strange to me," Rosie said for the second or third time.

"Well, one thing we know," Aunt Emily said. "Grandpa can't resist hiring unsavory characters to work at the marina."

They chuckled over the collective memory of him hiring a mob hitman the same summer Emily had fallen in love with Uncle Drew.

It was a valid point, though. Delia wondered why barge captain Durb Martin's great-grandson had not gone straight to Hickory Graham with his curiosity about the old structure. Sneaking around in the dark with a flashlight (even one he didn't appear capable of operating) seemed suspect, indeed.

Delia loved everything about it.

"Miles told Drew afterward that he wasn't excited for any of us to know he was descended from a villain," Emily put in.

"I have to say, it makes me like him a little better."

"Delia," Rosie admonished with exasperation.

"Grandpa told him he can make arrangements with Delia to explore it, so she's not scared next time," Emily said.

"I wasn't that scared."

"I heard you scream."

"That was Miles."

"What do you think the big mystery is?" Ruth asked. "What did this Miles fellow say, exactly?"
~~~~~

"It's some secret." Delia snapped a sheet and folded it before her, frustrated. "Miles doesn't even seem to know, himself, except that it's worth a great deal. I can't help hoping it's treasure."

"That's unlikely," Ruth said. "Why would the old captain just leave it there, then?"

"And how would some buried treasure clear their family name?" Emily asked.

~~~~~

The typewriter in the barge house stayed silent as that morning turned to afternoon. Delia had been silent, as well, as she'd casually and not-so-casually familiarized herself with the construction and re-construction of the freighter in which she was living.

By suppertime, she was stymied.

That was why she stood, arms crossed over her chest, just outside the marina when Miles Martin clocked out. He jumped a little when he found her there, but he smiled just as quickly.

"Well, hullo! I keep literally running into you around corners, don't I?"

"What does your great-grandfather's journal *say*, exactly, Miles?"

Instead of looking resentful, the man's face lit. "You want to help me, then?"

Delia made a non-committal sound, a little surprised that he'd welcome such a partnership with someone he barely knew. She imagined them engaging in a tug-of-war over a chest of gold coins.

Then, she was still more distracted when she heard his stomach growl.

Miles smiled sheepishly as he patted the front of his short-sleeved shirt with its panels of maroon stripes.

"We could go get dinner," he offered. "And then grab the journal from my place, if you like."

Alarms sounded within Delia. Yes, she longed to know what his "place" was like. After all, he was the first traitor-trespasser she'd ever known in real life. A handsome one, at that.

But being seen out to dinner in Millersport or anywhere near Buckeye Lake with a *teacher*?

"Never mind," he said with that same calm confidence. He must have read her response in her face. Delia figured he probably read a lot, and, anyway, alarms in her mind always tended to manifest themselves on her face. "I'll bring the journal back to show you in a bit, okay?"

~~~~~

Outside the cottage later, Miles examined the roof while Delia examined him. What would he be doing if he weren't out here tonight? Dancing? Did teachers dance? Again, she could easily imagine him reading plenty of books.

She liked books, too.

Had he read much Edgar Allen Poe in Teacher School?

"Of course, it would be easier if we knew what we were looking for," Miles said with a smile. He'd returned in a powder blue shirt this time, damp hair starting to curl a bit behind his ear. Not that she found that of interest.

She was interested in the mystery they had to solve, the leather-bound journal he'd brought back, and, admittedly, the paper sack he'd tossed her with a coney dog in it.

"I marked some spots in the journal that are of interest," he told her over his shoulder, sounding like a teacher again. "Mind if I pop inside to see how this board here attaches?"

She waved permission.

With her legs tossed over the arm of a lawn chair, Delia opened the century-old book. The thin handwriting within covered each page top to bottom, but she could make out most words. Enough to know Durb — short for "durbin," which was a common term for canal boat operators, according to a lecture from a certain history-loving teacher — was up to all kinds of mysterious activity up and down the Ohio & Erie.

A scrap of new paper marked one passage in which Captain Durb Martin referenced "collecting a hefty sum" for hauling something he couldn't even see once he got to the southernmost point of the canal in Youngstown. Some entries were comparatively mundane. Fish fries, brawls for priority entrance into a lock (which his crew usually won), decisions about whether to run after dark.

Miles emerged again from the barge house, and she looked up to find him staring wide-eyed at her.

"What?" she asked. "Did you find something?"

"I did. Some sketches and notes about the *Frogs of the Bog* book series?" His face lit, and Delia didn't know quite how to feel about being discovered. "You're *the author*! It just clicked!"

"My mother is the heart and soul of the series. The sketches are hers. I just put her ideas into words."

"Well, I *love* those books."

Delia smiled. "I'm glad you do." *So much for Edgar Allen Poe.* "Anyway, I read a little of what you marked here. The journal says what Durb's hauling, at least in part ... is something he can't *see*," she said, flipping through pages and glancing up at the captain's great-grandson. Miles crossed the grass to her and crouched beside her chair.

"Right. Whatever it was, I believe he wasn't entirely aware of what he was being paid to transport," he said, reaching over. "Based on the language he used. May I?"

He was so polite and smelled so good. More spicy soap now than engine oil. Delia watched him turn back a few pages.

"Look here. He notes that part of his biggest 'job' is to disappear from the barge for an evening up by Brecksville, at the far north of the route."

"Disappear?"

Miles read aloud, his finger on some of the scrawled text: *"Crew doesn't mind being banished from My Gal …"*

"That's the name of this old canal boat? *My Gal?*" Delia considered the low-ceilinged little cottage with fresh eyes, imagined it being tugged by a team of horses along the waterways. "Huh."

"He says just below that: *Hate leaving her unoccupied for whole evening, but instructions very clear. Money waits down in Youngstown. Have to leave her alone an evening again when down there.* See? I think he's not entirely sure what he's hauling."

"Something they can't touch? But why would he and his crew have to disappear for it to be loaded and unloaded if it's not able to be touched? Do you suppose it could be something to do with the Underground Railroad?"

Miles stood and joined her in staring at the whitewashed wood of the barge. "Don't think so. Only because he was known in the North as a suspected traitor in the years that followed, so that doesn't match. Plus, he seemed to be making the delivery down south, *from* the north."

"True."

"That was a good thought, though," the teacher said, causing her to smile in spite of herself.

They were quiet for a moment, and Delia found the silence surprisingly comfortable.

"He didn't burn the barge or anything, but also, he needed to keep it a secret. So, did the barge prove his guilt, or did it prove his innocence?" She looked up at him. "And if it was his innocence, why didn't he offer it up as evidence?"

Miles turned a chunk of pages to another bookmark. "Here, this is the part that's so important." He read: *"The game is lost, over. Soldiers in wait in Balt. Am suspected."*

"Is that Baltimore, Ohio, as in just south of the lake here?"

"Seems like it. He goes on to say: *H.G. helped haul My Gal to towpath. Disguising as house. Pleasure boats around it. Heading north with horse team. Crew disbursed, sworn to silence. Staying off water.*"

More quiet.

"H.G. must've been Henry Graham, Hickory's dad. 'Other boats' must have been the marina he was starting here on the towpath. It would've been a decent hiding place," Delia mumbled aloud, thinking. "So, it had to be northern soldiers waiting for him just below this part of the canal as he headed south."

"Yes. Which means whatever he hauled had to be dangerous to the Union Army."

"Hence, the traitor rep."

Miles sighed. "Yes. Interestingly, he returned just a couple days later and helped build the foundation for the barge as a home. It says here on this page that he exacted a promise that it would never be moved."

"That matches what Hickory said the other night, but I think he just was raised thinking the old captain was sentimental about the thing. What did the man end up doing? I mean, after?"

"Durb Martin went off and used his loads of money to establish his family on prime real estate in Lancaster, Ohio," Miles said. "But folks spread rumors about him. Nothing clear. Just that his money had come from betraying his country."

"That's where you were raised, then?"

"Lancaster, yes."

"It seems like whatever information was hidden with this barge would have gotten him killed, Miles. We need to imagine what that could be."

"Perhaps, but why didn't he simply burn it, then? I just need to know. No one has ever known."

Delia got up and considered the barge. *"My Gal,"* she said softly. "Miles. Why was it important to Durb to put it on a stone foundation? What if there's a body hidden or something?"

He didn't react much to that. "Seems unlikely. If the cargo were human, he'd have simply off-loaded it here. There'd have been no reason to hide the entire barge from the folks waiting for it to float down, you know?"

Delia sighed. "It really doesn't add up."

"No."

"But I feel like there could be *some*thing under it. Some clue. Why else wouldn't he want it moved?"

Together, they bent and pushed some growth aside to consider the stone blocks and the mortar between them.

"If we took just a few stones out, we could get under there and check."

Miles straightened and shook his head. "No. I promised Hickory I wouldn't harm or change the integrity of the barge because of his own father's promise."

"You didn't say anything about the foundation," Delia wheedled. "Besides, we can easily put the stones back. If there's nothing under there, he'll never know, but if there's treasure ... well, he won't care that we moved a few blocks."

"I think we should ask."

"I'll take care of it," Delia hedged.

That was when a small herd of children came pounding over the footbridge and across the lawn, basically a tribe of scraped knees and missing teeth. Delia watched them running toward her: Aunt Emily's boys, and then her own brother and sister, the twins. They were all eight to ten years old, and they were usually seen traveling in a wild pack all over Liebs Island, happy to leave their younger siblings and cousins behind.

Delia braced herself for the impact of them, worried they'd frighten poor Miles. But then they bypassed her completely, and she realized they were yelling, "Mr. Martin! Mr. Martin!"

She might as well be invisible!

Turning, she found Miles on his knees, receiving hugs and summer updates. He asked them about fishing, and they told him short, frenzied stories, one on top of the other. His laugh was warm and rich, his blue eyes so kind that it was easy for her to see why a child might be drawn to him.

Or anyone, for that matter.

Eli finally noticed her. "Del, we came to see if you'd make us up a fireside story. The sun's setting!"

"It's too hot for a fire, but I always have a story."

They stumbled to the nearby fire pit, just ash and half-burned logs right now. Delia watched her little sister take Miles' hand and lead him over to the benches where they sat on cool nights. The canal water sat mostly still beside them, lit here and there by floodlights and colored by Rosie's glasswork.

"We want a story that will really scare us," Bobby demanded.

Delia watched Miles blink in surprise at that request, and she heard Charlie's advice echoing in her mind: *You can't be so strange right away.*

"How about a nice *Frogs of the Bog* tale, you guys?" she suggested.

"Booooo!" It was a morbid chorus.

"We want a story with skeletons in it. Like last time."

"A new one, though."

"But we still want there to be, you know … stuff hanging off the skeleton's bones."

Well, it seems the strange ship has sailed. Or the strange barge had been pulled out of the canal? Delia sighed in defeat. "Okay, okay. But remember the rules."

"We won't tell Mom and Dad the story unless they ask," Ginny recited.

"And if any of us starts having bad dreams, we're done," Jimmy put in. "We *know*!"

Delia settled in on the mound of rock between two of the benches, still captivated by *My Gal*, the barge, just behind her little audience.

"Once upon a time," she began slowly. "A century ago, there was a man who captained a canal barge, and his name was Captain Martin."

"Ooh, like *Mister* Martin! Go on!"

"Well, it looked to everyone that he hauled mounds of black coal, which was very important during the Civil War. But underneath the black coal, guess what he really hauled."

"Ponies!" Ginny exclaimed.

"I thought you wanted a scary story."

"Ginny, it was prob'ly canons!"

"It was actually gold," Delia said, ignoring the fact Eli's suggestion made more sense than her own.

"Gold? Where'd it come from?"

She bit her lip. "Alaska, of course." They all hummed in approval. Delia knew their grasp of geography was shaky, and she knew they loved stories of Alaskan adventures. There was talk now of the place being added as the 49th state. "Gold from the north, floated down the canal to the Ohio River. He employed the toughest crew around to make sure the treasure stayed safe."

"Were they mean?"

"The meanest."

"And rich prob'ly."

"The richest and meanest crew of canallers on the Ohio & Erie, mark my word. Until one dark night in late summer."

Delia waited for the ripple of anticipation.

"What happened to 'em?"

"They floated into *a trap* set by other greedy boatmen ... in fact, four other barges of canal pirates, lying in wait just south of here, in Baltimore."

"Oh, no! Where the soda shop is!"

"Oh, yes. As they approached a curve in the canal, there was an ambush from the trees. Word is the fighting was so fierce the canal waters ran red all the way to Youngstown the rest of that week!"

There was a delighted gasp, and Delia knew she'd delivered. She hazarded a glance at Miles, only to find him watching her *not* with the horror she expected but, rather, with a kind of ... appreciation. Something warmed inside of her.

"Did they all die?" whispered Ginny.

"Every last one. Captain Martin too."

"Nooo!"

"And every piece of gold was stolen by the crews of the other four barges."

"They got *away* with it?"

"Well, yes and no. You see, each man involved in that massacre went missing within a year. One of them disappeared with every full moon, never to be heard of again." Delia paused as their little blue and brown eyes went wide. "Legend has it Captain Martin's ghost skims along over the smooth, green waters of the Ohio & Erie Canal, looking for his lost gold."

"Can you still see him?" Bobby asked, looking over at the leftover canal channel beside them. "Is his ghost still there?"

"Nope," Delia said, suddenly completely dropping the foreboding in her voice. "Because souls don't float around on waterways here on earth, do they now? Have you all been paying any attention in Sunday School?"

"No, souls don't do that," Bobby agreed.

"Captain Martin went to heaven, probably," Ginny put in. "He's not over there in the canal or anything, you know, scaring people."

"Of course, he's not," Delia confirmed. "A lot of that has to do with the fact I made him up."

"He's not *real*?" Eli moaned.

"No. You asked me to make up a story, so I did. But it was scary, right?"

"Well, it used to be," Eli mumbled.

"I just heard something over there, though," Jimmy said, eyes huge. "Over by the water."

"*The captain!*"

Two of them screamed, two of them sighed, and they all tore off across the yard in the direction of home.

Except for Miles Martin, whose ancestor she'd just made into a murderous ghost. He looked delighted. "They really keep your bedtime stories a secret?" he asked, hands in his pockets as he rose.

"Sometimes. Sometimes not."

"You don't get into trouble with their parents?"

"Oh, sure I do. I get lectures about my imagination all the time, believe me."

"Well, I love it. It's like Poe got his hands on my family tree!"

He did read Poe. Delia felt like flinging herself at this man just as the children had. Instead, she played it cool. "Some people don't love it. Some people think I should stick with the happy little frog stories and keep the scary stuff ... buried."

Miles shrugged, hands still in his pockets. "Why can't both be true about you? Why can't you tell happy frog stories and murderous pirate tales? Life doesn't have to be simple."

"But you don't think that's ..." she cleared her throat. "... misusing my gift?"

"Your gift from God?"

"Right."

"Not sure how that would be. There's *a lot* in Scripture about being afraid."

Delia couldn't help the breath of a laugh that escaped. "Yes, but it's about *not* being afraid because God's got us."

Miles smiled his exceedingly pleasant smile. "Seems to me like, if there's nothing to be afraid of in the first place, God wouldn't be offering quite such a wonderful thing, would He?"

She blinked. He was putting to words what she'd been quietly convicted of since she was young. "I saw both my real parents die," she said softly. "Life can be scary. I've always thought pretending it's not is just silly."

"Do you think scary is going to win?"

"Well, *no*. I'd never say scary wins … exactly."

"But it sometimes puts up a real good fight, doesn't it?"

"Yeah." He got it, and she let out another breath. "Yeah, it does. And then God lets you finish growing up in a safe, solid place with safe, solid people who love you, and you come to understand His bigger plan. But that doesn't mean it's all sunshine and butterflies in your head, you know?"

"Or it's not all frogs in neckties."

"Not all the time, anyway. Scary happens, too."

"We're all made differently, anyway," he said, tipping his head to the side. "Given that, I don't think all Storytellers are supposed to be telling the exact same story."

He called her a Storyteller, which meant maybe God did, too. The God who already knew the stories in her heart weren't all pretty.

To keep herself from sliding into love with him, Delia cleared her throat. "Find something that will chisel away mortar between the foundation stones, Mr. Martin. Tomorrow night, we dig."

~~~~~

The next evening was perfect for treasure hunting. A storm rumbled in the north, and the sky over the lake was draped with low-lying clouds. Having spent a guilt-free day pounding out pages of her novel, Delia was in a fine mood as she held the Coleman lantern for Miles.

She was so convinced they'd find something fascinating and horrible under the old barge, she knew Hickory wouldn't mind them removing a few little stones. Just the same, they went about the task on the side that faced *away* from the other house. And in the dark.

"So, I've been meaning to ask, Miles. Did you take the job at the marina just to poke around over here at the barge this summer?"

"No." He was stretched long on the already dewy ground, hammering an awl into the crumbly mortar before scraping it away. "I
~~~~~

came to see about the barge, yes, but I saw the Help Wanted sign. I was looking for a summer gig, anyway, so it all just fell into place."

"Teaching not paying enough?"

"Got my eye on a house on the water," he said, grunting a little as he pried with another tool. "Right now, I'm boarding with the superintendent and his wife, so I don't have to drive back and forth from my family's place in Lancaster. Here, help me guide this out."

Delia was disappointed the work was going so quickly. They'd found a second layer of stone behind the outer, but they could move that easily to the inside once they'd broken up the adhesive. Miles had brought a masonry saw, but they hadn't needed it yet.

As the heavy stones came loose and were removed, one after another, the pair of them filled the night with soft conversation.

They debated whether American or British literature was better. Whether Cary Grant was more talented than Jimmy Stewart. One of them would invariably have to shush the other when the debate grew too heated.

Then, suddenly, the dark hole in the foundation appeared big enough for a body to crawl through. They fell silent.

A dank coolness seemed to come from within, the scent of old wood. When they touched the flat bottom of that barge, it would last have been touched by the flowing water of a working canal.

For the first time, she considered what might live in the soft, unseen ground beneath the barge house.

Delia slanted Miles a look.

"C'mon, Nancy Drew," he said playfully, reaching for the lantern. "Thought you liked creepy stuff."

Delia dipped her head to peer in, taking the light from him. Before her was a space that almost refused to be lit. She stretched a tentative hand within. The dirt was, indeed, soft.

"I won't let anything bad happen to you," he whispered.

Another strange thing happened in Delia's heart over that, so she ducked and shimmied into the tight space. She led with the lantern, aware that she was doing an unfortunate amount of wiggling. She wondered how Miles would fit through.

Delia imagined him *not* following her. She imagined him re-positioning the large stones like that one story by Poe, the one in the catacombs, burying her alive under the barge. Did she really know him that well? Wouldn't this be the ideal premise for a murder?

She didn't believe any of it, but her line between reality and imagination had always been a little blurred.

Then, Miles was grumbling and scooching just behind her. He seemed to have trouble and took longer than she had, but at last they were both stretched long in the darkness, barely able to raise their heads above their shoulders.

It was silent in the cavern between the ground and the barge's bottom. Miles had suggested they examine the wood above them and the earth below them in systematic quadrants. He did not seem optimistic.

As it turned out, he was right not to be.

After an hour, Miles and Delia had very sore necks, were covered in mud, and had found nothing more substantial than a tin mug half-buried in the ground.

The cicadas seemed loud as Delia made her way slowly back out through the hole, where starlight and fireflies seemed unusually bright compared with the grave-like air within.

"I know I can use this in a book," she whispered to herself. Once her torso was far enough out and the grass was once again wet on her hands, Delia turned over and pulled her knees up, scooting backward as Miles's head emerged.

"Don't be discouraged," she told him. She didn't like the idea of him giving up on his romantic quest to learn the truth about his family.

Yet, his face didn't emerge looking like the face of a quitter. She settled the lantern near him, noting a smudge of dirt along his nose.

Self-conscious, she touched her own hair and found a cobweb. He watched her pull it out in the lantern light, and they laughed together.

"We're a real fright," she said.

"Not you. You're lovely."

"Please. Don't," she said, rolling her eyes. "If growing up with Charlie and his friends has taught me anything, it's not to be taken in by fresh talk from boys."

"Good mantra," Miles said. "But don't mistake an honest compliment from a man for whatever banter those boys subjected you to." He winked, and her heart thudded.

She watched him shimmy his forearms out beneath his head. Then he twisted, scooted back, moved forward again, twisted the other way.

"Miles?"

He looked up. "Delia. I'm sorry to say … I'm stuck."

There was a silent beat between them. "What do you mean?"

"I mean I cannot move forward. The inner layer of stones is narrower than the outside, and my shoulders won't pass."

"But you made it *in!*"

"Barely. I think the unevenness of the blocks was working for me a little more in that direction." He'd backed up and was feeling around with his hands. She heard more grunting, and then his head emerged again. He was muddier now. "I might have to try to saw off the edge here."

"That will take a long time, won't it?"

"Especially with zero leverage from within this space," he said. He rested his chin on his fist, then, and smiled at her. Like nothing in the world was wrong.

"How do you manage to be so pleasant all the time?" she asked, stretching back out on her belly to see into his eyes. Just inches away.

She'd find the saw for him, but not yet.

"What do you mean? I'm having a grand time with you tonight," he said, the corners of his eyes crinkling with his grin.

She scooted closer still. "It occurs to me that I have all the power here."

He regarded her. "You do, at that."

"I have the saw out here. The lantern."

"Why do I feel like this isn't going to turn out well for my character in your novel?"

"Who says you're a character in my novel?"

"After ending up half-entombed below your mysterious house, how could I not be?"

She inched forward again. Eyed his delicious face in the shadows, smudged with dirt and who knew what. "I wonder what would happen if the heroine tried to ... steal a little kiss while your character was helpless?"

He didn't miss a beat. "Why just a little kiss? I mean, who would I tell, since I'm stuck here forever?"

They were both smiling when Delia pressed her lips experimentally to his.

And then, in that soft, sweet moment ... they were flooded in light.

"What in the *world*?" Uncle Drew's voice boomed from somewhere behind that blinding beam.

~~~~~

It was rare for the family to gather at seven in the morning, fog still clinging to the waters of Buckeye Lake.

It was even rarer, these days, for them to all be in the tiny barge house at the same time.

Yet, dawn found them—Hickory, Rosie, Aunt Emily, Uncle Drew, Miles, and Delia—crowded into the front room space. Some had coffee steaming in cups once more. Others—well, Delia and Miles—were still red-faced with humiliation.

Miles, at least, had been freed by Uncle Drew's help with the saw. Drew was now clad in his watercraft officer uniform, his service gun at his waist.

"And you've got nothing to show for disobeying me," Hickory was saying sadly, confirming Delia's suspicion that a bag of priceless gems would've changed their reception.
~~~~~

"I always figured from the first time I met you that I'd have to cuff you one day, Delia," Uncle Drew declared.

"Now, Drew," Rosie scolded, hand on her daughter's shoulder. Her mother had brought muffins to this bizarre gathering, of course.

"The day I met her, she threw a dead fish at me and then demanded I figure out how it had died," he defended.

"I don't see what's so wrong about the second part," Delia muttered.

"Please. This is all my fault." Miles slumped against the wall. "I knew you wouldn't have wanted us to remove part of the foundation. I'm sorry."

"No, it's my fault," Delia said. "I implied I would get permission."

"I assume you didn't, or we wouldn't be here," Aunt Emily said dryly, gulping another mouthful of coffee.

"I was going to ask."

"Afterward?"

"I haven't been in here for years." Hickory stood, running a hand along one of the gigantic beams of white oak worn dark by time. He stooped a little, ran his fingers over some grooves and chuckled.

Rosie made a sound of amusement, leaning over too. "Nice to know how tall I was when I was two. Look, here's your carved hashmark, Em."

"What are the other markings?" Drew asked, distracted from his interrogation. He moved closer to the beam.

"What other markings?"

"Grandma told us they were probably Hickory's heights and whatnot," Emily said.

"No, they weren't." The old man had his face close to them now, as well. "No one ever measured me in here. And look how high some of them go."

Delia and Miles made eye contact across from one another. Like the others, she had assumed that worn beam simply held a record of growth or marks made by a bored someone with a pocketknife. The marks were difficult to see, blending with the natural crannies of aged wood.

"This looks like …" Drew said, squinting and trailing off.

Miles was there, then, investigating alongside the others.

"What do you suppose 'XXI Corps 17T' means?" Drew asked, shining his flashlight where the beam joined the ceiling boards.

"Something to do with freight on the canal?" Emily asked, setting her cup on the table and crowding in.

Miles, who could see best at the top because of his height, said, "Corps. It's military."

The low-ceilinged space got silent.

"As in Civil War military?" Delia asked.

Miles turned, eyes gleaming. "Rosecran's army had three corps, and

I think this is referring to one of them."

"What's 17T?" Rosie asked.

"A location?" Hickory wondered.

"Or number. 17T," Delia said, rising now. "Seventeen thousand, maybe?"

Miles nodded, turning back to the beam, running his finger over carvings along the natural grain of the wood. Time had rubbed them shallow in spots.

"I'd never even noticed those before," Delia remarked, finally getting a look. "Just Mom's and Aunt Emily's hashmarks, is all."

"I can't make them out very well," Emily mumbled. "You'd have to really be looking closely to see them. But here's the word *Dennison*, I think, and below it … muskets? See? I think that says muskets."

She deferred to Miles, and Drew handed him a flashlight. Miles started nodding with excitement.

"8T," he said. "I bet there were eight thousand troops stationed at Camp Dennison down by Cincy. That's where that was. And they had only a few muskets. Look."

"This is military intelligence," Drew said. "On a canal barge, of all things."

"A canal barge that was operating during the war between the states," Emily noted.

'That's right," Hickory said. "Here's the word Sheridan. The General, probably? Can't make out the rest at all. A bunch of numbers. Maybe coordinates. But look, here. Look. It says 'tell Polk.'"

"Polk was a southern general," Miles exclaimed.

"Was your great-grandfather … spying for the South?" Delia asked.

"That would explain the traitor business," Rosie said, patting Miles on the back sympathetically.

"Del, can I use some of your paper?" he asked.

Emily, Hickory, and Rosie investigated other beams for hashes or carvings. As Drew shone light on the grooves of the upper part of the beam, Miles recorded what he could make out on the paper.

Delia watched:

Moving mid-Tenn

Guard conf. Buff F No guard cross, capt, Clark

Miles startled them all when he smashed the paper into his pocket and announced, "I need to go! I'll be back before my shift!"

"Now, wait a minute, son …" Uncle Drew called in his best police voice, but Miles was out the back screen door.

"I've got to get to the library!"

The door smacked closed behind him.

Delia thought she'd never been more attracted to anyone than she was to the sight of Miles Martin the Third running from the law.

~~~~~

Having been raised at the Island Inn, Delia was always more comfortable pulling shifts there than she was at Graham's Marina.

Still, she missed another day of writing to cover the marina's office while Miles sat on a canvas-covered pile of nautical whatnots behind her, three thick books open around him.

Occasionally, she heard him mumble, and he'd follow that by scribbling on the piece of paper she'd lent him that morning.

"We have the term Mad Scientist, but I've never heard of a Mad Historian until today." Delia placed a Coke bottle beside him.

"He was transporting coded messages, Del," Miles said, not looking up. "Durb Martin was moving intel south."

"That explains why the secret cargo wasn't something he could touch. Do you think he knew what it said? Or meant?"

"I'm not sure he even knew where to find it. Remember, he said he had to leave the barge unmanned for a full evening at the northernmost docks and then again when he made it to Youngstown."

"So, he was just the go-between. But between whom?"

But Miles had already returned to one of the books, a crease between his dark brows. The heat increased in the afternoon, so Delia moved the electric fan into the open window of the marina's office. Miles's papers fluttered, and one scrap took flight.

"Sorry." She was, but she also felt a bead of sweat running down her back.

"No problem," he said happily, looking up. Above his tidy beard, his cheeks were bright red with the heat and — she hated to think it — possibly, excitement over *research*.

He grabbed the paper notes to fan in front of his face. "So, I think I know as much as anyone's going to about my great-grandfather's antics on the barge you live in."

Delia climbed onto the canvas beside him. "And?"

"Well. Look." He pushed the paper into her hands, but nothing on it made a bit of sense. "There were seven Confederate prisoners locked on Johnson's Island with the last name Clark."

"Island? There's no Johnson's Island on Buckeye Lake."

"Up on Lake Erie. Sandusky Bay, actually. There was a prison up there where they kept high-ranking southern officers who'd been captured. One of them was probably the Clark who sent that longer message from the beam. This one." His finger ran along the page:
~~~~~

Guard conf. Buff F No guard cross, capt, Clark

"There must have been a Union guard who was selling intel to the major generals, see?" He was so pleased with himself. Delia wondered if she'd ever known anyone more easily entertained.

"And then this guard would, what, send the info on Durb's canal barge down from Lake Erie?"

"That's right. He'd have probably come aboard the *My Gal* and notched the short message on the top of the beam, and this way they could get info south without censors spotting it in a letter out from the prison," Miles explained.

"The guard couldn't mail a letter?"

"He'd have been stationed on the island. Besides, would you put betrayal in a letter you mailed from your military post? When all mail was being checked?"

"I guess not. Then there'd be someone in Youngstown waiting to board the barge while Durb and his crew went out carousing in the town," Delia said with a nod.

"Right. But the best part is," Miles went on, his eyes shining, "My great-grandfather would not *necessarily* have been a traitor!"

"Uh ... how do you figure?"

"I figured this message out!" He poked his fingertip again at the words he'd jotted from the beam of wood. "It's about Buffington Ford. That's what the 'Buff F' is referring to, and it's one of the only real well-known battles that happened in Ohio."

Delia blinked sheepishly. "I'm afraid it's not *that* well-known. I've never heard a thing about it."

"Were you not paying attention in school, Miss Adams?"

She debated kissing him now that she knew he wasn't opposed to it.

But he was already moving on with his lesson. "See, in July of 1863, a Confederate named Morgan led his cavalry north to raid, mostly to distract troops in southern Ohio who were poised to invade eastern Tennessee."

"A diversion."

"Right. Except, this brigadier general was ambitious and thought it would go well for him if he could find a good crossing of the Ohio River for other Confederate troops, so he took his raiding cavalry to what *someone* had informed him was an ideal spot: Buffington Ford."

"Things couldn't have gone great for them when they got there," Delia guessed, trying hard to be a good student. "I mean, since the South didn't exactly invade Ohio. I do know that."

"Yes, right. When Morgan got there, three hundred Union soldiers were there, and the Confederates were pinned down by gunboat fire," Miles said enthusiastically. He pointed to the scribbled message. "It was a trap! I think Morgan could have been operating off this message, which could be indicating 'no guard.' And 'capt' could be short for 'capture.'"

"So, the info on the beam of the barge was wrong?"

"Or it was a double-cross," he said with a vaguely satisfied, small smile. "There's a good chance the Union officer who carved the message was deliberately sending bad intel, you know? This captured Confederate Clark was probably paying, sure, but *he* didn't know what message ended up carved and floated down the canal!"

Miles closed the thick book on his lap and set it aside.

"So, there's no way to know," Delia offered, "what the intentions were of the person who sent the message."

"Nor the one who carried the message," he noted.

Delia scrunched her nose a little. She was coming to adore Miles, but she recognized a far reach when she saw one. "Well … let's consider. I mean, you yourself said Durb Martin probably had no idea what he was taking down the canal. Only that he had to disappear for a few hours at the farthest-flung towns."

"Right."

"And that he was being paid very handsomely to do that."

"Right."

"He definitely knew himself to be up to no good, though. The fact some piece of information might have been deliberately wrong hardly redeems him. I mean, he flipped his lid when he heard there were Union officers waiting for him in Baltimore. Enough to disguise the barge and try to disappear."

"He was probably overly cautious," Miles decided, and Delia giggled.

"Can we at least agree that the man was … morally gray?"

"I can live with that," he replied. "It's better than *traitor*. This information might redeem him, right?"

Delia tried to find a nice way of saying she didn't care. She cleared her throat. "Regardless, he's a far more complex character now. What will you tell your family, though? This hasn't exactly exonerated him, so what is there to say?"

"That I've got a girl."

Delia blinked. "Huh?"

With his usual confidence, Miles reached over and twined his fingers — freckled with ink today — with her own, which had been stained with ink for years. "I'll tell them I've got a girl who likes me *better* because I hale from a potentially traitorous and mercenary scoundrel."

Delia smiled. It was so nice to be understood. She decided she liked people who allowed life, and people, to be complicated. "I suppose all this business does water down your wholesomeness so I can almost stand you."

"You can more than stand me."

"Maybe."

"Enough to let me take you dancing up at the pier?" He smiled. "You know, to celebrate?"

"And be seen out with a *teacher*?"

"A teacher who's eager to read your scary stories and your sweet, little amphibian adventure stories, both."

Delia pretended to consider. "All right. But don't tell Charlie when he gets back. Knowing him, he'll think this whole thing was his idea."

The End

Kim Garee is the author of the award-winning *Together* series, which includes several beloved characters who made an appearance in this anthology. Check out *Pressed Together*, the start of the series, wherever books are sold. Kim has been a reporter, teacher, and school librarian (sometimes at the same time). Either because of or in spite of working every day with teenagers, she is a hopeless romantic. She's married and lives with/near her three children and plenty of other family members! When she's not writing or reading, she's doing socially acceptable things like cycling and kayaking or cuddling her pets, along with more perplexing things like crafting teeny, detailed miniature scenes that have no practical purpose. Visit Kim and leave a "hello" at *kimgaree.com*

Shovels and Spilled Peas
Owen Ferdig
Student First Place Winner
Cuyahoga Valley Christian Academy

Steve stepped from the truck and into the driveway. Having been unused for years, grass had long since grown between the loose gravel. Their assignment stood at the end of the overrun path.

No one had lived in the house for years. The bay window was chipped, curtains torn. The top row of panels lining the garage door had fallen in, detaching itself from the rail that at one point would have been opened manually. Once a pale yellow, the siding had faded to the color of a page stricken by time and water.

And it was time to say goodbye. That's why Steve was there. Steve and Martin and Gene.

The three had been commissioned to remove the public eyesore, and so that Tuesday morning, they had clambored into the truck hauling that excavator and made their way to Crescent Street.

"It's beautiful," Gene said.

"Get your glimpses now, cause it'll be gone in a matter of hours," Martin stated.

"Gives me the creeps," Steve said.

They stood for a moment.

"Okay," Martin said, climbing into the excavator and driving it off the trailer, leaving Gene and Steve coughing in a cloud of exhaust. "Where we startin'?"

"Right to left?"

"Affirmative."

The metal shovel slammed into the garage.

~~~~~

"Sorry!" Xavier cried as the metal paintcan hit the cement floor with a *clang*, a cool gray covering the worn garage floor usually shaded by a 1946 Volkswagen Beetle that had been pulled into the driveway. Elijah sighed, stepping off the ladder. The house was in need of a little patching up.

"Alrigh', son."

"I had it in my hands, Pop! It just slipped through and —" He broke into tears.
~~~~~

"Xavier, look in ma eyes." The six-year-old looked up at his father. "Imma sure that there's a valuable life lesson in this, like holdin' onta whatcha got while you got it or not takin' nothin' for granted."

"Mmmhmmm," Xavier sighed, wiping his nose with his sleeve. Father and Son looked at each other for a moment.

"But your pops don't know what that lesson is. So we's not gonna worry 'bout it."

They hugged. They laughed. They cleaned up the spill. They resumed painting.

~~~~~

The garage crumbled with a few brief swings of the steam shovel. The panneled door crumpled like a piece of paper, falling at the slightest nudge. In a matter of moments, the chipped concrete was covered in the roof that had once sheltered man and vehicle from the wrath of the earth.

Steve, leaning on the handle of a sledgehammer, sighed as he watched Martin and Gene clear the wreckage. A few concrete steps remained, connecting what was once the garage to the kitchen. Steve waved his hands. Martin advanced.

The shovel went clear through the bay window.

~~~~~

"But I don't *like* peas!" seven-year-old Moody pouted, staring knives at the fork sitting on her plate. It was Friday, the one day of the week where, regardless of commitments, the African-American family sat down to have dinner together.

"You can't even taste them," her nine-year-old sister Perlie scoffed.

"You just eat them," Xavier piped up, agreeing with his sister.

"Of course you and Perlie like peas. You're twins," Moody huffed.

"What does being twins have anathin' to do with it?"

"It has everthing with it!"

"Nu-uh. It ain't got nothing with it."

"Does too!"

"Hey, hey," Elijah interrupted. The kids looked at him. "It might have somethin' to do with it," he said after a moment.

"*See!!*" Moody hollered. Her mother gave Elijah a dirty look and playfully smacked his arm.

"Settle down, hon'," Billie said, giving her husband a look. "I know chicken pot pie ain'tcho fav'rite, but it'll help you grow big and strong. It has peas and carrots."

Moody looked at Billie. "So I can do the cartwheel and flip, Mama?"

"So you can do the cartwheel and flip."

Moody thought for a moment. *I could do the cartwheel and flip,* she thought. "Then I'll eat my peas!" she said, shoveling her meal into her mouth.

"Careful now, you gon' choke on Mama's food goin' that fast," Elijah warned, laughing.

"I'll be strong tomorrow, won't I," his daughter said between bites.

"Sure will, hon'," Billie smiled. The clock struck seven. "But only if you get a good night's sleep," the mother continued. "Go get ready for bed, all of ya," she said, sending her three children shuffling from the table to the bathroom.

Her husband suddenly grimaced. The couple sat in silence for a few moments.

"It's getting worse, isn't it?" she said, looking to Elijah.

"Yes."

"War-related?"

"They don' know. It's likely."

"Do you have an appointment made up?"

"On the wall. Next Thursday."

"You're worried."

"We don' have the money. It's too expensive."

"*That's* what's worryin' you?"

"Already had to pick up extra shifts. You might here soon too."

"And the kids?"

"Gon' have to just wait a'school for one of us." Straight-faced. Mouth in a thin line.

Billie sighed. "When you gon' *tell* them what's goin' on?"

"When they has to prepare to say goodbye."

~~~~~

The garage was gone. The kitchen was gone. The house now split into a larger section that branched off into bedrooms and bathrooms.

"Where we starting, Martin?" Gene hollered from around back.

"Let's go left to right this time."

"Not back to front?" Steve asked.

"Do you want to go back to front?" Martin responded.

"Gene asked you, not me."

"Then why'd you speak up? Let's go back to front." Martin drove the excavator behind the house, now facing two small windows. Gene peered in.

"Kinda spooky. What is that, the kids' room?" Martin joined him.

"Must be. Three beds?"

"Eh. I had bunk beds. They weren't that exciting. Get back in the excavator. You said we couldn't break for lunch till we were halfway there, and I'm getting hungry."

~~~~~

"Pop?" thirteen-year-old Perlie hollered from the top bunk. "I'm hungry." Elijah appeared in the doorway.

"Didn'tcha eatcha dinner?"

"Well, I did, but now I'm hungry again," his daughter replied.

"Me too," a small voice piped up from the darkness.

"You too Moody?" the father asked.

"Yeah."

"What's goin' on?" Xavier said, sitting up in his twin bed across the room.

"You hungry, son?" Elijah asked. His other thirteen-year-old thought for a moment, then shook his head. The father led the three kids back into the kitchen.

Bellies full, the three McClain children returned to their room, Billie and Elijah flipping on their bedroom light as they clambored back into bed.

"You ready to sleep now?" Billie asked, laughing. Three "yes"es came in reply. "Then I'll tuck you in again." And their mother made her way to each of the three beds—though it was a small stretch up to Perlie. Comfy spots found, pillow nests made, and sheets pulled tight like a hug from their Mama, Billie hit the lightswitch. "Should we sing for you again?"

"Ok, Mama, the tuckin' in and the fairy tales I can live with, but the singin' is for babies," Xavier said.

"Shh!" Moody aggressively whispered from the bottom bunk. "I want them to sing!"

"Gon' have to be quiet, now," Elijah said. Even Xavier stopped talking almost immediately.

"You are my sunshine, my only sunshine," Billie started. Elijah joined in.

"You make me happy, when skies—" He stopped singing suddenly and grunted, putting his hand over his heart and leaning dependently on the doorframe. Billie moved next to him and wrapped his arm around her shoulder, helping him from their room.

"Good night, kiddos," she said, closing the door behind her as she helped Elijah into their own bedroom.

The three children stared at each other in the dark.

"I'll go check," Xavier said. Leaving his nest once more, he made his way to his parents' room.

"Pops? You alrigh'?" Elijah looked up from where he was sitting on the edge of the bed.

"Sure am, son," he smiled weakly. "Just startin' to realize the extent of the 'old' in your old man." Xavier walked over to his father and gave him a hug.

"Love you, Pops," he said. He went back to bed. Elijah watched him leave.

~~~~~

"Hold on a minute, Martin!" Steve said, raising his hand. Martin stopped. Steve walked over to a small pile of debris and pulled an old leather book titled "Bedtime Fairy Stories" out of the rubble, brushing dust from the faded, smooth cover. Opening the front cover, a label read, "Property of the McClain twins," and scrawled next to it in purple crayon, "And Moody."

Steve stared at the book for a moment, then set it aside. A keepsake. "Keep goin'," he said. The shovel swung; the bathroom mirror fell with a loud splintering sound.

~~~~~

"Let me fix your tie, hon," Billie said, staring at Elijah's mishapen necktie in the bathroom mirror.

"It's fine."

His wife scoffed.

"Your daughter is singin' for service today and you don' want me fixin' your tie?"

"I ain't the one singin'. How come I's gotta be the presentable one?"

"So that when the congregation comes up to us to tell us what a mighty fine daughter we raised and how angelic her singin' voice is, you don' look like you just rolled right outta bed and came to church havin' called yesterday's clothes a day."

Elijah laughed. "Fine, fine, you right. As always."

"And Moody gon' get *lots* of attention today seeing as Xavier and Perlie are both off at college. No older siblings to be compared to."

She finished fixing his tie. She smoothed her dress.

"You still haven't told them," she continued.

"Don' wanna add another thing to their plates," her husband said.

"Or you just don' wanna accept what's happenin' to you?"

Her husband said nothing.

"Hard to believe the war will do somethin' like this to you," he said quietly.

"Is it?"

Her husband thought. "No, I guess it isn'."

"The doctors gon' do anythin'?"

"They gon' try."

"Expensive?"

Her husband said nothing.

~~~~~

"**By Jove**, is that a mudroom?" Gene hollered.

"Gene, why you always gotta be hollering nonsense?" Martin asked from the excavator. "I'm right here."
~~~~~

"Think we can save those washing machines? Even if they don't work we'd get good money for the metal."

"Sure. Steve saved a storybook. Why not the washing machines?"

"Really?"

"No! They get gone with the rest of the house! You know how much extra work it'd be trying to save those old things?"

"Fair, I guess."

Martin moved for the mudroom.

~~~~~

Billie sighed as she opened the washing machine, pulling strands of wet clothes from the drum. *Another day, another dollar*, she thought. Moody's graduation was less than a week away. Elijah had a follow up appointment for his diagnosis. Sitting next to her was a stack of papers, unopened letters. The monthly mortgage. She sighed. Medical bills. Her brow furrowed. She slid her finger under the seal. She pulled out the paper.

Coronary Heart Disease caused by war-related trauma. The next letter was an assisted living pamphet.

Billie broke down and cried.

~~~~~

One room. The majority of the house stood in a pile of siding, shingles, and broken glass. All that was left was a fireplace, a cobweb-covered rocker, and a dust-ridden rug atop the remaining rotted wood floorboards. Steve and Martin and Gene did not hesitate. They were tired. They were hungry. And a house was just a house.

~~~~~

Elijah and Billie stood next to each other staring at home. Home they had loved, disciplined, eaten, grown, cried, laughed, celebrated in. Their house had a heart. The assisted living van entered the driveway as the couple gazed longingly into the house's eyes, Billie beginning to slouch with age and Elijah in his wheelchair, and said goodbye for the last time. They could see their children in the windows, running through the sprinkler, fighting over a toy, stressing over report cards, singing in the bedroom, laughing with each other, crying with each other, praying with each other. And as watery memories slipped down their cheeks they bid a final farewell to a piece of themselves and stepped inside the van.

~~~~~

With the final slam of metal into concrete came a child's laugh; a parent's tears; furrowed brows and wondering minds; a mother's lullaby; spilled peas; a couple standing on the steps of what had once been home. What was once is gone, years erased from select minds.

Where a house had once stood now sat an excavator surrounded by a pile of echoes.

Gene and Martin and Steve returned the following day to clear the mess. They stared quietly at their work.

"Gives me the creeps," Steve said. And by day's end, there was no house.

There were no echoes.

There was only end.

And grass.

The End

Raised and residing in Northeast Ohio, **Owen Ferdig** is a senior in high school who enjoys the theatre, playing the piano, and of course, creative writing. *Shovels and Spilled Peas* is the first work he has published, though he aspires to publish more. His favorite book to read is *Alice's Adventures in Wonderland*, and, looking forward, Owen will be attending Malone University with hopes of teaching high school English classes.

The Skeleton Key
Annika Klanderud

I squatted on the sidewalk and stayed that way — as still as possible. The humid Ohio wind rattled the corn in the field beside me. It was trying to distract me, but I wasn't falling for it. I just stared at the freshly cut blades of grass in my front yard. A dark curl fell into my eyes, but I didn't miss that subtle twitch on the ground. The grass moved. I was sure of it.

There. It moved again. I saw it. I couldn't hold back a smile as I pounced and cupped both hands around that critter. Macon was gonna be so happy. He loved everything that creeped and crawled — even the ugly ones.

Now my fuzzy hair was all over the place. Mom would probably be mad that my hair was a mess and my normally caramel-colored skin was now even darker — caked in mud. I could just hear her now telling me to act more like the young lady I wanted to become. Whatever that meant.

But none of that mattered because I got him. I was a hundred percent sure I did. I could feel the wiggly thing tickling my hands. But I should probably check to make sure. One quick peek wouldn't hurt.

I brought my cupped hands close to my face and, quick as could be, I peeled back my thumb, just a sliver, and snuck a look.

Yep! A tiny green frog with black streaks down its back. After closing my hands again, I tucked them close to my chest and leapt to my feet. Now all I needed was some sort of container to keep it in until I saw Macon again. Where was he, anyway? Probably at home playing Fortress Twilight or something.

I hurried up the porch steps, two at a time. My hands were full with the frog. No problem. I'd done this a million times. Using my elbow, I shoved open the front door.

But I froze at the yeasty smell of Mom's sourdough bread, drifting through the air from the kitchen. She sang so loud I could hear every word all the way across the entire house. "I come to the garden alone, while the dew is still on the roses."

Ugh! She sang those songs so many times, even I had all the words memorized. Like she thought she was a brown version of Taylor Swift or something. A brown version that only sang church songs. And we weren't even in church. It was so embarrassing. I mean, didn't she know that Cami's friends were here? What if they heard her?

Dishes clanged in the kitchen. "Piper! Piper, where are you?"

Oh, great, now she was calling me. That could only mean one of two things. Either I was in trouble or she had work for me to do.

Whichever it was, I wasn't about to stick around to find out.

Using my chin, I pushed the long handle to the hallway closet and nudged the door open with my head.

"And the voice I hear, falling on my ear, the Son of God discloses." At least her loud singing was good for covering up what I was doing. I quickly scanned the shoes, bags, and other random things on the closet floor.

A box. Perfect. I flipped open the lid with my pinky finger. It even had crumpled tissue paper on the bottom. Perfect bedding for Froggie. I plopped the little guy in there and shoved down the lid.

Now to sneak past Mom. I clicked the closet door shut and, gripping the box to my stomach, I pressed my back against the door while my heart thudded wildly against my chest.

Mom's voice sounded like it was the tiniest bit farther away.

Slowly I peered around the corner and across the living room. From this angle, I could only make out the sink and the stove. She wasn't there.

If I was fast, I could dash across this entryway to the living room and hide behind the wall attached to the kitchen.

I took a deep breath and went for it.

The box slid out of my hands, but I caught it before it hit the floor. Then I righted myself and flattened my back against the next wall.

Phew! That was a close one.

"And the joy we share as we tarry there, none other has ever known." Mom's voice came close. Very close.

I held my breath and stood as still as a statue.

Then the singing shifted. And her voice drifted off toward the living room. I exhaled. Good, she was going the opposite direction.

I craned my neck just in time to see her slip into the living room. "Piper! Where are you? You have chores to do."

No. Not chores. I glanced toward the back door. If I was fast, I could dart behind that far wall and then slip out the back when Mom's singing got loud again.

I closed my eyes and exhaled silently.

One. Two. Three. Go!

I dashed down the hall while Mom hummed. Clenching the box to my chest, I slid behind the wall.

"Piper, now I know you probably don't feel like working, but being a responsible young lady means doing what you know you should, even when you don't want to." Sounded like she was in the far corner of the living room.

This was my chance to escape out the back door. Crouching low, I reached for the door handle and slowly turned it.

Why did adults always talk about responsibility? That was the furthest thing from my mind right now.

I cracked open the door and tiptoed out to freedom.

I took a silent step onto the screened-in back porch. But before I closed the door behind me, I froze at the sound of Dad's voice. Inside the house, he shouted Mom's name.

"That wallet," he said. "Have you seen the leather wallet I just made?"

I should've guessed. Work was all he wanted to talk about. Boring. He spent all day every day in the shed out back working with leather. Why was work the only thing Mom and Dad were interested in these days?

Anyway, his leather wallet, or whatever he was worried about, was definitely not worth getting caught over. Besides, I had to get this frog to Macon before Mom or Dad caught me with it and made me release it back into the wild.

I clicked the door shut behind me and turned to see Cami and her friends sitting around the glass table on the back porch. Fairy lights twinkled along the ceiling above them. Nothing said *summer* like fairy lights. It wasn't completely dark outside yet, but the sun had begun to go down, and the storm clouds made it seem later than it was. The lights gave off the most amazing glow.

"I'm just saying, don't you think it's odd that you and all your neighbors out here in the country live in these really big, fancy houses, and then—right across from your backyard—is this rundown shack from like a hundred years ago?" Cami's friend sat with her back to me, so I wasn't sure which one she was.

But it really didn't matter what her name was. If she was Cami's friend, she wore the coolest clothes, she knew how to drive, and she could go wherever she wanted whenever she wanted. Must be nice.

"It's not a shack." Cami rolled her eyes like she was frustrated with her friends. "It's a two-story house just like this one. It even has a basement."

"And look at that big treasure chest on the back porch." The girl on Cami's other side leaned forward. Her long, straight hair cascaded over her shoulder as she strained to look at the old house through the back screen. "What do you think's in that thing?"

"I'm pretty sure Conner and Beck know what's in it." Cami's curly hair looked so chic piled on top of her head the way she had twisted it. She was brown like me, but she looked so much more grown up than I did. It didn't matter that both of her friends were white, they were all so fashionable and fun. They fit so well together.

"You mean Conner Smith and Beck Randall?"

Cami nodded before pointing at the rundown house that had always been there but just looked like a dump to me up until now. "That chest is locked, but Conner says there's a skeleton key in the basement behind the furnace that will open it."

A skeleton key? "Woah. Cool." *But what is a skeleton key, anyway?*

While Cami and her friends stared out the back screen at that old house, I wandered toward them and dropped the box on the table.

Is it a key for skeletons? No, that would be stupid. What does that even mean? Skeletons don't need keys. Maybe it's a key shaped like a skeleton.

"Piper. Where have you been?" Cami stood from the table and glared at me.

I guess her nagging voice must've made me jump, and I bumped into the box. It tipped over, but before I could pick it up, the frog hopped out, leapt from the table, and landed on the painted toenails of one of Cami's friends.

The girl shot to her feet and squealed.

Yikes! I lunged for the frog before she squashed it in all her excitement.

"So disgusting!" She snatched up her slides and headed for the back door with Cami and her other friend.

I dropped the frog back into the box. The tissue paper crinkled beneath its weight, and I slammed the lid shut before it tried to escape again.

I stepped toward them. "Wait. Where are you guys going?"

"Ice cream." One of the girls gave me the sweetest smile, and I just knew we'd be amazing friends if they gave me the chance to hang out with them.

"Can I come?"

"You're too little." Cami shoved open the screen door.

"No, I'm not. I'm twelve years old."

She stopped and faced me. "Really? You're carrying a frog around in a box like a kindergartener would do."

My insides burned — hot — like my bare feet on the driveway earlier today. She didn't have a clue what she was talking about. The frog wasn't for me. It was for Macon.

"If you think you're so big, go do the dishes like Mom told you to." She shoved open the door and marched out.

I locked eyes with one of Cami's friends — the one who ended up with the frog on her toes. "You don't mind if I go with you, do you?"

She scrunched up her face and shook her head wildly. "No. Just don't. I mean, sorry, but that whole frog thing kinda creeped me out."

She hurried out the door and a lump lodged in my throat. This was all Cami's fault. In front of her friends, she practically called me a baby who plays with frogs and doesn't obey her parents. How was I ever going to live this down?

They all shuffled out the door and into the grass of the backyard, and my eyes stung with unshed tears. But I blinked them away and stared down at the brown cardboard box on the table.

I couldn't let Cami boss me around in front of her friends. And I was definitely not gonna go inside and do the dishes like she told me to.

It only took about two seconds before I knew what I had to do. I was going to prove that I wasn't a baby like she said. And I knew just how I was going to do it, too. I had to get that skeleton key. And the frog I just caught was going to help me get it.

~~~~~

The screen door of the back porch creaked as I pushed it open. With the frog box tucked under the other arm, I stepped into the grass and let the door slam shut behind me. Cami and her friends were long gone, but that didn't bother me because now I had a plan. A plan that would blow their minds. And in no time at all, they'd see that I wasn't a baby like my big sister thought.

I wandered to the side yard. Did I really want to drag Macon into this? I mean, he wasn't always as brave as I was. And the last thing I wanted to do was traumatize my best friend.

From this spot beside the house, I could see the road that ran along our front yard. A cute little SUV—just like Cami's—sped past. My sister and her friends were never gonna see me as anything other than a little girl who played with frogs unless I did something to prove how grown up I actually was.

No time to doubt myself now. I had to go through with this plan, even if it scared Macon a little.

"Piper?" Mom sang my name like it was the chorus of a church song or something. And that familiar nagging sound shot ice through my veins. I couldn't see her from where I stood in the grass—which meant she probably couldn't see me either. But I could tell she was close. Probably on the porch.

I'd come this far, and I wasn't about to get roped into doing a bunch of chores. Especially not now that I had this genius plan to pull off.

I raced off in the direction of Macon's house. As fast as my feet would take me. Down the sidewalk. Past Melissa's house.

Good thing he only lived three houses down, because I was out of breath by the time I got there.

But there was no time to waste on catching my breath. The box in my hand rattled as I sprinted up the steps. And after tucking Froggie under my arm again, I banged on the door.
~~~~~

It only took a few seconds for Macon to swing open the door. His freckled face looked tired. And when he yawned, I knew it was gonna take some work to get him excited about our mission.

"Good thing you opened the door fast because we don't have much time. I have a plan." I made sure to hitch up my eyebrows really high so he knew this was a big deal.

"Well, yeah. I knew it was you because of how loud you were knocking. I had to get you to stop before my mom heard you and got on my case about making you quiet down." Now his green eyes didn't look as tired as they did a few seconds ago. I could see he was feeling my urgency.

I swatted my hand at the air. "You worry way too much about what your parents think."

He stepped onto the porch and closed the door behind him. "Okay, so where are we going?"

I turned, skipped down the steps, and landed on the sidewalk, hoping he would follow. When he did, I sighed with relief.

"Oh, you know." I continued down the sidewalk. "Nothing big. Just exploring."

Great! We were closer to that old house now. But when I stepped into the grass of his side yard, he stopped.

No. No. No. Why was he stopping?

"Wait a second. What do you mean by exploring?" He crossed his arms, and I knew it was almost time to pull out the big guns.

But I couldn't let on that I was concerned. "What? I told you it's nothing big."

"Piper, the last time you took me *exploring,* I ended up grounded for a week. And there's no way I'm gonna survive another week without Fortress Twilight."

I backtracked a few steps and with the box perched on my left arm, I gently grabbed his arm. "Come on, it'll be fun."

He shook his head, and his blond stringy hair swooshed across his forehead. "I'm not moving until you tell me where we're going."

My heart picked up its pace. This was it. I had to tell him. But in a calm and cheery way. I had to make him think that he wanted to do this.

"The biggest adventure of your life."

"Piper."

"Okay, we're going to explore that old rundown house across from my backyard."

"No way." He turned his back to me.

But I jumped in front of him—the box jostling in my arm. "Wait."

"No, Piper. There's no way you're getting me to step one foot in that old house. The sun's going down, and you know the dark creeps me out."

"But, Macon, I have to do this. My sister and her friends are going to think I'm a baby for the rest of my life unless I can get into that basement and find the skeleton key that opens the treasure chest on the back porch."

I paused to check his reaction. It was a long explanation, I knew. And the words just kind of bumped into each other as they came out of my mouth. But he was my best friend. He had to help me protect my reputation.

He chewed on his bottom lip, and for a few long seconds, I thought I'd convinced him. Then my whole world collapsed when he opened his mouth. "Sorry, but I can't. A dark house like that ... way too creepy."

He tried to shuffle around me, but I shoved the box into his chest before he could leave.

"I'll give you this if you help me."

"What is it?"

"Open it." I raised the box just slightly.

He lifted the lid, and the most amazing smile spread across his face. "Why didn't you tell me you caught a frog?"

He reached his hand toward it, but I slammed the lid shut before he could touch the critter. And I snatched the box away from him.

"Okay. Okay. I'll help you sneak into that creepy old house. Just let me get a flashlight before we go."

My smile had to be just as big as his as I watched him head back into his house.

See how easy that was? I knew I could get out of doing boring chores so I could have fun with Macon, all while proving myself to Cami and her friends.

~~~~~

The grass rustled as I tromped across my backyard. Dad must've really been distracted with whatever leather project he was working on — what did he say it was, a wallet? Whatever it was must've been taking up all his time because this grass looked like he hadn't cut it in weeks.

"Can I hold the frog box now?" The faint beam from Macon's flashlight swung around and around behind me while Macon hurried to catch up. It wasn't even all the way dark yet. So why was he flashing that thing?

"No. Not yet." I squeezed the box to my chest even tighter. Okay, so I know that *sounded* mean, but I wasn't about to give him the frog and then watch him wiggle out of his side of the deal.

"But you said you caught the frog for me."

His swinging light was starting to annoy me, so I spun around and glared at him.

He stopped in his tracks and raised his eyebrows like he didn't know how annoying he was being with that light.
~~~~~

Turning back around, I headed for that old house across the yard. "I did catch it for you. But I'm not gonna give it to you until we get inside the rundown house. A deal's a deal."

"What, you don't trust me?"

"No, I don't."

We crossed into the weed-filled yard of the crumbling house, and my chest tightened. This was it. We were really doing this. The glass of the window closest to us had been shattered—probably years ago. And the white boards on the side of the house were all busted and falling off. Now that I was close enough to see it clearly, I could see that the paint had chipped off the pillars on the back porch.

Macon's light swung to the enormous treasure chest on the back porch.

I swiped at the flashlight in his hand. "Give me that thing."

But he hid it behind his back before I could snag it.

"Come on," I said. "You're wasting the battery. And it isn't even that dark out here."

"I'll trade the flashlight for the frog."

"Not until we're inside the house."

His eyes zeroed in on the darkened back door. He looked terrified. Oh, boy. His fear of the dark was starting to kick in.

I slapped him on the shoulder in what I hoped was an encouraging way, but he jumped as if the slap scared him.

I exhaled my frustration. "Better get in there while we still have light." And I marched right up to the back door.

When I didn't hear his footsteps behind me, I lifted the frog box. "Once you get inside, this frog will be all yours. Besides, with that light, it'll be like the middle of the day in there. Nothing to be afraid of."

He nodded and followed.

Better get inside while I have him excited about it. I reached for the door handle, hoping this dump wasn't locked. When the door handle turned and the hinges creaked, my insides bubbled, and I slipped into the house. The floor kind of shifted with my first step. And I nearly gagged on the thick smell of dust and fifty-year-old wet wood. But I covered it with a cough. Couldn't let Macon think I was scared.

He stepped in behind me and shone his light on what used to be a kitchen. Ancient white wallpaper dotted with bright yellow lemons covered most of the walls. In places it had peeled back.

"Ahhh!" Macon's squeal forced me to turn just as a mouse scurried across the floor.

I grabbed his shoulder and squeezed. "Knock it off, Macon. It's just a mouse. I thought you liked mice."

"I do. I just . . . I thought it was something else, that's all." He shone the light on the mass of cobwebs in the corner and then at the doorway that looked like it led out into the living room or something. "All right, we're inside. Give me the frog already."

I lifted the box but pulled it back real quick. "Promise you won't run screaming out of the house."

He cocked his head. "Come on, Piper, now how am I supposed to promise something like that? I mean, a creepy house like this? Who knows what kind of creature will jump out at us next?"

"But you promised."

"Well, I'm here, aren't I? I'm exploring. *We're* exploring together. I'm doing it. Now give me the frog."

I held the box just out of reach. "You promised you'd trade the flashlight for it."

He held out the light, and I snagged it. Then I gave him the box. I didn't have to shine the light on his face to see that enormous smile of his. It was brighter than any light. I knew he'd like the gift I caught for him.

"All right. Now let's hurry up and find what we came for so we can get out of this creepy place."

My heart picked up speed. Now that he had what he wanted, I could get what I wanted — that skeleton key — so I could prove myself to Cami and her friends.

"Right. We gotta find that skeleton key." I swung the light from one side of the room to the other. "It's gotta be this way." I pointed the beam at the doorway and hurried out of that musty old kitchen.

Clang! The sound came from behind me. I pointed the light at his feet just as he was righting himself. Some clunky thing that looked like a piece of the outside gutters was on the floor beside him. He must've tripped over it.

"Hey, slow down." He clung to the box as I turned forward again. "If you had been shining the light at our feet, I never would've tripped on that piece of metal."

I didn't want to slow down. But I didn't want Macon to get hurt either. That would definitely be the end of this little expedition into the creepy rundown house.

"Right. Okay." I pointed the light at our feet.

"How are you gonna find some key in this enormous old house, anyway? It's too big." The floor creaked as his feet shuffled behind me.

"Oh, I know where it is. Cami told me. It's behind the furnace." I hurried through the living room and down the hall. A spider web brushed against my nose, and I batted it away.

"Okay, so where's the furnace?" His voice shook, and I could tell he was ready to leave. But we were just getting started.

"There." I aimed the light at a door that had fallen off its top hinge.

Now the middle hinge was bent, and it was basically hanging by only one hinge at the bottom. And beyond that door was a wall of darkness. Or maybe it was just a wall. "That's gotta be the way to the basement." I raced toward it—the floor feeling flimsy and uneven beneath my feet.

"What? The basement? It's probably even darker down there."

I reached back and shone the light on his feet. "What does that matter when we have this?" I stretched my hand out in front of me and pushed the dangling door out of my way. Then I brought the light in front of me and, sure enough, there was a staircase leading down into a lower part of the house.

Macon's chattering teeth behind me sent a chill down my back. What if something *was* down here?

Stop it!

Boy, this phobia of his sure wasn't helping any.

I swallowed and made sure my voice was upbeat. "We'll go down together." I stepped down, and the wood of the first step made a cracking sound. Great, what was I getting us into?

But the next step down was better. Shining the light on each step, we made our way to the basement without any problems.

"It really is a lot darker down here than upstairs." He tapped on the box in his hands, and I was so sure he was trembling.

"Right. Cami said the key would be behind the furnace." I swung the light around. Spiders and other tiny bugs clung to pipes and scurried across wires. I shuffled over to a box on the wall and swiped a hand all around it. Nothing was there.

"Here. Shine the light over here. This has to be the furnace."

I aimed the light in the direction of Macon's voice. The contraption he stood beside was made of metal. It had knobs on it. Definitely looked old. It could be a furnace.

"That's probably it." I brought the light closer. "Reach your hand behind it and try to find a key."

He worked fast—almost frantically. Like he wanted to just get it over with and get out of here. "Nothing. There's nothing back here."

"Looking for this?" A girl's voice sliced through the stale air of the basement.

I swung the flashlight in the direction of her voice.

But before I could get there, Macon shrieked. There was a clatter, and it sounded like he bolted up the stairs.

"Macon," I heard myself say.

The beam of my flashlight landed on a dirt-faced ghost of a girl with tangled hair. Her hand was stretched out to me.

My breath lodged in my throat, and I backed away. Everything in me said to run like Macon did.

But before I could, she spoke again. "Is this the key you were looking for?"

Sweat dripped down my neck. But, wait. What did she say? A key?

The small object in her hand was silver. And it glinted in the light. The key.

I swiped it out of her hand and took off. The sound of her wild laugh chased me up the stairs.

That was messed up. But as I burst out of the house and into the dim light of the setting sun, it hit me.

I did it. I had the key.

"That was awesome!" The flashlight beam ahead of me bounced as I raced toward Macon.

He leaned against the back of my shed with his arms crossed.

"Did you see that?" I stopped when I got to him. "I can't believe we actually made it out of that place in one piece. We did it."

Well, at the very least, he could try faking a smile. My cheeks were burning I was smiling so much. Then I noticed his hands were empty. So I used the light to search the grass around his feet. Nothing was there.

"Hey, where's the box with the frog in it?"

He tossed up his hands. "I don't know. I dropped the thing and sprinted out of that horrible place as fast as I could." He brushed past me, and I turned to watch him pace the grass. *Reer!* A bit grumpy, are we?

But I guess I'd be grumpy too if I lost my brand-new pet frog. "I'm sorry you lost your frog."

"It's okay."

Behind him the old house wasn't much more than a shadow now. A bat flitted around the rundown place.

Then something moved on the ground. I pointed the light at it.

The girl with the messed-up hair from the basement.

She waltzed over to the treasure chest on the back porch and sat down on it. Was she grinning at me?

"I'm going home." Macon swiped the light out of my hand.

"Huh?" Without the light, I was plunged into darkness.

He lumbered off toward his house.

"Hey, Macon, don't worry about the frog. I'll catch you another one. At least we got the key. That's the important thing." I held it in the air, but he didn't bother turning around to look at it.

"Yeah, okay. See you tomorrow." He was moving faster now.

"Right. Tomorrow. Then we'll test out this key together, right?"

"I don't know, Piper. Maybe not."

"Come on, Macon. You have to." But it was no use. I was practically shouting now, and he was way too far away to even hear me.

So I just shoved the key into my pocket and headed for my house.

I'm not gonna lie, I wasn't looking forward to facing Mom after running away from my chores, but it was late, and I had to go inside.

Just in case she was still mad, I opened the back door slowly and crept into the kitchen.

"Are you sure you didn't see that wallet?" Dad followed Mom as she slid a knife into the sink.

"No, I haven't." She turned and leaned up against the sink. "Where did you say you put it again?"

"In the closet. Right next to the front door." He went from pointing at the door to motioning wildly with his hands. "I'm pretty sure I put it on the floor of the closet. No, I'm absolutely sure I did. One hundred percent sure. I wrapped it in tissue paper. Then I put a layer of crinkled paper on top of that to protect the leather."

"And what kind of box was it?"

"Just a plain old brown cardboard box."

My heart stopped. Crinkled paper in a cardboard box? That had to be Macon's frog box.

I wandered away from Mom and Dad's conversation. Mom was always telling me not to interrupt adult conversations anyway. So I dropped into a chair in the dining room.

"That was a custom-made wallet."

Sweat trickled down my back. I knew right where that box was — in the basement of the creepy girl's old house. I pulled the skeleton key out of my pocket and ran a thumb over it. But it wasn't like I could do anything about it now. No way was I stepping foot in that creepy house again. Macon was right about that much. That place was a freak show.

Dad would just have to make a new wallet.

"You know how long it took me to make that thing? Full grain leather. *And* I personalized it." What was Dad doing? Reading my mind? "Arghhh!" Dad roared and stormed off.

Woah. I'd never seen Dad that upset.

His bedroom door closed, and Mom ran the water in the sink. "Savior, Savior, hear my humble cry. While on others Thou art calling, do not pass me by."

Oh, great. Now she was a singing diva again.

I stood with the key in hand, ready to get as far from her singing as possible. Tomorrow I'd test this thing out.

"Let me at a throne of mercy, find a sweet relief."

I tiptoed toward the hall, but the key slid out of my hand and clattered to the floor.

Mom spun around, holding up her soapy hands. "Piper, there you are. Have you seen the wallet your dad was making?"

"Wallet?"

"Yes. It's made of brown leather. And he engraved a customer's name into it."

I could've told her that the wallet was probably in a box in the basement of the creepy house behind ours. But she had asked if I'd seen the wallet, and I hadn't.

"No," I said. "I haven't seen it."

"Okay." She turned back to the sink. "Savior, Savior, hear my humble cry. While on others Thou art calling, do not pass me by."

After scooping up the key, I hurried off to my room. *Phew!* That was a close one. I got out of doing chores *and* I got away from Mom's singing.

~~~~~

Everything felt better in the morning. Once I used the skeleton key to open the treasure chest at that old house, Cami wouldn't dare call me *too little* ever again.

I sat at the kitchen table, spooning the last of my soggy Fruity Loops into my mouth.

I checked the clock for the millionth time. *Come on, Cami. Where are you?* It was already past ten o'clock. I knew it was summer break, but this was late—even for her.

"While on others Thou art calling, do not pass me by." Mom swooped in wearing overalls. Her curly hair wrapped around the top of her head.

She'd been singing that song all morning long.

"I'll be out in the shed, helping your father find that wallet." She grabbed a piece of paper from the counter, folded it, and shoved it into her pocket. "Piper."

I met her eyes so I wouldn't get in trouble for not paying attention. "What?"

"You'd tell me if you saw that wallet, wouldn't you?"

The back of my neck tingled with a cold shiver. Why was she picking on me all of a sudden? Did she know that I took the box?

Then she swatted a hand at the air and smiled. "What am I saying? I know you would." And she was gone—out the back door—just as fast as she'd appeared.

Phew! Another close one. But at least now I could prove myself to Cami. It would be nice if her friends were here to see me shine too, but we didn't have time to find all of them.

I leapt from the table, dug the skeleton key out of my pocket, booked it up the stairs, and banged on her bedroom door. "Hey, Cami!"

"What?" Her voice was muffled through the closed door, but it didn't sound like she was just waking up.

I swung open the door and saw her sitting on the edge of her bed, reading some fashion magazine. It must be nice to be able to look at all those cool clothes and then just drive your own car straight to the mall
~~~~~

whenever you wanted and buy them.

Well, at least she was dressed. Now we could head over to that treasure chest on the back porch of that creepy house. After we found that treasure, she'd be begging me to go to the mall with her and her friends.

I held up the key. "Look what I got."

She tossed the magazine on the bed beside her. "What's that?"

"The skeleton key from the basement of the creepy house behind us."

"No it's not." She shot to her feet and crossed the room to me.

I knew I had a cocky smile on my face, but I just couldn't help it. This was going to be the moment that would change everything between us. And she'd know for sure that I was just as smart as she was. Just as mature as any one of her friends.

"Yes, it is." I let her take the key from me.

She turned it over in her hand. I couldn't control how giddy I was at how big and round her eyes were.

"Macon and I snuck into that dark and filthy basement last night. We even saw a ghost girl while we were down there."

She shoved my shoulder. "Shut up."

See? I knew I was going to blow her mind. But I wasn't about to let her steal the key from me and act like she was the one who unlocked the treasure chest. So I snatched it out of her hands and started down the hall.

"I don't believe you." She crossed her arms and tilted her head. But I expected this reaction. Of course she wouldn't believe me.

"That's what I thought you'd say. All right then." I dangled the key between us. "Let's go to that treasure chest right now, and I'll prove it to you."

~~~~~

My legs were trembling by the time Cami and I had trudged through the grass to the back porch of that old house.

"Okay, so there's the chest." Cami pointed at it. "Let's open this thing and get out of here. This place creeps me out."

My chest tightened as I stared down at the rusty hinges on the clunky black thing. This was it. I exhaled and stepped closer.

"What do you think's inside?" she asked.

I tugged at the lock to see if it would open without having to use the key. No such luck.

"Whatever it is, I know it's gonna be amazing." I held up the skeleton key to the light to make sure I was putting it in the right way. This was it. My heart raced. A part of me wished Macon could be here to see my moment of glory. But, oh well, his loss.

I shoved the key in the hole, turned it, and it made a clicking sound.

"You did it." Cami crouched behind me. "Open it. Open it."

I knew this skeleton key was going to change everything. With a
~~~~~

hand on each side of the lid, I thrust it upward. The hinges creaked. But then it stopped.

"What?" Cami was practically breathing down my neck. "Why'd you stop?"

"I didn't stop. It's stuck."

"Well, what's in there?" I could feel her leaning even farther over my shoulder. But there was no way she was seeing the treasure before I did.

I peered inside. I couldn't see much. It was dark in there. But something silver glinted off the light pouring in through the small crack I'd made. Then, as my eyes adjusted, I saw something gold and round. Coins. And paper too. No way!

"Money!" I shouted. "Tons of it."

"No way! Let me see."

That's when I noticed the string attached to the lid of the chest. And some other round thing. What were those circles? Bubbles maybe?

Cami reached a hand toward the chest, but I shouldered it out of the way.

"Just a second," I said. "I think I can get the lid to open more. A couple pieces of string are stuck to the top." I gave the lid a good shove while Cami pressed even closer. Then I shoved it again — really hard.

The lid flew open. *POP! BANG! BANG! POP!*

Cami shrieked, and I jumped back as balloons popped inside the chest and color splattered all over. Something like paint sprayed across the contents of the chest. Splashes of red, yellow, and blue coated all that rich stuff.

"No!" I shouted. "My money."

"Ha! Ha! Gotcha!" That creepy girl with the messy hair leapt out from the side of the house. "I got you real good."

Huh? What was she talking about?

While Cami screamed again, I got to my knees, crawled back over to the chest and peered inside. Sure enough, all that paint coated the money. I reached a hand inside and pulled out a coin.

"Hey, wait a second. This is all play money." I glared at the cackling girl at the side of the house. "None of this is real."

The girl's face was red from laughing so hard.

"You did this." I pointed a finger at her, but she raced off. "Wait. Come back here." I hopped to my feet, ready to chase her down. "Who are you, anyway? I bet you don't even live in this neighborhood."

"Cami. Piper?" Mom's voice made me turn. "Cami, is everything all right?" After Cami nodded, Mom continued, "Cami, I came to tell you that you need to get an oil change in your car today." Then Mom turned to me. "Piper, what's that mess all over your hand *and* your new shirt?" She did not look happy.

I glanced down at the yellow and blue on my arms that was mixing together to make green and dripping onto the wood of the porch. "I . . . I don't know."

"Cami, are you sure everything's okay?" Mom placed a hand on her shoulder.

Cami nodded, even though she looked like she might cry. Then she shook out of it. "I'm fine. Piper's just acting like a baby again."

What? I was not a baby.

Mom clenched her hands in front of her overalls and hummed her go-to-church song, which did nothing but annoy me.

Cami sneered. "I can't believe I wasted the whole morning on a bunch of fake play money." She turned and walked toward the house. "I guess I'll go get that oil change."

Fake play money? Those words burned me up inside. Made me even more mad that she called me a baby. But I wasn't a baby.

Mom just stood beside me, humming.

I'd gone all the way into that creepy basement and had to deal with that strange girl. I found the key. I even found the treasure.

"Savior, Savior." Mom just kept singing that song, but that creepy girl's cackle was all I could hear. Everyone was laughing at me.

"Hear my humble cry." That song.

I swung around to face Mom. "Stop it! Stop singing. You're always singing those church songs. And we're not even in church."

Mom was silent.

And right away, I wished I could take back every word of what I just said because I wasn't really mad at her. I was just frustrated.

She stood there for a second, staring with the saddest eyes I'd ever seen at the messy chest beside us. "I'm sorry," she finally said. "I didn't realize you hated those songs." She turned toward home. Then she stopped. "Oh, I just wanted to let you know that wallet your father is looking for, it was personalized. One of a kind. He was going to meet the customer and give it to her this morning. Just wanted to make sure you knew. It's worth $145. And we need the money to pay the electric bill. So if you ever do see it . . ."

I felt so bad about what a jerk I'd been that I couldn't even talk. All I could do was nod.

She rubbed at her arms and didn't even bother to lift up her head when she said the next part. "You know, I don't sing those church songs because I'm trying to be a rock star. When I sing those songs, I'm talking to God. I've been asking for help finding your dad's wallet. Then I was asking God to help you girls with whatever you were screaming about over here." She glanced at my painted hands and hurried off, making me feel like the worst person in the world.

~~~~~

I wandered around the yard, feeling terrible until Cami came out of the house. Of course, she didn't look at me while she pulled her wallet out of her purse and counted out a few tens. She hopped into her car, slammed the door shut, and sped off.

That was right, Mom told her to get an oil change in her car. I guess she wasn't going to the mall, after all. Man, I sure wouldn't want to waste my own money on oil for a car. But I guess we all need to do things we don't want to do sometimes.

I kicked at a stick on the ground as she drove off down the street.

Ugh! We *all* have to do what we don't want to do sometimes. Just because it's the right thing to do.

I turned back toward that creepy house, knowing what I had to do.

All this time I blamed Cami for thinking I was a baby and Macon for not wanting to join me in that dark basement. But they were both right. And I was wrong. If only I'd obeyed Mom and Dad from the start, I never would've lost Dad's wallet in that old house, and I never would've made Mom feel terrible by telling her to stop singing.

I forced my feet to move quicker as I trampled the grass in the yard of the old house behind ours.

I paused at the door and took a deep breath. This time I had no flashlight. But at least I scared off the girl with messy hair.

I charged straight into that creaky old house. More light shone through than last night. That was a good thing. But my heart still hammered against my chest. I hurried to the staircase where a spiderweb clung to my face.

Swatting and tugging at the sticky floss, I navigated the stairs with a hand on the railing. Daytime or not, it was still dark down here. I inched forward through the dark, trying to remember where Macon had dropped that box.

Finally, I dropped to my hands and knees, swooshing my hand in front of me until it bumped into something that felt like cardboard. It was the box. I felt around the edges. It had opened and the tissue paper was all over the cold floor. Good thing, too, because that meant the frog had probably escaped to freedom.

Blind, in this dark place, I felt around until my hand landed on what had to be leather—the wallet. *Yes!* I shoved it and the tissue paper back into the box. Then, carefully clutching the box to my chest, I booked it out of that creepy place once and for all and headed home.

A seed of joy sprouted somewhere deep inside of me. Yes, I had messed things up, but I was fixing it now. I was going to make this right.

Hugging the box to my chest, I stepped into my house and closed the door behind me. The smell of coffee swirled through the air, reminding
~~~~~

me that it was still morning. I still had time to get this wallet to Dad so he could meet the lady this morning.

But the second I shuffled down the hall and into the kitchen, I knew something was wrong.

It was too quiet. Dad sat at the counter with his head down, and Mom ran water over her hands at the kitchen sink.

"Sorry, Dad." I stretched out the now dented and dirtied box to him as he turned my way. "I guess I did know where the wallet was."

"What? You found it?" He jumped up, took the box, and kissed me on the forehead. "Thank you, Piper." He squeezed my shoulder and zipped down the hall, looking back for half a second to shout to Mom, "I'm heading out, honey. Probably be home in about an hour."

It did feel good that I was able to help, but the sound of the door closing left the kitchen in an uncomfortable silence all over again.

I thought about taking a seat at the counter, but then I headed to the sink instead. When I got there, Mom headed for the coffee maker. She didn't sing or even hum.

After washing my hands, I dried them on a towel and began emptying the dishwasher. The whole time, the only sounds Mom made were the refrigerator door opening and her spoon clanging against the inside of her cup while she stirred cream into her coffee.

Then she just sat on a stool at the counter, sipping her coffee without humming a note. The whole thing left me feeling like I had swallowed a handful of rocks and now they were crashing and smashing together in my stomach.

I closed the door to the dishwasher and turned toward Mom. I couldn't look right at her face. I felt too horrible to do that. But nothing was going to stop me from saying what I had to say.

"Uh, Mom . . ."

"Yes?" Both her hands held tight to her coffee cup.

"I . . . I'm sorry. About what I said. And did. Or didn't do." I swiped at the sweat on my forehead. The words weren't exactly coming out the way I wanted them to. "Cami was right, I acted like a baby yesterday. I guess I'm not as mature as I thought I was. I should've done the dishes after dinner."

"Well, that's all right. At least you are doing them now." Mom's gaze wandered all over the room. I guess she was having a hard time looking me in the eyes too. "Making it right is the most mature thing you could've done. I'm proud of you for that."

I went back to the sink and started loading the dirty dishes into the dishwasher. But I still had that kind of sad feeling inside. Which made no sense, because Dad had his $145 wallet and my chores were finally getting done.

It was just too . . . quiet.

So while the dishes clanged, I sang, "I surrender all, I surrender all. All to Thee—"

"Piper," Mom whispered, "you might not want to sing so loud. You know your sister's friends are out on the back porch waiting for her to get back from town."

I didn't know they were out there, but I didn't care. I actually sang even louder. "I will ever love and trust Him." I dropped a fistful of spoons into the silverware slot of the dishwasher. "Come on, Mom, sing with me." This time I did look into her face. Right in her eyes.

"Are you sure?"

I didn't know why, but my eyes watered just a little. But I blinked it away. "I'm sorry I told you to stop singing. I was just upset about everything else."

She tilted her head like she was really listening to me now.

"The truth is, you're not a bad singer."

She smiled then.

"But even if you mess up the words sometimes, I'd still rather have you happy and singing than quiet and sad." I grabbed a bowl and continued my song, "In His presence daily live."

Then, right there at the counter with her coffee mug in her hand, Mom joined in. "I surrender all, I surrender all. All to Thee my blessed Savior, I surrender all." Her voice was prettier than I ever remembered it.

And even though I was just doing boring old chores, I was kind of having fun. At least I didn't have to waste my own money—and a perfectly good summer day—at some greasy old oil change place.

The End

Annika Klanderud's MG novel, *I Lived Through A Wind Chill Advisory*, won the 2024 Cascade Christian Writers Contest. Her YA novel, *Red Rock*, was the Cascade Christian Writers Contest winner in 2022. And her YA novel, *Qualify*, was a runner-up in 2024. Over forty of her articles have appeared in numerous publications such as *Keys for Kids*. In addition to seeking traditional publication for her novels, she is passionate about revolutionizing the Christian publishing industry. She has worked with numerous Christian authors to start a book fair in the state of Oregon, facilitate critique groups, and host events like the Author Spotlight and book clubs.

Visit Annika on Twitter/X and Instagram *@annikaklanderud*, and *aklanderud* on Facebook. Her website is *annikaklanderud.com*. When she is not wrestling with words for her novels, you can find her in the utility room battling her twelve children's mountain of laundry.

The following songs quoted in the story are in the public domain:

In the Garden
By Charles Austin Miles
Publication Date: 1912

Pass Me Not, O Gentle Savior
Lyrics written by: Fanny Crosby in 1868
Music Composed by: William H. Doane in 1870
Published: in Doane's publication, *Songs of Devotion*, in 1870

I Surrender All
Words written by: Judson W. Van DeVenter
Music Composed by: Winfield S. Weeden
Published: in the hymnbook 'Gospel Songs of Grace and Glory' in 1896

Surprise Inheritance
Heidi Glick

What was wrong with him? Why couldn't he tell people no? Neal Miller huffed as his boss walked away from Neal's desk. With a shaky hand, he ran his fingers through his hair. He couldn't stay late. He'd lose his other job. Quickly, he rose to his feet, and his boss turned, glaring. Neal forced a smile, sat, and started his computer. He'd just skip dinner. The drive from downtown Cincinnati to the west side took roughly thirty minutes. Longer in the winter. Thankfully, fall had arrived, and winter only loomed on the horizon. If he hurried, he still might make it to the camping store for his shift.

Somehow the thirty-mile move away from his mom and stepdad still hadn't helped him find a way to assert himself. Oh well. Staying late at work meant more overtime. And more money meant being able to buy the camping store sooner.

His boss cleared his throat and tossed a stack of folders on Neal's desk. "I need you to go through these as well."

"But—"

The man glared. That same look Neal's stepdad had given him.

"Yes, sir." Neal sighed once his boss meandered out of sight and texted the camping store's manager, then shut his phone.

Mindy chuckled and stopped in front of Neal's desk. She worked in accounting, and with her medium brown hair and tall height, she could pass as his twin. Today, she wore a pale blue dress and had her purse slung over her shoulder. "Goodnight, Neal. Someday, you'll have to learn to say no. I'm glad I did. Otherwise, the boss will have you staying late every night." She waved and walked away.

Easy for her to say. He massaged his right temple.

After wrapping up work two hours later, Neal headed outside to his car. He'd barely turned onto Fourth Street when the cars in front of him slowed to a halt. He maneuvered his car to one side but couldn't detect the source of the delay.

Minutes later, traffic moved again. He turned right onto Central Avenue and then left onto Sixth Street/U.S. Highway 50. He'd made up for lost time. Things were looking up. He enjoyed the scenic view of the Ohio River, catching glimpses of several red, orange, and yellow-leaf trees along the way. Farther he traveled, making a right onto Fairbanks

Avenue/Delhi Avenue and progressing into Delhi Township.

A few streets later, he arrived at his westside bungalow. Nothing fancy, but his neighbors took pride in the appearance of their older homes and their manicured lawns. He inspected his leaf-littered yard as he pulled into his driveway. His grass stood several inches higher than acceptable. He stepped out of the car. Better mow tomorrow.

"Hi, Neal," a female voice said.

He turned to face his neighbor, Lydia Miller—a perky yet kind woman he'd known since middle school, when her family had moved to town. Something was different, though. He'd been busy. Hadn't seen her for a while. She'd done something different with her hair. Pulled her long blonde locks away from her face. Looked nice. Very nice. A small gold locket hung from a thin chain around her neck.

Neal had always liked Lydia, no matter how she wore her hair. Too bad she didn't feel the same way. At least, she'd never expressed an interest in him. He found her to be empathetic and caring—someone who was easy to be around.

She walked her tan and white corgi, Wags, who yipped a greeting. Lydia waved at Neal as if she were flagging down aircraft. "Are you working late again?"

"Yes." He kept his head low and headed toward the front door.

"That's good, isn't it? Soon, you'll have enough money to buy the camping store. That's always been your dream."

How did she know? He hadn't told that many people. Neal smiled. "I hope so." Overtime was overtime. So he missed work at the camping store. His office job paid him extra. "You should stop by. I have a friends and family discount."

"You probably like to camp a lot, don't you?"

"Well, yeah."

Lydia's face drooped. "I'm not really much of a camper. I just walk the dogs and then go home." Using one hand, she fidgeted with the locket, and with the other, she maintained a grip on the dog's leash.

Was it something he'd said? "Oh. Okay, well, I'll see you around."

As he waved, his phone rang. "Hello?"

"Hi, I've been trying to reach you all day," an elderly-sounding male voice said.

"Sorry, I've been working. I've had my cell on do-not-disturb mode. Who is this?"

"I'm with Gersheim and Leiberman and Associates. Your great-uncle passed away and left you his estate. Would you be free on Monday to stop by my office?"

"Monday? I'm working two weekday jobs right now, and I had been working Saturdays."

"Had been ... Will you be free tomorrow? Normally, I'm closed on the weekend but make a few exceptions."

"Thank you, sir. I appreciate your flexibility. How about 1:00 p.m.?"

"Sounds good. I'll see you then."

His shoulders drooped. He'd never see Great-Uncle Larry again. But the old man had been in pain. At least now he was in a better place.

Maybe Neal could sell the property and acquire the camping store even sooner. The home was older, but he could fix it up and resell it, like those house flippers did on home improvement shows. First, traffic cleared up on his way home so he could get there sooner, and now this. He turned to tell Lydia, but she'd gone back inside. As he should, too.

He hurried into the kitchen, grabbed a small package of peanut butter and crackers, and filled a metal water bottle. He'd snack on the way to work.

His phone rang again. Caller ID displayed the number for the camping store. Maybe a call from his manager, Tom Wardley. "Hello?"

"Neal?" Tom asked.

"Hey, how's it going, Tom?"

"Neal, you canceled on me yesterday. We need to talk."

Neal fidgeted with his collar. "I know, I'm sorry, my other boss —"

"That's the third time this month. I'm going to have to let you go."

"No, please, wait. I'm so sorry —"

"I am too, but my wife's been sick, and I can't be at the store as much. I need someone who's reliable. Besides, my new hire has expressed an interest in the store. I need to sell the business soon. Sorry, bye."

"Wait ..."

The only response was a dial tone.

No more second job. Fine, he had overtime at the first. But if Tom sold the camping store to the new hire ... This wasn't just about money. Neal's dream was on the line.

Perhaps he could convince Mr. Wardley to hold off on selling the store. That and he'd have to fix up his great-uncle's house sooner rather than later.

Neal stumbled inside his house and retrieved the mail that had fallen on the floor from the mail slot. Bills. A flyer for the music store on the corner. A political ad. A letter. He opened the envelope and peeked at the paper inside, then unfolded it. A letter from his mom. She'd written and included a newspaper clipping of his great-uncle's obituary.

Neal set the letter on his kitchen counter and settled into a comfy wingback in his living room. He folded his hands behind his head. Why had Great-Uncle Larry chosen him? He'd visited the man's place a few times over the years and had fun, but they weren't exactly close. Then again, Larry had never married or had children.

~~~~~

At 1:30 p.m. the next day, after he'd left the attorney's office, Neal headed over to West Price Hill. Per the attorney, the city had condemned the property and planned to tear it down in accordance with eminent domain laws. The city would provide him with compensation for the property but not much.

Neal lowered his chin to his chest. He'd taken a second job to help him buy the camping store, and then his boss fired him. He'd inherited a property, but it was condemned. Every time Neal tried to get ahead, something prevented him from doing so.

With his trusty camping backpack slung over his shoulder, he trudged to the old, brick Tudor-style house Great-Uncle Larry had once called home and trotted up the first set of two flights of stairs toward the front door, leaves crunching beneath his feet. Wrought-iron rails framed the sides of the stairs.

He paused at the top before jogging to the peak of the second set of stairs, framed by two ornate concrete lions on either side. A cool breeze blew, and he wrapped his coat around him tighter, then zipped the front.

Before taking a step further, he turned and admired the view across the street. Three empty lots enveloped two homes — one had been restored to its former beauty — the other stood on the verge of collapse. He turned again and stepped toward his great-uncle's house.

The door was several feet ahead. Neal navigated around the bright yellow caution tape wrapped around the columns and onto the porch. An official notice stuck to a front window. He felt around in his pocket for the key the attorney had given him.

His belly fluttered, and he paused, recalling what the house had once looked like when built. Great-Uncle Larry had shown him photos from the previous owner. Over time, his great-uncle had traveled and failed to maintain the home.

Larry had traveled a lot and collected sports memorabilia. That might be worth something. Neal's first task was to look for anything of value.

Large clouds loomed across the gray sky. Better get inside soon.

With increasing pressure, he jostled the old key inside the lock several times before the old metal item turned. He opened the door, but a familiar female voice nearby stopped him from entering.

"I thought I saw your car parked in the driveway. Are you moving?"

Neal turned around and absently toyed with his shirt collar. "Lydia? What are you doing here?"

Lydia held up two leashes. Wags pulled on the end of one. A second dog, a black pug, tugged at the end of the other. "I walk dogs on the weekend. For some extra cash. To pay my bills."
~~~~~

Neal nodded. Lydia had a second job too. She taught online classes to elementary school kids. No commute that way. Must have been nice.

She cleared her throat. "So? Are you moving? I hope not. I like having you next door." Her cheeks reddened.

And he liked being next door to her. He took a deep breath, contentedly. "No, no. I'm not going anywhere. My great-uncle passed away. This was his house."

"Oh, I'm sorry to hear that."

Neal gestured to the dilapidated home. "Apparently, he left the place to me. The house is, um, condemned."

"I'm sorry. Too bad you couldn't fix it up. It looks like it was a nice place once." Wags yipped and pulled in the opposite direction, toward the stairs. Lydia followed. "Bye. Hurry home before the rain starts."

Neal waved to her. "Bye." He opened the front door, allowing a musty smell to emanate, then closed the old, white wooden panel behind him.

Inside the home, strong hands grabbed him from behind. "Don't make a sound," a male voice whispered. A hard object, presumably a pistol, pressed against the small of Neal's back. Would the robber take Neal's wallet and release him, or was he in greater danger?

Lydia was right outside. He could yell, and she could call for help. Or he might end up endangering her life too.

"Move it," the man said, pressing the gun further against Neal's skin.

He made up his mind. He'd go along with whatever the man said. Maybe if he did, the crook would just take his money and let him go.

"I have some cash in my wallet. You can have it," Neal said.

The doorbell rang.

"Answer it," the man said. "And don't try anything."

Neal opened the door, revealing his beautiful neighbor still standing outside. "Lydia?" he said, maintaining composure. She was the only one nearby. She and the two dogs. No one else. Not a police officer or a jogger or even a mail carrier.

She smiled and made strong eye contact. "You know ... If you need assistance to go through your great-uncle's things, I could help."

"Make her leave," the man whispered.

"I-I'll call you later," Neal said, then bit back a whimper as the gun pressed deeper against his skin. "I, uh, can't afford to pay anyone to help me right now. Maybe you can pick up more dog walking jobs."

"Oh, I mean, I'm not looking for a paycheck. Just trying to be neighborly." A look flashed across her face. What was that? Hurt?

"I've gotta go," Neal said curtly, and shut the door.

As he turned, the man directed Neal toward the other end of the house. He marched in that direction and continued for two more steps.

The doorbell rang again.

Go away, Lydia.

The door opened, and his neighbor popped inside. "Neal, I can lend you money if you ..." Lydia looked over at Neal, with the man pointing a gun at him, and she gasped.

The man stepped away from Neal and now pointed his pistol toward Lydia. "Stand next to him. Oh, and toss your cell phones on the floor."

Lydia retrieved a hot pink phone from her pocket and tossed it onto the old hardwood floor. Her Corgi growled at the man. The pug joined in too.

"Get rid of the mutts. Or else."

Lydia released the leashes, and the man let the dogs outside. Maybe someone would find the pooches and realize something was wrong.

Neal fidgeted with his phone. Should he pretend he didn't have one?

"C'mon, I don't got all day," the man barked. "Your phone too. On the floor."

Neal tossed his phone. The object crashed onto the old wooden planks. Regret washed over him the moment the device left his hands. He should have found a way to call for help first.

The man held up his gun, as if to remind them who was in control. "We're gonna take a walk downstairs."

Neal narrowed his gaze. The guy looked familiar.

Lydia gasped, and Neal moved closer to her. He gestured for her to go downstairs first.

He should do something. Now? Maybe later. Perhaps he could find a weapon downstairs.

After flipping the light at the top of the stairway, Neal followed Lydia down the old stairs. His foot wobbled on the second step. His skin prickled as the coldness of the basement overtook him. In the far corner stood a large, three-sided, gated cage.

Huge, from floor to ceiling. Maybe eight feet long by eight feet wide. Didn't Great-Uncle Larry have a dog? Perhaps he kept it in there in the winter. Judging from the appearance, he'd used the space for storage as of late. A bench, stool, old chair, various boxes, and odds and ends sat inside. At the far end of the cage, a basement wall, reinforced by concrete, containing a window, made up the fourth side.

"Get in there," the gunman said.

Lydia obeyed, climbing in the cage first.

Mildewed walls lined the basement cavern. Old roots poked holes through the sides of the space. The single ceiling light near the top of the stairs flickered. The only other light peeked through two small windows.

Neal entered the cage. What would happen next?

The man shut the gate and padlocked it, then walked away. "I'll be back later," he said before clomping up the stairs and shutting the door at the top.

Lydia turned to face Neal, eyes wide open, one hand fidgeting with her locket. "What are we going to do?" She moved closer and leaned on his shoulder.

He set down his backpack on a bench and put an arm around her.

"How will we get out of here?"

We? No one ever looked to him, the youngest of five children, for advice. This was a first. Hopefully, this wouldn't be a last. But the way things were headed, he wasn't sure.

Neal embraced Lydia tighter. "We'll find a way."

Thou shalt not bear false witness. His statement wasn't exactly a lie. Though chances were slim, they might find a way out of their dank dungeon.

"Let's look around. What can we find? Maybe we can pick the lock on the cage."

"Good idea." Lydia looked through boxes nearby. Neal checked near the shelves on the bench, near the back of the caged cell.

He swiped a cobweb to examine a toolbox on the shelf, then opened the metal container and examined the contents. A hammer. Some nails.

Lydia stood. "I found something. Some paperclips. Maybe we can use them to pick the lock. Like in the movies."

"I found a hammer." Neal held up the tool.

He moved closer to the cage lock and gestured to Lydia. She straightened the paperclip and inserted the small metal object into the lock. After several attempts, she gave up.

"My turn," Neal said. He gripped the hammer, but the lock sat on the outside of the cage. Maybe he could push the tool through the openings in the gate.

Why did his great-uncle have this cage? Couldn't he keep his dog outside? Did he really use this for just a dog kennel?

Voices came from upstairs.

Lydia put her finger to her lips.

The hair on the nape of Neal's neck stiffened. The man said he would return. Then what? Neal and Lydia still hadn't found a way out of the cage.

He gripped the hammer and hid the tool behind his back. "Go sit near the bench. In the back," he whispered to Lydia. "I'll, uh, I'll handle this." He wasn't sure who he was trying harder to convince. Himself or Lydia. The way she looked at him earlier, like her hero. Well, he'd need to act like one.

His older brother, Vince, served the local community as a police officer. His other brothers owned a martial arts studio. Neil had attended

Boy Scouts. That was it. He wasn't prepared for this.

The voices from upstairs grew louder. Could there be more than one person? Who was the man from earlier arguing with? Light shone at the top of the stairs. The door opened, and the man who'd trained a gun on them now had a weapon pointed at his back. Guess now he knew what the fear of being held up felt like.

The man with the gun snarled. Was he more deadly than the first?

The first guy stumbled downstairs, and the second rushed back upstairs and slammed the door behind him.

The other man reached the bottom of the stairs and opened the lock on the cage. "My boss isn't happy you're here." He removed a pistol from his waistband and shrugged. "It's nothing personal." He pointed his weapon at Neal.

Neal bit back a snort. Not personal? Maybe not to him. Neal's hands shook as he steadied the hammer. For a few seconds. Until the man's hands came into view. They shook too.

The man's name finally came to him. Ty Barrone. Neal had seen the guy's name in the newspaper. What was he wanted for — robbery?

"Ever kill someone before?" Neal asked.

Ty's right hand and the gun he was holding fell to his side. "I … What?"

Neal gripped the hammer with confidence. Ty might have stolen. Ty might have acted tough. But the dude didn't seem like he wanted to add murder to his rap sheet.

Neal swung his hammer at Ty, and the guy darted backward, then slammed the gate shut. He locked the gate as Neal pushed against it. "Where ya' get that from?" Ty shouted, then rubbed his head. A scowl spread across his face.

A siren blared, interrupting them. "The cops?" Lydia asked.

"Tornado," Neal said.

Ty raised his gun and aimed at Neal, then shifted his hand at the last moment and shot into the wall. Five times. He put his finger to his nose.

"Thanks," Lydia mouthed, as she stood up.

"Don't thank me," Ty whispered. "The city plans to demolish this house soon." He headed upstairs and shut the door.

"Should we yell for help?" Lydia whispered.

Neal shook his head. "Not yet. We'd only alert his boss we're still alive."

"For now. Do you know when the city plans to demolish the house?"

"My great-uncle's lawyer mentioned the house was condemned. I was going to come by and grab any family heirlooms before, um, before —"

"When, Neal?"

"Two days from now." He gulped. "But we have bigger problems."

The siren blared again.

Lydia sat back down on the bench. "At least if there's going to be a tornado, we're in the right place."

"Good way to focus on the positive." He took a seat next to her and grabbed her hand. "No matter what, we're in this together."

She squeezed his hand. "Together."

Neal chuckled.

"What's so funny?" Lydia asked.

"I always thought a heart attack would kill me. Never suspected a tornado."

Her face contorted.

"I'm sorry. I'm kidding. I guess now's not a good time to joke about something like that."

"Do you think the men will return?"

"Tonight? Nah. That gives us some time to figure our way out of here."

"Once the storm is over."

"Right."

The wind howled. The rain outside pounded harder against the small basement windows. Rain leaked in through the bottom of one window.

The wind continued in intensity. The rain remained constant.

The building shook.

Lydia sat there.

Neal paced. He should do something, but what? He wasn't the hero of the family.

A noise like a train approached. Rumbling and roaring. Only Neal was fairly certain they were nowhere near any tracks.

The house made an ungodly, twisting, wrenching sound. Were pieces of the old, condemned house being ripped apart by the tornado?

Neal sat next to Lydia and gripped her hand. "Please, God. Help us."

"Amen." She squeezed his hand in return.

The door at the top of the stairs blew open and off its hinge. The basement ceiling caved down onto the cage.

"It's good the cage was there. The metal protected us."

"Yep." Except now, they were not only locked inside a cage. They were buried under rubble.

~~~~~

The wind raged for a long time, and rain pelted the mutilated structure, but the storm cleared after nightfall. Somehow, they managed to get a few winks. Thank goodness for the wooden bench to sit on and keep them off the damp floor. Overnight, the basement ceiling fell in large enough chunks to provide shelter from the last of the rain. At least for
~~~~~

now, they were dry, if not exactly warm.

One more day until demolition. They still had time to escape.

Sun peeked through the glass block window, and Neal gently touched Lydia's shoulder.

Gesturing toward the window, he said, "Help me clear this stuff so I can get closer."

Lydia helped him move boxes and other clutter away from the sill.

Neal crept closer and reached toward the window. Small glass blocks covered the area instead of one large pane. No crank. No opening. Now what?

He spied a hammer. "Stand back!" Neal picked up the tool and smashed the glass blocks until he'd made an opening. Though bowed, the surrounding wall remained intact. "Help!" he yelled until his voice grew hoarse.

The street was unusually quiet. No sound of cars or people's voices. Not even a dog barking. Had the neighborhood evacuated?

Neal's stomach ached. He reached in his coat pocket and removed the candy bars he kept for emergencies. Like having to work late without dinner or commuting to his second job.

Lydia smiled when he produced the slightly squished packets of chocolate and peanuts then stared at him the same way as when they'd first been captured, looking at him as if he were a hero.

He beamed. "I used to be a Boy Scout. Always be prepared, right?"

Too bad he hadn't packed more food though. Two chocolate bars wouldn't hold them for long. Then again, tomorrow the city planned to demolish the house. Food wasn't their highest concern at this point.

Lydia ate half of the chocolate he gave her but saved the rest. "Are you sure you don't want any?"

"No, thanks. I don't really have much of an appetite. But I am thirsty. I bet you are too. Hold on." Neal located his backpack and removed two water bottles from inside. He handed her one and took a sip from the other.

"Let me guess," she said then grinned. "Just in case. For emergencies."

"Yep. I'd say this counts as one."

Lydia drank some water, then tugged on her necklace locket.

"Have you heard from anyone since graduation?" Neal asked. "I haven't kept in touch much."

"Oh, well, Tom Anderson works for a bank downtown. Kevin Brunswick got a job with an insurance company and travels all the time. My friend, Megan Hafner, has a salon on the westside. She's getting married in a few months."

"Vince is a police officer."

"What?" She clasped a hand to her mouth but failed to stifle a chuckle.

Neal nodded. "Yep, the brother who was always in trouble."

"What about Chuck and David?"

Crossing his arms, he said, "They opened a dojo in Oakley."

"Interesting ... So, what about your camping store idea?"

"It's still just a dream for now. I had hoped to find my great-uncle's sports memorabilia. I'm afraid anything left in this house worth saving is probably ruined by now."

After sitting and reminiscing for a while longer, Neal stood and stretched his legs then moved nearby debris, expanding their living space.

As the sun set, he studied the rubble atop their cage. Was there a way to lift it? Maybe if he could use something long for leverage. He spied a wooden board on the ground. Snatching the wet piece of wood, he pushed against the weight of the material above him, moving it slightly but not enough.

"I can help," Lydia said.

She moved toward him and held onto the board.

"On the count of three. One. Two. Three."

They shoved upward, but Lydia slipped on the wet floor. Falling backward, she hit her head on the bench.

Neal let go of the board, and more surrounding debris caved downward. A jagged piece slipped through the cage and scraped Neal, cutting his left bicep. He winced and moved toward Lydia.

"Are you okay?"

She nodded. "I'm sorry. I think we made things worse."

"It was worth a try."

Rubbing her head, Lydia rested on the bench.

A siren blared in the distance. Could someone be coming to rescue them? Neal sprinted toward the window and shouted, "Help! Help!" But the siren grew fainter until it disappeared altogether. His shoulders slumped.

Shadows danced inside their cage, while a rat scurried by his feet. A musty odor filled the space.

Neal sat on the bench and scooted closer to Lydia, putting his uninjured arm around her.

Her skin was cold to the touch.

He rubbed warmth into her right arm. *Please, God, help!*

The wind picked up, and droplets of rain fell. Pitter patter. The house creaked and groaned. *Not another storm.*

If he and Lydia could just stay warm through the night, maybe tomorrow, they could get the worker's attention before they started tearing down the damaged house—assuming the old home didn't completely topple and pancake them beforehand.

~~~~~

Sunlight peeked through the basement window. Finally, Monday morning.

Neal glanced at Lydia. She rubbed her eyes. At least she'd gotten some sleep. No way he could get any rest. Today was demolition day. Maybe they could scream when the demo began. Then again, could anyone hear them over the noise? It was worth a try.

A vehicle rumbled outside.

"That's probably the demolition crew. They're here to knock down the house. But maybe if we yell loud enough, they'll hear us."

"Help!"

More noise.

Footsteps. A form appeared at the top of the stairs. Ty Barrone again. What did he want?

"You're still alive?" Ty asked.

Lydia quirked a brow.

"I forgot something." Ty walked over to the first pile of rubble and dug through the debris. What was he looking for?

Neal dipped his head. He hadn't protected Lydia from entering the building. He hadn't protected her from being trapped in the wreckage. The demolition crew would come soon. Could he protect her from them? What if he couldn't?

If he and Lydia made it out of here okay, could he risk telling her how he felt? Would she even want to go out with someone like him?

Neal sighed. At least they could move around. No body parts were trapped. In an odd way, the cage had protected them. If he and Lydia worked together, they could dig their way out.

A bigger problem lingered. Why would Ty come back? Would he shoot them this time?

Neal felt in his pocket for his flashlight.

Ty continued searching through the surrounding ruins. Could he have left jewels stashed here?

Last month, Neal read about a crook stashing his loot in an abandoned warehouse, so why not a house? But his great-uncle had only died recently. Except, he'd spent some time in a nursing home before that.

Lydia breathed raggedly. Neal moved toward her and bent down in front of her. "It's gonna be okay."

She looked away, then opened her locket, revealing two photos — one each of her mom and dad. "How can you say that? My parents were ..." she whispered, "murdered." She sobbed. "I didn't want to leave my house, but my pastor and therapist said getting out would be good for me. Now I'm not so sure I'd agree." After studying the photos, she closed the
~~~~~

locket.

Neal nodded toward Ty, who continued to search frantically through the rubble. "Lydia, I don't know what he's up to. But he's leaving us alone. We're stuck under here, but I think we can try to dig our way out again."

Ty stood and left the basement. He wasn't holding anything that Neal could see. Either he'd taken something small that could fit in a pocket, or maybe he didn't find what he'd been looking for. Either way, he was gone.

Lydia cleared her throat. "What if the construction crew arrives first to demolish the house? With us inside?"

"We'll have to find a way to signal for them to find us." Neal reached with his left hand and grabbed her hand, squeezing her fingers gently.

On his own, the problem was insurmountable. But he wasn't on his own. Lydia was there. And God too. He'd solved problems in Boy Scouts. He could do this. With God's help. He'd remain levelheaded and avoid panicking.

~~~~~

An hour later, motors hummed, whirred, droned, and rumbled. The ground shook.

"What's that?" Lydia asked.

"Probably the demolition crew."

Lydia blinked rapidly. "Ever since my parents were killed, I've been scared to leave my house much. That's another reason I took the dog walking job. To try to expose myself to the outside world slowly. And so I went out, and now I may die."

"I don't want to die either, but if I do, I know where I'm going."

"I know I'd go to Heaven, but I don't want to get crushed."

He took a deep breath. "I figure if we die in here, God will give us grace to get through even that."

Nondescript construction noise loomed above them.

"But," he said, "I don't think we should give up and plan our funerals just yet."

"You have a plan?"

Hurrying toward the window, Neal shone his flashlight outside. He turned the object on and then off.

"What's happening? Is your battery low?"

"No. Morse code. Trying to send an SOS."

Lydia clapped. "Smart, Neal. Really smart." She moved closer to him. "Can I help?"

"Yeah. Here." He reached in his pocket and removed a whistle. "When the crew finds us, you should blow this. Make it easier for them to locate us."

The machinery continued. The team was getting closer.

"That's pretty loud. I'm not sure they'll be able to hear us," Neal said.
~~~~~

"Now what?"

Neal searched the shelves. Nothing. He sat down and closed his eyes. Lydia sat next to him, and he held her hand.

"Please God, we need help," he said.

"Amen."

Neal searched again, choosing another pile of rubble to sift through.

Lydia did the same. A minute later, she approached him holding a box. "Did your great-uncle have a boat?"

"Yeah, why?"

"I found a flare gun. It's old. I don't know if the old thing even works, but …"

Thank You, God. And thank you, Lydia. Neal held out his right fist and extended three fingers, one at a time. "One. Two. Three."

"What are you counting?"

"Those flares are only good for so long. I'm wondering how long it's been since my great-uncle last used his boat. Might have been three years. Might have been longer. Guess we'll find out if the flares are still useful."

He snatched the flare gun and loaded a flare. "If we weren't about to die, I could kiss you." He smiled, and she blushed, then frowned. The outside noise grew louder. The far end of the house appeared to shake.

"Neal, hurry!"

Neal leaned toward the window, held out the flare gun, and pulled the trigger.

Nothing.

No! Was this it? The end?

"Are there any others in there?"

"Wait, here's a newer looking set." Lydia ripped open the package and removed a new flare.

Neal loaded the gun, and the house rattled louder. He fired the flare gun out the window. Whoosh. A flash of light was followed by a pop and then a continual whooshing noise that sounded as the flare shot through the air. Seconds later, the machinery stopped.

Lydia cried.

Neal hugged her and pointed to the whistle.

She put the bright red object to her mouth and blew a tune for the construction crew.

"Anyone down there?" a gruff-sounding male voice said.

"Down here. In the basement," Nate yelled.

The male construction worker leaned down and peeked in the window. He yelled over his shoulder. "We got people down in here." He looked back at Neal and Lydia. "You could have been killed. We'll get you out shortly. Is anyone injured? Is there anyone else in there?"

"Just us. No injuries."

"That's good."

"Wait, there's one more thing. May I borrow your phone? I need to call the police."

"Huh? Okay." The man handed over his device to Neal.

Neal dialed his brother's number. "Vince? It's Neal. I'm over at Great-Uncle Larry's house. He left the place to me. Ty Barone was in the house."

"Ty? He's a criminal," his brother said. "Why was he there?"

"Apparently, when our great-uncle was in the nursing home, Ty must have broken in and stashed something here. I don't know what. But my neighbor came over. Ty locked us in the basement. A tornado hit. The house was set to be demolished, and we're still inside."

"Whoa. Are you both okay?"

"Yeah. We were able to communicate with the crew. They're going to get us out. But I wanted to tell you about Ty, so you can stop him. He was working with another man. Older. Had a mustache."

"Hmm. Could be his older brother. Got it. I'm glad you're okay. I'll relay this to the Sheriff right away."

Neal stared at Lydia. "One more thing. My neighbor's dog is loose. It's a corgi. And she was walking another dog. A pug. Both pooches are on the loose. Maybe you could alert animal control."

"Sure."

"Thanks." Neal returned the phone to its owner.

Lydia sat nearby and exhaled as construction workers came down the stairs and removed rubble from the top of the cage.

She leaned against him. "We're alive."

He grabbed her hand and squeezed it. "Yes, we are."

"We were in a house. Not even out in public."

"Bad things can happen anywhere."

She nodded.

"But good things too."

She lifted her brow.

"Lydia, I'd like to go out with you this week. Would that be okay?"

"Yeah, I really like you, Neal."

He faced her. "You do?"

"Mm-hmm. Have for a long time, silly. Why do you think I hung out with you and your friends over the years?"

"Really? I assumed you liked one of them." The corners of his mouth turned upward. All these years, and he'd never known. Well, now was better than never.

~~~~~

Neal finished his dinner and washed dishes afterward. As he exited the kitchen, he passed the wall calendar. An entire month had passed since
~~~~~

the incident in his great-uncle's house.

The money the city had given Neal wasn't much. Too bad he hadn't found his great-uncle's memorabilia. Even if he had more money, the camping store owner had agreed to sell to someone else. He slumped into his armchair and rested.

A minute later, his phone rang, and he jumped.

"Hello?"

"Hi, Neal, it's Tom Wardley. I'm calling because the offer I had from someone else to buy my store fell through. The other guy had a family emergency and backed out. If you don't have the money or aren't interested, that's fine. But I wanted to ask you before I put the store up for sale with a realtor."

Neal pulled himself into a sitting position. "I'm still interested, but I don't have the money. Thank you for thinking of me though. Bye."

The doorbell rang, and Neal hurried to the front of his house. He flung the door open.

His brother Vince stood outside and held three large metal boxes.

Neal stepped toward his brother and held out his arms. "Let me help. Those look like they're about to topple over."

"Thanks, considering they're yours, anyway."

Neal grabbed the top two metal boxes and carried them inside, setting them on his coffee table.

Vince followed and set the remaining box next to the others then plopped onto the couch. Neal settled into his armchair nearby.

"What do you mean they're mine?" Neal asked.

"They're fire safes found at the crime scene. The police have gone through them. They don't pertain to the case, and they're yours now."

"What's inside?"

"Open 'em and find out." Vince grinned.

Neal unlocked the first box. Baseball cards were stacked inside. Tons of them. He shifted his gaze to his brother. "And the others?"

"Same thing. Some of them look pretty old." Vince reached in his pocket and withdrew a card. "Here's the name of an antique dealer who's trustworthy. If you want, you can show him the cards and see if they're worth anything."

"Thanks, Vince."

"You're welcome."

Neal walked his brother to the door and then outside.

Lydia stood near her front door and waved to them before entering her home.

Vince raised a brow. "You live next door to Lydia?" He smiled. "She's nice. Have you spoken much since the whole ordeal?"

Neal sighed. "I'd asked her to go out with me tonight, but she had to cancel."

Vince patted Neal on the back. "Maybe another time. Take care."

Neal waved and walked inside and into the living room. He lay on the couch, with his hands interlaced behind his head. Could the cards really be worth something? Enough to help him put down money on the store? Should he dare to dream again?

~~~~~

Dusk settled in, blanketing the sky with a thin cover of darkness.

Neal's insides danced. How surreal. Could his dreams really be coming true? *Thank You, God.* Though the last two months had felt disastrous, God still had control of Neal and his situation.

He chuckled. Who knew rare baseball cards were worth so much money?

Neal knocked on the door to the light pink and white Victorian home Lydia rented. The house's gingerbread trim had seen better days.

A yip came from inside. Wags sat atop the back of Lydia's couch and poked his head through the curtains.

Animal control had located Wags and the pug not long after Lydia and Neal escaped. A kind elderly neighbor had taken the dogs in and cared for them in the meantime.

Lydia opened the front door, and a vanilla scent wafted in Neal's direction. "I'm ready."

Together, they walked to his car. He opened her door, then hurried to the other side.

"How was your interview?" he asked.

"Good. I got the job. I'll be teaching in person next year. And how was your meeting?"

"Great. I'll be leading a scout troop next year."

Within minutes, they arrived at the camping store. His store. One hand busy holding a brown paper bag from his car, he used his other hand to unlock the front doors of the store, and Lydia followed him inside. He set aside the brown paper bag on the counter and showed her the fridge and other food items in the employee lounge area. She followed him into the main part of the store and helped him set out snacks on a long table for the store's open house.

"What time will everyone else get here?" she asked.

"Six o'clock."

Decorations covered the room. He'd worked on them earlier.

"Anything else I can do?"

"Why yes. Can you sit here for a moment?"

She raised a brow. "Sure. What are you up to?"

He smirked. "Whatever do you mean?" In a hurry, he set off for the employee lounge and retrieved the paper bag from the counter. Then he
~~~~~

grabbed two water bottles from the fridge and stuffed them inside the bag.

As he walked back into the room where Lydia sat, she stared at the sack. "What's inside, Neal?"

"You'll see." He removed the bottles from the bag, setting one each in front of them.

While Lydia twisted the top of her bottle, Neal held two entrees in plastic containers in the air. "Ziti or lasagna?"

"Mmm. Ziti, please."

Neal set a container of ziti in front of her and placed the lasagna-filled container by his place setting. He reached into the bag for plastics utensils and napkins, then divvied them up.

He sat across from Lydia. "Let's pray," he said, then reached across the table.

Lydia stretched her hands and grabbed his.

He smiled, then said, "Lord, bless this food to our bodies. Thank you for keeping us safe. Thank you for this opportunity. Bless the people coming tonight. Amen."

"Amen." Lydia grinned, then grabbed her fork. She stabbed the ziti and took a bite. "Takeout from Razelli's?"

"I hope that's okay. I don't cook much."

"I love their food."

"Me too." He took a bite of the lasagna and savored the zesty marinara sauce covering the alternating layers of cheese and pasta.

She chuckled.

"What? What's so funny?" Had sauce dribbled down the side of his face? He grabbed his napkin and dabbed his cheek.

"My aunt and uncle are the owners. I spent a lot of time there growing up. That's why I like the food so much. Maybe next weekend you could come over, and we could make lasagna together. If you're not busy."

"I'd love that."

"Me too," she said, then blushed, as if the last part wasn't to be spoken aloud.

Neal's stomach fluttered.

He and Lydia enjoyed their meal together.

Afterward, Neal stood and moved near the front door of the store, and as guests poured in, he greeted them.

"Hello, welcome."

Lydia stayed by the refreshments area, replenishing food as needed.

Neal counted over a hundred guests over the course of the next two hours. By eight o'clock, the last person filed outside. Neal locked the front door, then helped Lydia clean up the food.

"You had a nice turnout," she said.

"Thanks. I couldn't have done this without your help."

"Oh, you'd manage."

"Maybe, but I preferred having you here with me."

She smiled, and he walked her outside.

On the drive home, Lydia remained quiet.

"Are you tired?"

"A little. But I had fun greeting people. I needed to get out."

He pulled into his driveway, parked, and then walked Lydia next door to her house.

"G'night, Neal." She removed her key from her purse and turned away.

"Lydia, wait."

She turned to face him.

He leaned over and pressed his lips against hers. His heart beat, aware of the closeness between them. "Good night, Lydia."

He waved and walked back to his home, a new man. One ready to take on all challenges with God's help, and Lydia by his side.

The End

Heidi Glick has a B.A. in biology from Cedarville University, a Master of Technical Communication from Utah State University, and a passion for writing romantic suspense from a Christian worldview. Additionally, she is a member of American Christian Fiction Writers and Faith, Hope, and Love Christian Writers. She has an eye for detail and includes law enforcement particulars in her stories, grounding the reader in scenes. She's attended Writers' Police Academy and the Hancock County (Ohio) Citizens Sheriff's Academy to ensure accuracy of story details. Before becoming a romantic suspense writer, Heidi taught science to middle and high school students and edited science documents. Though she grew up in Southern California, Heidi now considers rural Northwest Ohio her home. When she is not busy discovering unique ways to wreak havoc upon the lives of her fictional characters, she spends quality time with her husband, two kids, and eight pets. Readers can learn more about Heidi on her website, *authorheidiglick.com*

This Old House
Lily Hubbard
Student Finalist
Toledo Christian Schools

Prologue

March 15, 1945, the day it all began for me. The world was amidst a world war, the second of its kind. On that fateful, supposedly cursed day, I took my first breath.

~1~

My parents were the conservative, traditional type, so my name obviously had to reflect that. I was christened Eden Mary Gilbert three months to the day from my birth. My father was overseas for my welcome into the world, but managed to get leave in time for my christening. My mother, Nancy Robin Gilbert, was the most iron-willed woman around. She managed a part-time job at the local general store while being pregnant with me while my father was away fighting for his country.

On June 15, 1945, my parents were finally together again after five straining months of being separated due to the war. They realized that their one bedroom, studio style apartment would not do for a small but growing family. We lived in the basement of my maternal grandparents' house for the next nine months of my infancy until my parents could afford the mortgage on a house. According to my mother, the day I took my first step was the day my father burst through the door and rushed down the stairs to tell her the news that he had just found the perfect house for our family.

The next day, my parents loaded me up in the stroller and walked the two miles to a quaint, three-bedroom house in Cleveland. My parents later told me that as soon as they walked up the block and arrived at the house, I started speaking in rapid-fire gibberish and clapped my hands. They looked at each other and shared a look that this was the right house for them.

~2~

After a long and painstaking process of getting approved for a loan, my parents were given the keys to their new house, which amazingly, had been finished on March 15, 1945. The same day I was born, so was our House. We moved in when the House and I were both a year and a half, and our family settled in fairly quickly.

When I was two years old, my mother thought it would be the greatest thing since sliced bread to mark my height on the door jamb of the kitchen. My father developed a tendency, whenever he left the House, to pat the wall in a loving way and with as much gusto as his voice could muster would cry "Hoooeeyyy hooooeeyyy," because he claimed that it, "imbued the House with love and protection for your mother and you."

The next six years in the House with my small family were the best growing up years I had, full of love and laughter. But that was before the rose-colored glasses were forced off my innocent eyes, exposing them to the harsh light of reality.

~3~

After my father came home from overseas, my mother was able to quit her job at the general store. He managed to find full-time work at the local machine factory, assembling parts for farming equipment. The pay was minimal, but it was the best he could provide for us during that time. One random Saturday, my father left the House with his routine farewell to us and to the House. After he left, my mother's and my morning routine began with a quiet breakfast together. After we ate, she started her chores and told me to work on homework.

I finished my work for the day, so my mother allowed me to go play outside. She kissed me on the head and said, "Make sure to find some joy out there." I would always respond to her by running to her legs and give her the biggest squeeze I could muster with my small frame and tell her, "I love you, Mama, to the moon and back!" and then squeal with laughter while running to our backyard.

I spent most of my free time outside, with the birds and the animals talking to me in their own languages. On that particular day, it was slightly gray outside with the clouds announcing a brewing storm on the horizon. Of course, I did not let that stop me from relishing the crisp air while I swung in the tire swing of the old oak tree in our backyard.

Something felt off in the air as I was playing, like the weather was a bad omen for what was to come. I marked that day as the last time I felt peace and security in my childhood.

~4~

After playing for about an hour, I ran inside to eat lunch because the cold weather had awakened a hungry stomach and I was excited for some hot chicken noodle soup my mother had been making. I entered our House through the back kitchen door, but I couldn't find my mother anywhere in the kitchen or the washroom. I walked out of the kitchen into the living room and in a panicked state, started calling, "Mama, Mama? I can't find you!"

I rounded the corner to find my mother at the front entrance of the House with the door cracked open, talking in hushed tones with a strange man on our front porch. I felt my panic subside momentarily, but then I had to watch as my mother's chest started violently heaving and she bent over at the waist while holding her stomach like she had just been punched.

She started shaking with sobs as she cried, "Please God, not him, anyone but him."

Over and over again she said this. I felt physical pain watching my mother, and in my childlike innocence, wanted to make it better, so I bolted to her and squeezed her leg while looking up at her with wide eyes and saying in a small voice, "I love you, Mama...to the moon and back."

This worsened her sobbing and she didn't reply, so I just crushed her leg even more with my arms and squeezed my eyes shut, thinking that would make it better so I wouldn't have to watch my strong mother crumple like a fallen leaf being stepped on. The man at the door, who I later found out was one of my father's coworkers and friends, passed through the doorway and scooped me up in his strong arms.

He looked at me with tears in his eyes and had to swallow twice to be able to speak, then finally said, "Eden honey, your daddy ain't comin' home no more."

I instantly felt rage rise up in me and balled my hands into tiny fists and started beating at his massive chest. "**Stop lying!** My daddy said he would be home tonight, so why are you lying? My daddy said goodbye to my mama, the House, and *me*. You are lying!"

The tears slipped from his eyes and rolled down his cheeks and landed in his bushy beard. He once again had to muster his voice to say, "I know, hun, I know. I ain't lyin' 'bout your daddy. He had an accident where he works, and he ain't comin' home no more."

I was furious.

Who was this man to come into my home and make my mother hurt like that and have the audacity to lie and say my father was not coming home? I managed to shimmy out of his arms and scurried to my mother once again.

"Mama, this man said Daddy isn't coming home, tell him he's wrong. Please Mama, tell him."

My mother managed to lift her head and met my gaze with her own red and tear-stained eyes for a second before dropping her head again and groaning like she was hurting. It finally hit me right in that moment that what the man said was truth. My father was not coming home anymore.

He was dead.

~5~

On October 22, 1953, a week after his sudden accident, we laid my father to rest. My mother was the driving force behind my parents' religious tendencies. She was raised Catholic and had just stayed in that denomination the rest of her life. The service seemed to last forever at our church, and afterwards the reception was even worse. My parents were friendly with everyone, which meant that there were so many people lining up to give their "condolences." The day is burned into my memory because of the fact that my mother was silent except from having to say, "Thank you" to **every. Single. Person.** She did not even attempt a smile, but rather kept her cool the entire insufferable time.

The last person left our House when it was pitch black outside that night. As soon as my mother shut the door, she turned and walked past me as if I was an apparition just standing there. She walked right up the stairs, and I heard her go to her bedroom and shut the door. I was so confused. How could my mother forget me like that? I decided to go in search of a snack while I was thinking of possible reasons she had forgotten me. I took some leftover "grieving" food from the table and sat on the floor in our living room, hoping that she was just changing and then would come down to get me.

I couldn't read clocks at that point, so I just sat there until my eyes drooped with exhaustion, then I climbed up the stairs and shuffled my way down the hall to where her room was and cracked open the door. She lay there on their bed with her back turned to me while still in her clothes from the funeral. I walked around to the other side and saw that her makeup had run in streaks down her slim face that was puffy from crying for so long. I did not know what to do at that moment, so I just leaned over the bed and kissed her cheek and said in the quietest whisper, "I love you, Mama, to the moon and back." She started stirring, so I quickly ran out of her room and into mine.

After I shut the door, I stood there feeling strange. My father was not coming home anymore, and my mother seemed to be slipping away. At that moment, I remember feeling helpless to keep my mother with me. I climbed into bed, finally allowing myself to feel the pain and realization that I had lost my father, and life would be completely different from then on out. I was lying on my back, drifting off into a deep sleep, when I remembered that the House was still standing, just like I was, and every day the House lived, so did I.

Sometimes I look back on those times and I am completely baffled that my young self could comprehend all that. I guess that is what reality does to someone: it forces them to grow up faster than they should.

~6~

The next few weeks felt like trying to run through a messy sludge of life. My mother was a human zombie, barely rising from her cocoon of a bed, only to get food when the moon had risen to its peak and the faint hoots of the owls could be heard. My grandmother on my mother's side came to stay with my mother and me for a while until things could "return to normal" or whatever normal could be in her eyes. She always seemed to have a cheery disposition about her, like she was putting on a fake, doll-like mask of togetherness. People had begun saying that I was a lot like my father, stubborn and ambitious about what we decided. So when my classmates and the nosy mothers from down the block got what I called the "pity face" look, it made my skin crawl and I would get the sudden urge to flee.

A year after my father died, on the anniversary of that horrible day, my mother and I made the trek to the cemetery to visit his grave. I had not talked to my mother for three days at that point, with her still retreating to her room and me doing everything I could to ignore the shell that she had become. In the middle of our walk, I wanted to make an effort to remind my mother that I was still there, so I reached up and grabbed her hand. I was met with bony fingers that were as cold as a block of ice. This person next to me was not the loving, carefree mother who had always been a beacon of light and warmth to me, but had transformed into a cold husk of a human. My small hand could not bear the cold feeling from hers, so I dropped it and just quickened my pace so I would not have to face her anymore.

We finally reached the final resting place of my father, with a light marble tombstone that read "Beloved husband, father, comrade." I looked away in utter disgust. How could my father's entire life be summed up in four heartless words? Once my mother caught up to me after a minute, she crumpled once more and knelt sobbing at the foot of the grave. She began muttering words under her breath through her hiccupping crying, but the only phrases I could catch were, "why me…can't take it anymore…broken…I don't want to live like this…please take me."

I just stood there with a face that felt stone cold at the weakness in my once-strong mother's voice. I was so bitter in those moments, rage running through me constantly at having to part with my father and my mother, both physically and emotionally.

My family used to be so involved in our church, going to mass on Sundays and helping with various charities and events through it. Now my mother and I barely left our House, only for the bare necessities of socialization or supplies. I did not have anyone to turn to, with my mother becoming something Other, and my grandmother constantly pretending

163

like my grief was not a tangible thing. My grandmother would refuse to speak to me if I cried at all, and she would always tell me that, "This too shall pass." So, I turned to our House. That may seem odd, but I felt a special connection to it, being the same exact age and all. On days that were warm and sunny, I could be found roaming the yard and our overgrown garden in the back, and on the cold, wintery days, I was always searching the House for its hidden treasures and the secrets it was keeping.

One particular day, about three months after visiting my father's grave, on a freezing January morning, I was in the attic of the House, looking for anything that might prove to be an adventure or escape. All of a sudden I heard a faint noise.

"Eden, Edennnn, where are you, sweetheart?"

I thought I had fallen asleep and was dreaming because that voice sounded like how my mother used to talk, before my father had died. I quickly slipped from my hiding spot and managed to shimmy down the ladder to the hallway. I crept along the wall and made my way down the stairs, being careful to miss every creaky spot that might give away my entrance. I army-crawled my way to the kitchen doorway and peeked my head around the corner. Like in a vision, I saw my mother there, cooking up a storm and looking like an actual human being. I shot up to my feet and inched my way into the kitchen, holding my breath so as not to disturb or frighten her into returning to her zombie-like state.

"Ma? What are you doing? What's going on?" I couldn't keep the quiver from my voice at that moment and nearly burst into tears at the sight.

My mother's head swiveled quickly to look at me and got the most concerned look on her face before she dried off her hands on her apron and rushed to scoop me up in a hug.

"I am so sorry, sweetie, I am so sorry."

We were both crying heavily at that point, a harmony of sniffling noses.

"Why are you sorry, Mom? Did you do something wrong?"

"Yes, honey, I didn't give you enough love."

Those simple words caused my heart to crack just a little more with the remembrance of all I had to endure when she had emotionally abandoned me.

"Why? Why did you leave me with Grandma!? I needed you, and you left me. I wanted to hug you and you just ignored me."

My heated words cause her to cry even harder. I was at a loss for words. I was caught between my love for my mother and the bitterness that had been caused by her careless actions. My thoughts were spinning so fast I felt ill. In an effort to break the solid wall of ice between us, I offered up a small olive branch of a peace offering.

"Mom…it's okay. I forgive you."

The look of pure relief on her face was worth my obvious lie. I felt sick to my stomach but tried to convince myself that it was the right thing to do.

My mom laughed while drying her eyes. "Eden, I will do better, I swear. After visiting your father's grave, it made me realize that I needed to change, for you. We're going to start by going to mass this Sunday!"

~7~

The rest of the week was strange. I was still adjusting, and a bit skeptical of how happy my mother was acting. Then came Sunday morning and I was made to put on my frilliest dress and have my hair yanked into a tight bun. The drive to our church was dead silent, except for the traditional hymns my mother played on the radio. We walked into our church and were greeted by floods of "concerned" parishioners crowding around us and asking ten million questions per minute about our personal lives. We finally broke free from the mob of people and managed to find a seat close to the front. Our priest came up to the altar and started the service, but my mind was drifting into oblivion. After droning on for about an hour, the priest finally led us through the prayers and it was finished. My mother decided to leave me sitting there in all my girlish finery to go talk to the other adults. I laid down on the pews, not caring that I was crushing my poofy skirt, and started to close my eyes. Right before I fell asleep, I looked across the room to where my mother was and saw her giggling like she was a teenager and touching the arm of a man who I did not know.

~8~

I awoke abruptly when my mother shook my arm suddenly.

"Eden! Wake up, we're going to lunch."

I groggily rubbed the sleep from my eyes and sighed. "Is it just you and me going?"

"No, sweetheart, we're going with the nice man over there, he invited us."

I looked to where she gestured and saw the same man she had been laughing with earlier. Something was off in the smile aimed at me. The hair on my neck tingled and I felt the sudden urge to flee from this strange man.

"Mom, please, can we just go home?" I didn't even attempt to keep the panic from my voice, trying to subtly warn my mother about how I felt about this man she had found.

She clicked her tongue at me, "Eden Mary, that is *not* how we treat

165

new people. We are going to lunch with him, end of discussion."

"Fine, Mother."

I had never called her "mother" before, and especially after everything that had happened, she looked like she had been slapped at that simple word. Instead of engaging, she turned on her heels and put on her fakest smile to greet the man. I saw them chatting quietly while I saw there, fuming. They eventually decided to go to the fancy Italian restaurant two blocks from the church, which was a lot more fancy than our usual lunch spot. Since it was extremely windy outside, we drove the short distance to the restaurant.

When we were seated at our table, both the man and my mother ignored me and continued to talk and laugh. I kept noticing how close the man kept trying to get to my mother and how often she batted her eyelashes at him and laughed while ducking her head. As soon as the food came to our table, it was like a veil was lifted off their eyes and they realized I sat across from them. My mother seemed slightly embarrassed and flustered at having ignored me for so long.

"Eden, honey, this is Brad Thompson. He has been going to mass for about two months now. Introduce yourself!"

That sickly sweet smile of hers had been pasted on her face again and I immediately lost my appetite.

"Hello."

"Eden! Be. Respectful." she hissed while still smiling at me.

"Hello, sir."

Brad decided to chime in. "Oh, what a cute little girl."

"I'm not cute and I'm not little!"

I had gone from stoic and collected to red in the face and screaming. Everyone in the restaurant swiveled in their chairs to look at the spectacle I made of myself. My mother was mid-bite when I erupted and dropped her fork with her mouth wide open. In a split second after my tirade, she managed to grab me by the back of my dress and with superhuman strength, hauled me out of my chair and started dragging me outside.

"We're done here. I can't take you anywhere, can I? I just wanted one nice afternoon with you and Brad, but no, you just had to spoil it all."

She practically threw me in the car, and stormed around to the other side and got in. She glared daggers at me through the rearview mirror while she started the car. We peeled out of the parking lot and drove home without the music this time.

As soon as we got back to the House, my mother sent me up to my room, without having eaten lunch, and went into the kitchen to call *Brad*. I felt tears come to my eyes and threw myself on my bed. After crying for about five minutes, I dried my eyes and decided to go back into the attic to get away. I could still hear her voice echoing up the stairs, indicating that she was still on the phone with Brad.

I climbed the steep ladder and found a warm spot in the corner and started to sort through some of my father's old belongings. I brought an old uniform up to my nose and breathed in his familiar scent, which made me begin to cry again. I felt so betrayed by my mother who seemed to have moved on too fast from my father.

After about an hour, I had had enough of my self-pity party and found my way downstairs. Lo and behold, who should I find next to my mother on our couch? The very same slimy Brad. Before I could go unseen back upstairs, they managed to spot me and my mother called me into the living room.

"Eden, I want you to apologize to Brad please."

What in the world? I was so angry because she was the one who had originally pushed me to like this guy and now she wanted me to *apologize* to him? I decided to take the high road and inhaled deeply before I spoke.

"I am sorry for blowing up." Hopefully she was still bad at recognizing my noticeably clear lies and would just accept it.

Then he was so "gracious" as to forgive me. "Eden, right? It's okay, no harm, no foul."

Gosh, I really hated his smile. It gave me the creeps every time I saw it. My mother, on the other hand, looked very pleased with me, so I just ignored him.

"Eden, Brad and I are going to go to dinner, but your grandmother will come stay with you for a little while we're out, okay?"

I just mumbled in agreement and managed to excuse myself to go do my homework. They left the House a little while later. As I stood in the doorway watching them go, I ran my hands up the wall where my height was notched in the wood every year. I sadly realized that the House was the only friend that I had, but we would keep pushing through it until clearer skies came. I quietly ate dinner with my grandmother, then went up to bed.

~9~

My mother and Brad's relationship progressed very quickly. A little too quickly, in my opinion. Within a month, he had proposed, and they were married in a simple courtroom wedding two months after that. My life had gone from having no parents essentially, to one mother who randomly decided to make amends, then to having a new stepparent that I loathed. Brad attempted to become like my real father, even insisting that I called him "dad" and all, but I refused. The honeymoon phase was horrifying for me because my mother once again acted like I wasn't there, and Brad was the center of her universe.

Things took a turn for the worse around their six-month wedding anniversary. Brad and my mother started to argue more often. It escalated from bickering, to arguing, to full-on screaming matches between them. I cried myself to sleep most nights, torn between pity for my mother and anger at her for ignoring me so much. About a week and a half before the second anniversary of my father's death, I came downstairs to find Brad and my mother yelling at each other at the dinner table.

"Brad, stop accusing me of flirting with other men, I love *you*."

"Shut up, Nancy, I saw the way you smiled at the man in the restaurant yesterday."

"He was our **waiter**. It's called being polite. You would know that if you had any manners at all."

I had managed to sneak past without them noticing and was in the middle of grabbing myself a snack from the cupboard when I stopped for a second to listen to what they were saying.

"You lying piece of trash! I have manners, you're just a loose woman with no personality."

"Brad, stop it! Stop it! What is wrong with you?"

The yelling had progressed into a screaming match at that point, and I began to get scared as to what might happen if one of them snapped.

"Oh, you want to know what's wrong with me, huh? I guess I'll just have to show you."

With a wicked gleam in his eye, Brad stood up and grabbed my mother by the ear to make her stand face-to-face with him. I had never before seen my mother as terrified as in that moment. Brad wound up and slapped her so hard the sound could have been heard from down the street. I must have gasped so loudly that he pivoted toward me and started pacing toward me. I sank down the front of the counter, hyperventilating with pure fear, my eyes bulging and my heart beating faster than humanly possible. He had just reached me and wound up once again, but this time landed his fist into my face when....

~10~

"Eden! Eden!"

I screamed as I lurched up in my bed. It took me a second to ground myself and realize that I was in my room, in my bed, having just been shaken awake, with my husband's arms embracing me soothingly

"Eden...sweetheart, you were having a night terror again. Was it about when you were a kid?"

"Yes. I'm sorry." I could only answer through heaving breaths of panic that still raced through my blood.

"Honey, there's nothing to be sorry for. I'm here, you're safe, you're home. Do you need anything?"

"No, it's okay, I think I just need some warm milk. I'm going to go get some then I'll be right back up."

He didn't ask questions because he knew that I needed a second to be awake and process my nightmare.

I went downstairs and made myself a mug of warm milk and sat at our kitchen table. Sometimes processing through all my childhood memories came up in my dreams and I needed time to sort through them.

My mother and I had both been hospitalized after that incident, and she divorced Brad right after. I had grown up in a slightly more stable environment after that. I went through high school quite uneventfully and went to my dream college after graduating. I had met the man of my dreams there, who stayed so patiently beside me whenever my childhood trauma resurfaced, and he was willing to wait for my trust and to prove himself worthy of it before we got married. My mother passed when I was twenty-four due to heart failure, which I believe was due to the heartbreak of all she had gone through.

I am now twenty-nine, with my two beautiful babies upstairs sound asleep, a wonderful man I call my husband, and a House that I had grown up in and now lived in with my family. As I went toward the stairs to go back to bed, I patted the wall and softly cried, "Hoooeeyyy hooooeeyyy."

This old House was like another family member to me, and we had gone through everything together and were both still standing strong.

The End

Lily Hubbard is a current senior at Toledo Christian Schools. She plans on attending Spring Arbor University in the fall of 2025 to study business and entrepreneurship. Lily is a part of her writing club at school and loves to put her ideas onto paper. Whenever she finds a moment, she can be found reading books of all kinds. Lily plans to incorporate her passion for writing and literature into her everyday life by opening her own bookstore one day.

www.ingramcontent.com/pod-product-compliance
Lightning Source LLC
Chambersburg PA
CBHW010801310726
48974CB00006B/932